STONE OF FIRE

AN ARKANE THRILLER
J.F. PENN

Stone of Fire. An ARKANE Thriller (Book 1)
Copyright © Joanna Penn (2011, 2013, 2015). All rights reserved.
Third edition. Previously published as PENTECOST

www.JFPenn.com

ISBN-13: 978-1-912105-00-7

Requests to publish work from this book should be sent to:
joanna@CurlUpPress.com

Cover and Interior Design: JD Smith Design

Printed by Lightning Source

www.CurlUpPress.com

For Jonathan.
Growing together, but not in each other's shadow.

When the day of Pentecost came, they were all together in one place. Suddenly a sound like the blowing of a violent wind came from heaven and filled the whole house where they were sitting.

They saw what seemed to be tongues of fire that separated and came to rest on each of them. All of them were filled with the Holy Spirit and began to speak in other tongues as the Spirit enabled them.

Everyone was filled with awe, and many wonders and miraculous signs were done by the Apostles.

Acts 2:1-4, 43

PROLOGUE

Varanasi, India. May 1, 1.34am

IT IS SAID THAT those who die in Varanasi can achieve *moksha*, release from the suffering of repeated death and rebirth. So many people come to die here and be burnt on the ghats that the pyres burn continually day and night, even when rain lashes down, soaking the firewood. Wet bodies take longer but eventually they all turn to ash and are washed into the river that cleanses all sin. On this night, rain soaked the ashes into the winding Varanasi streets, rivers of leaden mud returning to the source. Beggars shivered on the steps leading down to Manikarnika, the main burning ghat on the banks of the holy river Ganges. The ragged ones huddled closer to the smouldering bodies for warmth, watching as they were consumed by the sacred flames.

Behind the ghats, streams ran down the pavements, leaving the excrement and rubbish of the day in the doorways and corners of the Old City. Sister Aruna Maria hurried down an alleyway behind the spice markets, forcing her old feet to move faster, stumbling a little as she pushed off the walls that loomed above her. She glanced behind, sensing that those following were close, but seeing nothing in the shadows yet. An hour ago, she had heard men come into the little church tucked away inside the holy Hindu city and speak to one of the caretakers of the convent. She had listened with growing fear as they asked about an ancient stone, and she had peeked around a pillar to see money changing hands.

She ran then, heading for the anonymity of the streets, but she knew that Christians were barely tolerated by the sadhus. Beggars would point her direction for a single rupee and the men would be on her trail soon enough. Aruna Maria pushed herself faster into the labyrinth of narrow streets. How they had found her after so many years she could not fathom, but she knew it was time to hide the stone again. For she was the Keeper, the latest in a long line stretching back two millennia, each one prepared for the day when evil men would come for what she protected. Now it seemed, they had found her.

Beneath the sound of the rain she heard running feet closing behind her. Aruna Maria clutched the soaked habit in her gnarled hand as she desperately searched for sanctuary, for some dark corner to hide in. She pulled the ivory material closer around her and splashed through the puddles. She had run through these streets since her childhood, she knew the markets well and was sure she could outpace this evil now. A tall figure stepped out before her, dressed all in black so he seemed to emerge as a wraith from the shadows that dominated these close alleys. It was the man from the church. His face was almost boyishly handsome but his gaze chilled her with the thinly veiled threat of violence. She gasped and turned to flee in the opposite direction but another man had run up behind her. The streets, so busy in the day, were now empty, shutters closed and eyes turned from her trouble.

"Calm down, sister, we only mean to talk to you."

She could tell the man was American by his accent, but although his words promised safety, she could see his eyes in the dim light. They were shining with a fanaticism she recognized, a hunger for something she and few others possessed in the world.

"I know you have an Apostle's stone. All you have to do is give it to me and you'll go free."

He reached towards her, but she stood her ground, heart pounding.

"Don't you dare touch me. I'm set apart for God. I don't know of this stone you seek."

"Oh, but you do, sister."

Aruna Maria felt strong arms pinning her, holding her still while the American advanced towards her. As fear tightened around her heart, she began to pray, ancient words handed down by the Keepers, spoken in her own native Indian tongue. High above her head, storm clouds gathered, forming a tight vortex in shades of midnight. She felt an upwelling in her spirit as the words ran together, strange tongues transforming her voice as she called to God in the language of the angels. One hard hand closed around her throat, forcing her head back and silencing her prayers. With the other, the man found the thin cord in the folds of her habit. He lifted the stone out and over her head.

Rain lashed down on the three of them now, soaking their clothes, running down their faces. The man looked closely at the stone in his palm, roughly carved whorls set in a deeper grey, as he held it with reverence.

"This is what I've been searching for, sister. Now tell me what it can do."

Aruna Maria looked up into the approaching storm and prayed aloud, her words stronger now. She was sure that God would hear her as he had heard the cries of the faithful since the days of Abraham. Thunder rolled across the sky and lightning crashed. Fire lit up the heavens above them and flashed down to earth as if to strike the heathen. Aruna Maria was transfixed by the storm but then the man slapped her face hard and her head snapped sideways. The stinging blow made her head reel and spin but she held her ground.

"Tell me how to use it," he demanded. "I must know."

She looked at him, her eyes holding the knowledge of ancient years and the secrets he so desperately wanted.

"The power of the stones was sent by God and forged in the blood of martyrs in the first century, by the faith of the early Christians. Such power cannot be taken by men like you. The only way for you to see the power is to gather all the stones of the Apostles together, but they are lost to time and history now. They haven't been in one place since Pentecost itself, over two thousand years ago. The Keepers were scattered and none of us know of the others, so you cannot gather what you seek."

She smiled at his rising anger as a peaceful calm descended on her. Was this how the blessed martyrs felt when they faced death? The shadowed man roared then, his rage quickened by the violence of the storm. He tore her from the grip of the other man and threw her into the mud of the alleyway, kicking her old body again and again, his boots crushing the breath from her. Aruna Maria looked up into the heart of the storm and as she sank into blackness she saw a pillar of fire coming down from heaven.

When she came to, Aruna Maria couldn't move, she couldn't see. She tried to scream but her throat was blocked. Her whole body was paralyzed. She could barely breathe, but a small amount of air seeped through the bindings that wrapped her. She screamed in her mind and panic overwhelmed her as she gasped for breath on the edge of consciousness. She attempted to rock in place but nothing happened. She tried to figure out where she was knowing that the men had taken the stone. She had failed in her sacred duty and perhaps she deserved whatever fate was coming, for God had surely turned his face that day.

She was lying flat, being carried by people who were walking around many corners. It felt like she was on a stretcher of some kind, wrapped tightly in material. The sound of chanting filled her ears and Aruna Maria inhaled sharply as she realized it was the death chant of Shiva and she was on a funeral pyre being carried to Manikarnika ghat. It was customary to burn the dead as soon as possible after death and the men were covering their tracks by getting rid of her body. They would have paid for a quick burning amongst the many genuine dead. Panic rose in her throat as she struggled against the bonds that held her. She had to tell someone she was alive, because the ghats were not far from the temple. It wouldn't be long before she was on a pyre, burning alive and watched by the tourists who came to gawp at the spectacle.

In the past, Aruna Maria had been fascinated by how the flaming pyres had hypnotized the visitors, some stared into the flames considering their mortality, others clicked away with close-ups of cracking bones sticking out from the smoldering fires. They wanted to see the spectacle of death laid out before them, for the experience was anathema to clinical western cremation, where the face of death was hidden. But she knew the tourists had no idea of the bodies that lay just beneath them in the water, weighed down by stones, and swaying in the current. For children, pregnant mothers, holy cows and sadhus were not burnt but sunk into the river Ganges to live again in the cycle of reincarnation. Corpses often surfaced on the east bank of the river, to rot in the sun and be eaten by carrion birds. This place existed for death and tonight was no different, but the tourists were unaware of the living flesh about to be burnt alive before them.

Aruna Maria's heart pounded as she considered the ritual to come for she had watched these ghats all her life. The corpse was brought to the burning ghat on a stretcher, wrapped in holy saffron gold and crimson material, then draped in marigolds. The pyre is built and tended by the Dalit, the Untouchable caste, who take the wrapped cadaver from the chanting family and dip it into the holy river Ganges before placing it onto the pyre. More wood is heaped on top and then it is lit. The fires take the soul to heaven and the dead are released from the cycle of reincarnation. If a skull remains unburnt, it is smashed, releasing the spirit. The ashes and bones are finally swept into the Ganges, mixing with the river of life as it flows to the ocean.

Aruna Maria smelled the pungent smoke of the fires, the heavy scent of marigolds and felt herself being laid down. The chanting reached a crescendo. If only she could scream or move but she was too tightly wrapped. She was lifted again and felt the shock of cool water as she was dipped into the sacred river. She began to pray desperately to her God as she was laid on the pyre and the fire began to lick her skin through the wrapping. Her prayers turned to silent screams as her throat burnt through, silencing her before she died.

A cloaked figure stood by the pyre gazing into the flames as the body crisped and charred. His fingers rose to touch the stolen stone around his neck as he turned and faded into the alleyways of night.

Extract from The Times of India, May 2.

A violent storm rocked the city of Varanasi last night, with lightning igniting fires across the city even in the heavy rain. Scientists cannot explain how the fires burned so fiercely in monsoon conditions, but witnesses said lightning was seen in balls of scarlet fire as well as forked flames. A pillar of fire was reportedly seen above Manikarnika ghat on the banks of the Ganges.

"It was as if a whirling djinn was in our midst," said Rajiv Gupta, a local tradesman.

Even more unusual were reports of miracles that occurred at the time the pillar of fire was sighted. Beggars living on the edges of the ghat, drawn to the fiery spectacle, have claimed to be healed of various diseases and one man allegedly regained his sight after twenty years of blindness. Hindu priests as well as the police are investigating the claims, reportedly attributing them to mass hysteria associated with the violent storm.

CHAPTER 1

Oxford, England. May 18, 9.46pm

DR MORGAN SIERRA SAT at her desk, finishing notes on her cases for the day. Glancing at the time, she stood up and stretched, rolling her neck to loosen the taut muscles. It had been another long day, she thought, but there was no one to go home to and time for just a few more pages. Crossing the office to the small kitchen, she refilled her coffee cup, the bitter black her only real addiction. The fledgling practice was slowly gaining clients as her expertise in dealing with religious and psychological issues became known, but the University still frowned on her specialty. She battled their criticism daily while balancing her lecturing and tutorial appointments. Morgan's clinical psychology practice dealt particularly with people whose problems related to religion in some way, those trapped in cults or who claimed supernatural experiences. She also increasingly consulted with government think tanks on the impact of fundamentalist religion in the country. It had been hard work but Morgan had built up her practice to supplement the meager number of students she taught at the University in anomalistic psychology. The field studied ostensibly paranormal activity and behavior under scientific conditions, analyzing why certain phenomena existed and how they could be explained. Morgan sometimes wondered what she was trying to prove to herself, let alone others.

She sipped the hot coffee as she gazed at her many bookshelves, her mind wandering. Even while she loved being there, Morgan knew that the issue with the University of Oxford was its age and the instant kudos the name evoked. It trapped scholars and all who worshipped at their feet into ancient thought patterns with no room for change or progress. She thought of the doors in the Bodleian library, the venerable institution just around the corner from her office. The names of the Schools were written above them, inscribed in an ancient hand, gold-leafed and stamped into thick oak, banded with copper. Divinity and Scientia were two separate doors and the problem was that her door sat between them, and neither entirely accepted her field of research. Psychology sat within the Faculty of Science and was concerned with measurement, the scientific method, statistical instruments, experiments, control, even animal labs. The Faculty of Theology sat within Divinity, among the monks of Blackfriars, the nuns of the convent of the Assumption at Headington and the Quakers of St Giles. The Theology curriculum still boasted St John's Gospel in Greek, Israel before the exile and Patristics, while students still debated the Trinity with arguments used by Origen and Augustine, unchanged since the fourth century. Dons wore black soutanes on Sundays, held the Eucharist and celebrated Mass while on weekdays they held forth on dogma and ritual. They were the faithful. Morgan felt she was an anomaly between the two faculties because she specialized in the phenomena between psychology and religion, the unexplained between science and faith, that which fell through the gap.

Thinking of the Faculty took her back to her father and growing up with him in Israel. She looked down at the picture of him on her desk, his smiling eyes forever captured in the silver frame. She traced his image with a fingertip. He would have been proud to see what she had become and where she sat now, although he had been taken from her too soon to see it. On the days she felt inadequate, an impostor in this eminent place, she remembered that he had always believed in her and she carried on in his memory. It had been his library and study of Kabbalism that had first inspired her. It had sparked her own search for divinity and truth. He had found peace in it, but she had yet to find her own. She had joined the Israeli Defense Force, as all young people were required to do but she stayed on after the mandatory period as they had funded her training as a psychologist.

Morgan had been employed to investigate how fundamentalism affected behavior on both sides of the ideological fence. She smiled to herself as she remembered how her studies had ignited such heated debates with her father. After several years of active service, she had believed that the key to any form of peace was an understanding between the faiths, a common ground rather than a divisive duality. Evil and violence could be found on all sides and virtue wasn't owned by anyone's god. That wasn't such a popular stand though and it was easier to think about such issues in the sterility of Britain, away from the religious melting pot of Israel. She sighed, leaning forward to complete her notes as the clock ticked towards ten.

Her assistant had left hours ago and Morgan was finishing alone before heading back to her little house in the up and coming area of Jericho. She had been expecting a visit earlier from an American academic who had an interesting proposition for her, but he hadn't shown up. She had agreed to talk with him because he had mentioned research affiliations with her old University in Israel as well as opportunities in the US which might serve her career well. Oxford looked favorably on academics who brought in their own research grants. Maybe she would call him tomorrow, but for now it was time to head home. She began to pack up her files, preferring to start with a clean desk every morning.

Morgan looked forward to her cycle in every morning. Her office sat at the end of Bath Place, a tiny alleyway opposite the Holywell Music Rooms in central Oxford, where medieval colleges jostled with modern city shops. May was a glorious time in the city, with rare sunshine bringing the city outdoors, punting on the river Cherwell and lazing in the botanical gardens. It seemed that summer had finally arrived, and Morgan was glad. She still found the endless wet winters difficult after the sun baked Israeli climate. When it rained too hard, water ran down the cobblestones and under her office door, soaking the carpet so it smelled damp. It had happened too much the last winter, but she still loved being in the center of the city and in this little nook between the Turf pub and Hertford College.

The Turf had low, dark beams the height of stooped old men and the walls leached the smell of stale tobacco. She had often finished a winter's day with a mulled wine in the tiny bar. She could hear the dark wooden kegs of beer being rolled down the barrel vault, the crackle of the fire in the small hearths lit on cold nights. But now it was almost summer, time for the lively chatter of students drinking Pimms with lemonade, spiked with mint and cucumber. Tonight a live band played folk songs, and strains of the music could be heard along with cheers from the happy fans. These noises were the background to her office, her rhythmic day, and Oxford had just started to feel like home.

A sharp knock on the door made her jump. It was far too late for anyone to be here now and the door to the practice had no peephole, no chain lock. Morgan felt a spike of adrenalin, her Israeli suspicion kicking in at this late night visit. She pushed the feelings down with a wry smile. This was Oxford, England, not Jerusalem. A late night visit was only likely to be an academic with a research proposal. She walked into the outer office and opened the door.

A man stood outside, clean shaven, dark circles under

his eyes emphasized by the shadow of a nearby street lamp. His indigo pinstriped suit was expensive but understated and he carried a large manila envelope.

"Dr Morgan Sierra?" The man asked with an American drawl; she heard hints of the south in it and thought she recognized the academic from the phone.

"Yes, and you must be Dr Everett?"

"Actually, Dr Everett is indisposed, but I'm his research assistant, Matthew Fry." He held out his business card to Morgan. She took it as he continued.

"I'm so sorry to call this late but he asked me to come by and discuss his proposal with you. We fly back to the US in the morning so we don't have much time. Would you have ten minutes now?"

Morgan didn't sense any threat from him. Fry didn't look like a research assistant but she knew she didn't look much like the stereotype of an Oxford professor either. The lure of the potential American grant was too much to knock back. She stepped aside.

"Of course; I still have some coffee on if you'd like some."

Morgan refilled her own mug and poured Fry a coffee in the small kitchen as he looked around her spacious office. The room was a treasure store of accumulated knowledge, walled with bookcases, with one window high up so the night sky could be seen. The books were an eclectic mix of ancient tomes with broken, unrecognizable spines and modern textbooks, all spilling from the shelves to piles on the floor. There was even a small reading nook, a cushioned space surrounded by towering shelves where a picture of a mandala hung on the wall, a circle in a square in hues of turquoise and garnet. Fry recognized it as one of psychologist Carl Jung's pieces from the Red Book, his private work recently revealed to the public after years of secret storage. A Turkish rug lay on the floor, a runner with woven animals in twin pairs. There was also a black and white photo on her desk, an old man, perhaps her father, his eyes crinkled in laughter.

Morgan came back with the coffee and in the light of the desk lamp he could see her features more clearly. Her long dark curls were roughly tied back from an angular face, alive with expression. She wasn't conventionally beautiful, but she had a gravity that commanded attention. Her sharp eyes were a keen blue with a curious slash of violet in the right eye. He found himself staring just slightly too long, and then said quickly, "Thank you for seeing me so late. Dr Everett is keen to have you work with us on a research project that you would be uniquely qualified for and we're sure you would find challenging."

He opened the envelope he carried and spread the contents out on her desk. Morgan walked around to get a better look. She shuffled through the photos and her eyes darted to one image, a roughly carved stone with a leather cord threaded through it.

"The stone. That's why you're here?"

Morgan's hand flew to her throat where the outline of a similar stone could be seen through her fitted shirt. "It was given to me by my father before he died. But why is Dr Everett interested in these stones?"

Fry shuffled the documents and pulled out a map depicting the ancient world with red markers on it.

"Our research shows that there are twelve of them spread around the world. They're relics from the early Church."

Morgan frowned. "Surely not? My father would have mentioned its provenance. If it's what you say it is, then it should be in a museum, not around my neck."

"Perhaps, but given that you have one already and you're

an expert in religious history and psychology, we'd like to employ you to find the rest of them. We'd pay significantly for your time, as this is a project that Dr Everett cares deeply about. We have two stones already and we want the others as fast as possible."

Morgan shook her head.

"I think you have the wrong academic. This stone has great sentimental value to me, but that's about it."

Fry frowned, taking a step towards her.

"If we can't have your time for the project, then we want to buy the stone from you. It's needed to complete the group. It's critical that we have all twelve."

Morgan stood her ground, her face stony. Her mind was reeling at the implications if it were true. This was something she felt drawn to investigate but the aggressive tactics of this man made her hesitant to become involved with his group.

"I think you should go now. Tell Dr Everett to put an offer in writing and I'll consider it but I can't promise anything." She indicated the way out. "Thank you for your time."

Fry started to walk towards the door, then turned.

"We know your sister has one too. The offer includes her stone. We need them both."

Morgan opened her mouth to answer him but was interrupted by the sound of glass breaking from the outer office.

"Get down," Fry hissed, flicking back his suit jacket and pulling a gun from a holster under his arm. Morgan instinctively ducked down behind her desk. Then the lights went out.

CHAPTER 2

As Morgan's eyes adjusted to the dim glow filtering through the skylight above, she could see Fry crouched low to the floor. A flash of silver from the gun in his hand indicated he was ready for a fight. She realized that he had been expecting trouble of some sort. She cursed under her breath, wishing she had trusted her earlier intuition as the adrenalin flooded her system. Once her military training had kept her alert at all times but she had lost her edge in this protected pocket of academia.

She breathed deeply, trying to still her heartbeat, memory flooding back as she analyzed the situation even as she knew there was no easy way out. In her mind, she was back in Israel, under fire in the Golan Heights. Her husband Elian was by her side, joyous in the adrenalin of battle, his eyes shining as he led his men to the front-lines. It had been a life they had both loved, defending their country together. But when he had been killed in a hail of bullets, she had left the military behind, swearing an oath on his grave to put away her gun and to live a life of peace. Three years had passed since she had left the Israeli forces, but her survival skills were still deeply embedded. She hadn't forgotten all her training.

Morgan could hear two sets of footsteps in the outer room. The men were careless, didn't seem worried about being heard. But who were they? She peered around the desk and saw Fry swivel the wingback chair to provide some cover as he prepared for the men's entry. She needed to defend herself as well.

Morgan felt around the base of the desk for the compartment she had fashioned in the old wood. She had hidden the gun there when she moved to this office, daring to hope she would never to have to use it. Despite feeling it was a crazy precaution and one that could get her arrested, she had cleaned it and kept it ready just in case. She had felt guilty at the possibility of betraying her oath but she couldn't stop the niggling doubts in her mind and she didn't trust the world anymore. There were passports there too, and money ready to leave, as if she had always known this life was temporary.

The hidden compartment clicked open to reveal her Barak SP-21 pistol. With one breath, it was back in her hand, the familiar weight giving her confidence against the invaders as she knelt at the edge of the desk, ready to act.

A voice spoke in the darkness with a thick Eastern European accent.

"We just want the Apostle's stone. If you give it to us, there will be no problems. Dr Sierra, you have a nice, quiet life here in Oxford. It would be a pity to upset it. All we want is the stone. Toss it towards the door and we'll leave."

Morgan heard both the threat and the promise in his voice. He clearly wasn't with Fry so who were this other group? She didn't understand why this stone was suddenly so important, but she knew hers alone was not enough. Her sister Faye had one too and the men would go after her next. Maybe they were already there? Thinking of Faye, David and Gemma in the house with no idea what was coming, she was determined to keep the men there as long as possible. She called out,

"Who are you? Why do you want the stone?"

She heard Fry's hurried 'ssh' trying to quiet her. But she

had never relied on anyone else to keep her safe. After Elian's death, she had learnt how to protect herself and her own.

"It doesn't matter who we are or why we want it," the voice replied. "But if we have to come in to get it, then I can't guarantee your safety."

Fry was preparing to fire at the door if they came in. He called out,

"Backup is coming, I'm not alone here. I'm warning you to leave now."

"Then we'll be quick," the voice continued. "I'll give you five seconds to throw the stone out. Then we're coming in ...1 ..."

Fry turned towards Morgan and whispered, "You have to get out. Just get the stone away from here."

"... 2 ..."

Morgan held the pistol out in front of her with both hands, her eyes on the door as the thumping music from the Turf next door seemed to resonate with her pulse.

"You must know my history, Fry. I'm sure you did your homework. I can protect myself and besides, there's no other way out. I have to go through them."

She moved quickly to the other side of the room, keeping low and out of direct sight of the door. She held a position opposite to where Fry crouched behind the chair.

"... 3 ..."

"Don't worry. I've done this before."

He saw the flash of her grin in the pale light, the first dark smile she had given him, her lithe body now moving with a fluid grace, seemingly transformed by the weapon in her hand. This was Morgan the soldier.

"... 4 ..."

The door burst open and a rattle of gunfire exploded into the room, followed by two men in camouflage gear. Whoever

they were, the bastards had no intention of waiting, they wanted them both dead. Morgan fired and moved position, back behind her desk as Fry squeezed off two shots. He killed the second man before being blown backwards against the oak paneled wall. Smoke filled the room and the smell of sweat and blood took Morgan back to the close quartered battlefields of Israel's borders. Now it was just her and the main attacker remaining. They were both breathing heavily. Morgan's vision narrowed but she embraced the effect of the adrenalin dump, reveling in the heightened sensation. It had been too long since she had surrendered to the rush but even now she resisted the pull of this dark thrill. She didn't want to go back to the way she had been, but this wasn't a fight she could run from. She peeked around the corner of the desk. The attacker was protected by the bookshelf that protruded from the wall in her reading alcove. It had been a shelter where she read and learnt, now it was full of cold intent in the form of a man prepared to kill her.

Morgan breathed deeply. This was her space; how dare they invade it with their guns? How dare they threaten Faye and the life she had created here? She could feel rage building. It was one of the reasons she had left the military after Elian's death. She had become separated from her own humanity, ambivalent to killing. Her life had changed but she could still summon that indifference. Now it would serve her well.

The man spoke, his voice less calm than before.

"I underestimated you, but your colleague seems to be indisposed, so it's just you and me. If you toss me the stone, I'll leave. Otherwise, you'll find it a slow and painful death."

His threatening words brought back memories long buried. Morgan had been tortured once, but they hadn't broken her then, and this man would not break her now. She sensed his fear, his easy operation had gone wrong and now he would pay the ultimate price.

The bookcase the man hid behind was actually a thin veneer and she knew the books on it by heart. Morgan looked at them every day, and she knew where each one sat. She could visualize their covers and knew which ones were tall and short on the shelves. There was a place where a shot would not have to pass through books or wood to hit the man, but once she stood to take it, she would be a clear target herself. She considered where the shot would need to go, mentally rehearsing it, then in one movement she stood and fired through the bookcase. Her first shot caught his ear and knocked him off guard. He returned fire but she moved again, ducking to the floor. The framed picture of the mandala smashed down behind him and glass crashed to the floor. She fired again. The second shot blew his head apart and he crashed to the floor.

Morgan walked over to the fallen body of her assailant and flicked on the lights. She looked at her beautiful books, splattered in blood as brain matter dripped down the bookcase onto the carpet. Her heart was racing from the adrenalin of killing, not fear and she pushed thoughts of her oath from her mind. She dropped to one knee and frisked the man for ID. Nothing, as expected, but it was worth a try. He was white, heavy-set, a typical low level bad guy, all brawn, no brains. Morgan noticed that he had a tattoo on his left forearm. She pulled up his sleeve to see a stylized horse's head, mouth open in a frenzied braying. The lack of color made it eye-catching, for it was ashen, almost as if the pigment had been leached from the man's skin to make it a paler shade. Morgan took a picture of it with her smart phone. Tattoos had a way of betraying the allegiances of their owners and it was all she had to go on for now.

She turned to Fry, whose dead body was resting against the wall behind the chair. She closed his eyes out of respect, but she hardly knew the man. She didn't know who this Everett could be, but clearly there was another group who also wanted the stones that she and others held. She had to go now - there would surely be another group after Faye. She needed to protect her sister and her family, her own guilt about the past fueling the need to be sure they were safe. It seemed that her quiet academic life was over for now.

Morgan grabbed the rest of her gear from the compartment under the desk: her passport, cash and more ammunition. She dialed Emergency 999 on her desk phone, leaving it off the hook as the operator repeatedly asked if she was OK. She would deal with the police later but now she had to get to Faye. She left the building, music still pumping from the Turf, that would have drowned out the noise of the altercation. She grabbed her bike and pedaled hard up Holywell Street. She headed towards St Giles and the pay phone there. She had to call Faye but wouldn't risk it from her own phone in case it was tapped. She had only reached the second lamp post outside the Sheldonian Theatre when a black van screeched to a halt beside her. Three men leapt out and pulled her and the bike inside, slamming her to the floor and driving off at speed.

CHAPTER 3

Oxford, England. May 18 10.33pm

MORGAN WAS HELD FACE down by the three men, pressed hard against the handlebars of her bike. She didn't struggle. There was no use. It was better to lie still, listen and think while she worked out what to do next. She felt her gun digging into her thigh where she had jammed it in her pocket. It would only take a second to draw it and she tensed, waiting for the ease in pressure that would surely come. They hadn't killed her, so they couldn't be the same group as the men from her office. Maybe they were Fry's backup team? The van came to a stop and the pressure lessened. A voice spoke, quiet but authoritative. She could hear a faint South African accent in the deep tone.

"Morgan, I'm Jake Timber. A friend. We're going to let you up now. Please know that we don't intend to hurt you. We needed to protect you and getting you off the street quickly was paramount. Please don't scream. We need to talk."

He must have motioned to the men to let her go because they loosened their hold and she could move again. Morgan curled and sprang up to a kneeling position, gun in hand pointing straight into the face of the man calling himself Jake. He was dark haired with a rash of stubble on his chin; his amber-brown eyes showed little emotion even though his mouth smiled in welcome. Her gun was inches from his nose but he didn't flinch. She was so close she could see a faint scar that twisted up, like a mini corkscrew, from his left eyebrow to his hairline. She was aware of his men hovering just behind her, but he wouldn't have a chance if he tried anything. Jake held his hands up.

"We need to talk about your stone, and Faye. Just give me ten minutes and then you can leave if you need to. We'll deal with the bodies in your office as well."

Morgan was unmoved and silent. He continued, "I'm going to show you something now so you know I'm telling the truth. Can I open my collar very slowly?"

She nodded, the weapon unwavering in her hands. Keeping one hand raised, he slowly peeled back the collar of his shirt, revealing a tan leather string which he pulled up to show her a stone hanging round his neck. It was not exactly the same as hers, but similar enough. If he had a stone, Morgan thought, then he must know more than her. Fry had not finished explaining the significance of the stones, let alone why her family was involved. She lowered the gun.

"OK, let's talk, but I need details quickly. I want my sister protected and I want answers *now*."

Jake nodded.

"You'll have them soon. Let's go."

The men opened the van door into a warehouse sized room. There were a few workstations, banks of computers and maps pinned to the walls. Morgan thought it looked like a police crime scene investigation unit, only messier. She climbed out, refusing the hand of one of the men. She turned to Jake, "So, where are we?"

"The Pitt Rivers, next to the Museum of Natural History. Don't worry, we're safe. Few people even know our base here exists."

Jake led the way up through the main gallery of the museum to the rooms beyond. Dim floor lights illuminated the black and white stone tiles and iron gratings, but the torchlight also picked out figures within the wooden and glass cases crowding the main hall. It was a higgledy-piggledy place that Morgan had explored before, each case stuffed full of items, some with tiny handwritten notes from the original curator. She knew it had been founded in the nineteenth century, recipient of the collection of General Pitt Rivers, an avid collector in the field of archaeology and evolutionary anthropology. What distinguished his collection were the objects used in daily life as well as the ritual and sacred artifacts of the various peoples of the world.

The overall sense was of a museum crowded and alive in some way; the gods of such different cultures stuffed into tiny rooms, separated only by the glass of the cabinets. Morgan could almost imagine them stepping down from their cases in the dark of night, to wage war upon each other. The many handed Nataraja from India, skulls dripping from her neck and blue skin gleaming, wielded a sword at the head of a tribal god from Benin as Incan priest icons menaced the Native American totems. A flash of torchlight illuminated a case of giant wooden birds of paradise, their spiraling feathers like huge tongues. They crouched next to crocodiles and the jet black head of a bull, horns sharply tipped and glistening.

Here was the agonized face of a Christian martyr, neck twisted towards his God, desperate for release, next to a case of ceremonial knives for stripping the flesh from sacrificial animals. There a macabre toy cabinet, full of stuffed creatures with beady eyes that seemed to follow them past. The ghosts of dead children hung in their wake, puppets on tall sticks with limbs like dead trees, broken and dangling. As they walked through the main hallway, a huge Native American totem pole loomed over them, a squatting amphibian over the eyes of a huddled figure. Morgan felt the power of these objects in the semi-darkness. What was mere curiosity in the day had turned to mystic awe in the dark. She loved to come here and wonder at the collections, but this was experiencing the museum in a different, visceral way. She followed close to the man in front as he led her to the back of the main exhibition hall and then down some stairs into the crypt. What did it all have to do with the stone her father had given her, she wondered.

Jake turned back, clearly trying to break the ice.

"You probably know that William Pitt Rivers was an explorer, that he roamed the British empire collecting artifacts from now lost civilizations." Morgan nodded. "What most people don't know is that Pitt Rivers worked for a secret government agency on behalf of Queen Victoria. That agency has been investigating the supernatural for hundreds of years now. Many of the artifacts you can see in the museum are fakes but the real items are down here, a source of ancient power we are still investigating. You'd know the public face of the agency as the ARKANE Institute."

Morgan ran her fingers along one of the dark wooden cabinets, her eyes widening at the name.

"I've been to some of the ARKANE conferences. I thought it was just an academic collective for research and publication."

Jake smiled as they reached a large wooden door at the end of the hall.

"That's just the official version. Welcome to the other side of ARKANE."

32

He opened the door and Morgan gasped as she walked onto a small balcony overlooking five more levels below her with large glass windows opened to the lightwell. Each level had workstations with different artifacts spotlighted upon them, and equipment for dating and analyzing. The place was empty now, but she could see that during the day it was a working lab combining technology with ancient manuscripts to fathom the secrets these objects held.

"I knew there were levels below Oxford, as I've been in the stacks under the Bodleian library, but how could this all be kept secret?" she asked Jake. He grinned, raking his hands through his dark hair, tiredness evident in his eyes.

"There's a whole city beneath Oxford, chambers of secrets from down the ages. Some were hollowed out by the early monks and used for teachings banned in the University, and others for the secret societies that have always flourished in the company of powerful men. Occult knowledge has always needed its protectors and the ARKANE Institute is just one in a long line. The secrets are only known to a few, but now you need to know about this particular one because the stone you're wearing puts you in danger."

Morgan touched the worn leather around her neck.

"So what's going on? We need to protect Faye and her family if those men are coming for the stones. We each have one."

Jake indicated the stairs leading down into the complex.

"A team is on the way to her house now so she and her family will be safe, but we need to talk. Come down to the research center and I'll tell you what we know about these stones and why the timeline is so critical."

Woodstock. Near Oxford, England.
May 18, 10.32pm

David Price took another long sip of the Chilean pinot noir. It was his third glass and only now was some kind of inspiration starting to swirl around him. This was becoming a habit. He frowned and put the glass down, trying to concentrate on the sermon in front of him. Even though the parish was small, he owed them the best he could give, even if some liquid stimulation was needed to write his thoughts these days. His flock relied on him to give them something to think about on Sundays and he was also trying to improve his speaking so he might be invited to lecture at larger parishes and conferences.

It was difficult to reconcile a certain amount of ambition with the call to humility his profession demanded. He preferred to frame his aspiration as the desire to share the wisdom of God with more people, but he knew his deeper motivations. The pulpit was a powerful place to stand, to feel both physical and spiritual authority. He reveled in being the center of attention for that short time each week, to feel the gaze of the parishioners on him and to look back into their eyes, some questioning, some devoted. If he was honest, there were eyes he sought to look into more often, God forgive him. If only the Church of England had something like Catholic confession, where he could repent, do penance and move on. Then he could believe his sins were washed clean every week. But his personal relationship with God had stalled, and so his sins were piling up in front of him.

David shook his head, trying to clear the thoughts that cluttered his mind. He was reaching the edge between insight and melancholy. The wine needed to stop, not least because he knew Faye had noticed how many bottles they were getting through in a week. He could hear her in the kitchen, the squeaking of the tea towel as she dried dishes from dinner. She was listening to some talk show on the radio but it was faint and he couldn't make out the words. She knew the noise bothered him when he was working. He frowned again. They had a wonderful daughter, his job as parish priest was respectable and Faye loved helping the community. They were seen as a loving, happy couple and even though David doubted the reality beneath the drama they played out, it seemed that Faye was content in her part. So he took another swig of his wine and carried on writing about the shade of Samuel appearing to Saul and how it related to the spirit world in the 21st century.

Pitt Rivers Museum, Oxford, England.
May 18, 10.45pm

Morgan followed Jake down into a sparsely furnished room with high tech equipment and a flat wall-sized computer screen. One of the men with them sat down to work a laptop. An image of a rough hewn stone appeared on the screen, similar to hers but carved differently. There were markings on it but it was otherwise unremarkable. Her stone still hung around her neck on the soft leather cord that her father had given to her. The one on screen had a silver chain and was also different to the one Jake wore.

She sat at one of the desks while he leaned against the wall beside the screen. His athletic body was relaxed but alert, muscles taut in tanned forearms that could be seen under his rolled up shirt sleeves. Morgan thought he gave the impression of a powerful jungle cat, his dark amber flecked eyes adding to the illusion. She watched him as he spoke,

"You need to understand the story behind the stones in

order to grasp their importance right now. It's tightly bound into the history of the early Church, so some is established history and some is myth."

Morgan half-smiled, "and the truth lies somewhere in between, I suppose?"

"Yes, whatever you call truth, that is. Let me tell you what we know."

The screen flashed to a map of Israel, then to Jerusalem's Western wall.

"The story goes back to the Resurrection itself. The gospels and the Christian tradition say that Jesus was crucified and the eleven remaining Apostles waited after his death, not knowing what would happen next."

Morgan cut in, "Yes, Matthew's gospel tells of an earthquake that opened the door of the tomb and the Apostles realized Jesus had risen from the dead. But how is that related to what's happening now?"

The screen moved on to show an open cave door in a garden. "The myth of the stones says that the Apostles took some of the broken rock from the tomb of the risen Christ, as a kind of evidence for the resurrection. They broke it into pieces and used it as the lots cast for the twelfth Apostle, Matthias."

Morgan said, "OK, so far that could fit with the book of Acts."

Jake pointed at the screen.

"The story goes on to say that the Apostles carved the pieces of rock into amulets to wear around their necks as a symbol of their brotherhood."

Morgan leant forward now, engaged with the story and the images that spoke to her of her own life obsession with religion and myth. Could it be possible that she wore a stone with such history?

"There's no extant tradition I know of this myth but I could imagine such a thing happening. The symbolism of the stone is pervasive in Christian myth, like Peter, the rock upon which the Church is built. Yes, I see. Carry on."

The picture on the screen changed to a fiery tornado, an image of wind and fury, fire streaming out in bursts as it whirled. Jake continued. "The myth goes on to say that the power of the stones comes from the occasion of Pentecost, when the spirit of God touched the Apostles and gave them the power of healing, speaking in multiple tongues and the ability to convert many to their cause. It's said that the force of wind and fire, combined with the power of Christ's resurrection, became embedded in the stones themselves. When the disciples died or were martyred the stones were hidden and passed down through a network of Keepers, who kept the Pentecostal flame alive through millennia."

"Kind of like the Christian faith of each man of God contained within a talisman of sorts?" Morgan said.

"Yes," Jake replied. "Over time, the stones became imbued with a mythic status and miracles were said to be performed when they were present. There were healings and mass conversions as well as the power of communication through strange tongues. The Keepers who wore them also found themselves possessed of a creativity so extreme that it was considered a God-given power."

"So why aren't these stones more well known?" Morgan asked.

"When the twelve left Jerusalem, they never met again, but took the gospel to the people and died at the far corners of the known world. Because of their latent power, the stones were kept secret, protected as holy relics and known only to a few Keepers in each lifetime."

"But the biblical traditions vary when it comes to where the Apostles actually went," Morgan argued. "Many of the Apostles just disappeared into history. How do you know where the stones ended up and who the Keepers are now, after so long?"

The screen changed to a map of the ancient world, with markers of different colors scattered across the near east, into north Africa, India and Europe. Morgan recognized it as similar to the one Fry had shown her.

"Exactly," Jake said. "These pins represent the possible journeys of the twelve Apostles after Pentecost, where the stones may have ended up after they died. But it's not known where they all are now or who the Keepers are, if indeed they still exist."

"So how did you get your stone?"

"The ARKANE Institute holds this one, supposedly from the disciple Matthew Levi but I'm wearing it so that you would trust me enough to come with us. It was given to us by the Keeper in Athens before the Second World War. He also told us what he knew of this scattered brotherhood and how the stones had become lost over the millennia. He was worried that the Nazis would seek the power in the stones and wanted it more securely hidden."

"So why the sudden interest in the stones now? Why the men in my office tonight?"

Jake signaled to the man at the laptop. The screen changed again to display an image of Earth, with a circling comet in a wide elliptical orbit.

"This is the Resurgam comet."

"Isn't that Latin for resurrection?" Morgan asked.

Jake nodded. "This comet is in a long orbit pattern around Earth. It's calculated to return into the atmosphere in the next two weeks, triggering a series of stratospheric events. Scientists are already predicting it will cause extreme weather patterns in many parts of the world."

"How is this related to the stones?"

Jake turned towards her, his eyes deep with concern. Morgan could see that something disturbed him deeply about this situation. "The comet was last in orbit in 33 AD."

"When Jesus rose from the dead," she marveled.

"And when the stones were empowered at Pentecost," he finished for her.

"You're sure of this?" Morgan asked.

"The comet is definitely coming and it explains the sudden interest in the stones. We believe that they're being sought by a fringe religious organization that aims to use them to invoke the powers of Pentecost again, perhaps to trigger a fundamentalist uprising. The return of the comet could be seen as a catalyst for the power of the twelve."

"But that's crazy. These are just pieces of rock, even if they are two thousand years old. They can't have any special power."

"You might be wrong about that." Jake turned and flicked open a file on the screen in front of them. It was an article from the Times of India dated only a few weeks before. The image of flames leapt out with a headline proclaiming miracles in the midst of a fiery storm. Morgan scanned the article quickly.

"Varanasi ... that could be the stone of Nathaniel."

"The ARKANE researchers agree with you. The Apostle Nathaniel, also known as Bartholomew, supposedly died in India after taking the gospel there. A Christian nun disappeared on the night of the miracles and may have been murdered. We believe she was a Keeper."

"But who took the stone?"

"We don't know yet, but a body was also found in Jerusalem at the church of St Matthias. He preached in Ethiopia but was killed in the holy city. Two mysteries relating to the Apostles along with the reported miracles was enough to get ARKANE interested enough to do some more research. Do you know why your father gave you and Faye the stones?"

Morgan stood up, rubbing her neck again to release the strain she felt both physically and emotionally in talking of her family.

"It's complicated," she said. "My parents were archaeologists, passionate about their work. They met on a dig in Turkey and fell in love amongst the ruins of Ephesus."

Jake smiled and waited for her to continue. "Apparently these two stones were found in a commoner's grave and considered of little value, so they kept them. Faye and I were conceived there, so the twin stones had an emotional value."

"What happened to your parents?"

Morgan hesitated. The truth of what happened long ago was a story repeated in so many broken marriages, yet it had meant her life was never normal.

"They couldn't hold a relationship together away from the dig, especially as their careers generated professional rivalry. My father hated the British weather and my mother just wanted peace, so they separated. My father took me to Israel and Faye stayed here. I don't remember us ever being a family."

"So the stones were separated and handed down to you both?" Jake questioned.

"Yes, my father gave me mine when I turned 21. I know he regretted the past but he just wasn't able to compromise. By the time I came back to England after he was killed, my mother had succumbed to breast cancer. I know she wore her stone until the end and now Faye wears it in her memory."

"That's a sad story," Jake said. Morgan shook her head.

"I think it's probably the story of many relationships. I had a happy life with my father in Israel. Now I'm trying to get to know my sister and niece." She looked at her watch. "Talking of them, have you heard back from the men sent to protect them?"

Woodstock. Near Oxford, England.
May 18, 10.47pm

From his study, David suddenly heard Faye's voice raised, a scream cut off quickly and a scuffle from the kitchen. He leapt up, grabbing the nearest thing at hand, a poker from the fireplace that hadn't been moved from last winter. He was a big man, having played rugby for years and still muscular. Striding into the kitchen, he saw Faye slumped on the floor and a man in black talking into a radio.

"Faye!" He ran towards her, raising the poker to hit her attacker. As he moved past the door of the kitchen he felt a powerful shock in the middle of his back and excruciating pain spread through his body. He fell to the ground, grunting as he lost control of his limbs and his bladder. Another man leant down over him, grimacing at the stink of urine.

"We've got at least ten minutes before he can move. Let's get the girl."

David lay there, his ears ringing, agony flooding his senses. In that moment, he cried out to God to save his family. He wanted to scream 'take me, not them' but he could only lie there, body jerking in his own piss, witnessing the abduction. The man holding Faye had taped her mouth even though she remained unconscious. He hoisted her over his shoulder and took her out into the night. David heard footsteps come down the stairs and then the other man walked past him, carrying his two year old daughter, Gemma, who was also, thankfully, unconscious. David moaned, an animal sound of desperation. The man turned and said, "Bye bye Daddy" in a falsetto voice. He waved Gemma's little hand at her father and tears welled in David's eyes as they left him there alone.

Pitt Rivers Museum, Oxford, England.
May 18, 10.50pm

A radio hissed, turning Morgan's attention from the screen. The man at the computer looked over to Jake.

"Sir, you need to see this."

Jake stepped over to the man's side as the radio crackled into life. The voice was desperate.

"Man down, man down. We're under attack. I repeat, we're under attack. Man down. Calling for backup, all units."

Morgan felt a chill of fear as she heard the chaos on the radio.

"What is it, what's happening?" she asked, her heart hammering in her chest. She should have gone straight there.

Jake turned, his eyes serious.

"It's Faye's house. They must have come for her already. I'm so sorry, my men didn't get there in time."

Morgan stared at the tiny computer screen. It showed her sister's house, but instead of the quiet scene of the little village, there were men everywhere. She tuned out the sounds of screaming and gunfire, watching in horror as she saw a man running out of the door with the body of her sister slung over his shoulder. Behind him ran a man carrying a small bundle that could only be Gemma. They had taken her family.

CHAPTER 4

Woodstock. Near Oxford, England.
May 18, 11.35pm

THE ARKANE TEAM ARRIVED at the house twenty minutes later, Morgan with them. She had spent the journey staring out at the landscape, unseeing, fear snaking in her gut. Police were thronging about the house. Jake showed his badge to the officer in charge and they were waved through. Morgan ran into the house ahead of Jake. This was her sister's haven, a peaceful retreat from the busy city life. Faye had cultivated it out here in Woodstock, far enough away for them to have chickens and fields to stride through with the dogs but close enough to have coffee in Oxford when the sisters had time to catch up. Anger simmered inside Morgan at the people who dared invade their home. This is quiet sleepy Oxfordshire, she thought. This type of thing happened in Israel but not here. Had she brought this terror to them?

David was sitting on the sofa in the lounge surrounded by scattered toys and upended furniture. He stared into a mug of tea as a medic examined him, a blanket over his shuddering shoulders. One of the policemen said to Jake in a low voice,

"They tazered him. He saw the whole thing so he's pretty

shaken up."

Morgan knelt in front of him, and spoke in a soft tone, "I'm going to get them back, David. I promise."

He looked at her with glazed eyes, shock rendering him barely capable of speech. Morgan reached out to him and then pulled back. There was too much history for this not to be awkward. Her guilt over what had come between them made her even more determined to solve this. David hunched over his mug, tea cold at the bottom. It said 'best Dad in the world' and was decorated with baby Gemma hand-prints. He looked at her, his voice breaking with emotion.

"They're everything to me, Morgan. Who would want to kidnap them anyway? We don't have much money."

He lent across and touched her hand. Morgan had a sudden flashback of that one night and she jolted away from him. Her guilt grew stronger as she remembered the promise she had made that night never to hurt her sister, to protect her and keep David pristine in her eyes. Morgan had felt helpless then, adrift on what had happened with her sister's husband and how he made her feel. Now David was the helpless one, unable to do anything to rescue his wife or daughter.

"She's not dead, Morgan," Jake said from the doorway, beckoning her into the kitchen so they could talk away from David. "There's no body and no demand yet, but no doubt it will come. They clearly want to use your sister as a bargaining chip for your stone and perhaps ours as well, so for now, they'll keep Faye and Gemma alive because they want all the stones."

Morgan sat down at the kitchen table, head in her hands. She was suddenly overwhelmed as the situation seemed out of her control. She should have been there and it was Jake who had stopped her. She looked straight up at him, her voice rising in anger.

"Who are these people anyway? You've told me about

the stones but who are this group who are murdering and kidnapping to collect them in one place? You know, I'd happily trade my stone for their lives. You don't even need to be involved."

Jake shook his head.

"You don't understand Morgan. This thing is bigger than just you and Faye now. You saw the paper from India and the potential of the stones. We can't allow them to be gathered together, especially with the Resurgam comet approaching."

"People will say anything. Varanasi could have been mass hysteria, you know that."

"But what if it wasn't? What if the stories of power and the comet event are true? Imagine the force of the stones demonstrated in a digital age, the phenomenal ability the holder would have to make people follow him, maybe even to start a holy war. ARKANE's job is to shield the world from such events, we hold the supernatural secrets that the world isn't ready to see yet. We can protect you and we can find Faye and Gemma, just give us some time."

Morgan laughed then, a bark of indignation.

"So much for your all powerful organization, Jake. You couldn't even protect one woman and a child in an Oxford village. This group know our names, they are informed about you but you don't know anything. I'm doing this alone. I don't need you. I'll take your stone with mine and I'll get my sister back."

Morgan stood up and strode out of the kitchen, running upstairs to gather her thoughts. She pushed open the door to Faye and David's room. Like her, Faye always wore the stone around her neck so it would have been on her at the time they attacked. The bedclothes were rumpled. There was a thick romance novel on the side cabinet by the bed, next to a well thumbed Bible. Morgan went to the antique dressing table and felt around the back of the pine framed oval mirror. This had been their agreed upon hiding place if anything bad ever happened. Faye had laughed when Morgan had suggested it over a year ago. She had said there was no need for such a thing, that England wasn't Israel and Morgan was just paranoid. Now they needed it, but there were no messages. Faye had not known what was coming.

Morgan sat on the bed and stared at the photo of the two of them that stood on the dressing table in an art deco frame. Their faces were similar in bone structure, but apart from that the twins were light and dark opposites. Morgan had inherited their father's Sephardic Jewish looks, the ebony hair and dusky skin from his Spanish descent. Faye had a Celtic look from their Welsh mother, blonde hair and fair skin with a sprinkling of freckles she tried unsuccessfully to hide. Only their eyes gave their kinship away. Both were blue with an unusual violet slash through them, Morgan's in the right and Faye's in the left. Their parent's personalities were equally separate in the twins; her own passionate, explosive nature and Faye's cool, calm demeanor were diametrically opposed. Their parents couldn't overcome these differences, but perhaps the sisters could succeed where they failed. Morgan traced Faye's face on the picture with a fingertip, willing strength to her sister who had helped her start again after Elian's death. Everywhere she walked in Jerusalem there had been memories of him, but here in England his ghost was silent. Here she could could reinvent herself as an academic, a sister and an auntie. Morgan knew she would give everything to bring Faye and Gemma home again. Then the guilt came flooding back and she put her head in her hands.

Morgan thought back to the night with David, wincing at the memory, but she deserved the mental anguish. It had been alcohol induced, pure and simple, but that didn't justify the mistake. Morgan had only recently moved to Oxford and Faye had gone away for a weekend before the baby was born. The sisters had not yet found a rhythm in their relationship. They were still circling each other, questions unasked and history still buried beneath their parents' skewed remembrances. Morgan knew, if she was honest with herself, that it was partly jealousy that drove her that night. Faye seemed to have domestic bliss, a haven of peace in comparison to her own life of upheaval. She had lost Elian and she was lonely, desperate for a friend and the touch of a man. It had been too long.

David had called into her office that Friday evening to see if she wanted to have dinner. She had started to spend Friday nights with him and Faye in an attempt at friendship and she knew few other people in Oxford then. They had gone to Browns for mussels and ended up drinking a couple of bottles of wine. They had debated religion and psychology, Jung, Freud and the Bible. Morgan found that she could often out-quote David, having studied so diligently, even though he was supposedly the learned Christian pastor. They had laughed a lot and it had been the most fun she'd had in a long time. He had walked her home to her Jericho flat and come inside for another drink.

As she reached for wine glasses in the kitchen, he had kissed the back of her neck. She had wanted him, and thoughts of Faye were furthest from her mind. She pushed back against his hard body, then spun in his embrace.

The kiss deepened and Morgan had teetered on the precipice of what could be. Faye would never know, after all. It would only be one night.

But then she had glanced up at the mantelpiece and seen a picture of the three of them, laughing at the Mansfield College summer tea party. They held champagne flutes and Faye wore a cherry red hat. The sun reflected off her own hair, loose about her shoulders. They looked like twins in the photo and in that moment, shame had washed over her.

She pushed David away.

Nothing was worth jeopardizing the nascent shoots of her renewed relationship with her sister.

Morgan had pulled away from David. They both wanted more but but they both knew this could never happen again. Faye was his wife and her twin. He was a pastor.

What they had contemplated was a sin even if you didn't believe in God.

When Faye returned, they acted as if nothing had happened and never mentioned it again, maintaining a certain distance. Since then, she and Faye had finally found the relationship that twins were supposed to have. They finished each other's sentences and picked up the phone just as the other called. Morgan was Gemma's devoted Auntie, who the little girl called for when she was sick, who brought her surprise presents. They were her family and Faye and Gemma were all that mattered to Morgan now. She walked into Gemma's room and saw the little girl's favorite teddy discarded on the floor. Tears pricked her eyes. She picked it up and hugged it to her, saying under her breath, "I'm coming, Gemma."

Feeling eyes on her back, she spun to see Jake in the doorway. "We can help each other, Morgan. We're working for the same outcome, the safe return of Faye and Gemma, and the retrieval of the stones."

Morgan held the teddy tightly in front of her like a shield.

"I don't think you care about them at all," she snapped. "For all I know, ARKANE want the stones for the Institute to study and you would have taken mine and Faye's anyway."

"Who would you believe, then, the man who has your sister and your niece, or me?"

In the moment's silence that fell between them, a voice called from downstairs,

"Sir, you should come and see this. We've found a package."

The parcel was wrapped in thick brown paper and tied up with string like an old style present, 'Morgan' written in black marker on the front. As Jake and David watched, Morgan untied the string and pulled apart the paper to reveal a number of items packed neatly within the paper square. There were two black Moleskine notebooks, a DVD and a cell phone. No note. Jake put the disc into David's laptop. It had one video file which they played immediately.

At first the image showed a flickering fire burning in a hearth and a close up of the fiery embers. They could hear the crackle of flame. Then a voice spoke, an American southern accent that lazily grated over them.

"Morgan, apologies for the intrusion but taking your sister and the little one was a necessary step. Time is running out. The myth of the stones will become a reality on the day of Pentecost when the comet reaches its zenith and I will call down the power of miracle. As it was two thousand years ago, so it shall be again. I'm inviting you to be my guest for the event. Of course, you'll need to bring the other stones, otherwise your sister and niece will become a fiery sacrifice just like the Keepers from Varanasi and Jerusalem."

The image flickered and changed to show two burnt bodies in gruesome detail. It looked like they had been filmed soon after their deaths, one still smoking, wet flesh hanging from the bones. David turned away, retching.

"I need all twelve of the stones for the day of Pentecost and you will bring the rest to me, Morgan, if you want your family back. I tried to recruit you but your refusal has forced my hand. It seems that another party is also interested in the stones, so you will need to stay ahead of them."

The screen changed again to display the image of a pale horse's head. Morgan recognized the tattoo from the attacker's arm but only now did its significance become clear.

"Before me was a pale horse," she whispered. "Its rider was named Death and Hell was following close behind him. It's from Revelation."

The voice continued.

"I know this group only as Thanatos. They approached me about the stones after Varanasi and now it seems they're following the same path. They are known to be collectors of occult and religious objects and they will stop at nothing to get the Apostles' stones. But you must stay ahead of them on this quest if you want your girls back."

Morgan could see Jake frowning, as if he knew of the organization and it troubled him.

"I found the first two stones from my Father's research. He was a biblical scholar and had been seeking the stones before he died. I continued the search but there are vital pieces missing. It needs someone with more knowledge and more ... motivation to find the rest of them for me. In the package you'll find information to start you off in the right direction. Your background in religion is fortuitous, Morgan. I've given you my father's key notebooks as you have the knowledge to go further than he could. See how generous I am already? Leave the husband out of it though; his emotion will slow you down."

At this, David sagged as if the breath had been knocked out of him.

"I want the rest of the stones here for Pentecost Sunday, May 27th. You'd better hurry. Only nine days' time and a lot of travel ahead of you. Keep the cell phone on you and I'll contact you with where to bring the stones. You'll have the help of ARKANE, and of course if you want your family alive, then you will do this. If not, I'll continue to experiment with the effects of fire on human flesh. Tick tock Morgan."

The screen changed back to the smoldering bodies and then went blank.

"Bastard!" Morgan said, slamming her hand down on the desk. She looked at Jake.

"It's Everett, the American academic. ARKANE must be able to trace his whereabouts."

Jake nodded, pulling out his cellphone. "We'll get started on it."

David gripped the back of the office chair, knuckles white, his voice low but insistent.

"But you have to do what he says, Morgan. You can't risk their lives. You have to bring them home."

"Of course. I'll do whatever it takes. We'll find them."

David turned and walked from the room, shoulders hunched. Morgan whirled round to face Jake.

"I will rescue my sister, but why does he want ARKANE involved? Did you send him to me? Are you working with him somehow?"

"Of course not. I'm sure he was already coming for you. No doubt you'll find your parents mentioned in these books. They didn't know to keep the stones secret."

Morgan looked puzzled.

"Is that how ARKANE found us as well?"

"Yes, after Varanasi our research uncovered the dig report of the stones which was linked to your parents. Unfortunately we were just behind the Thanatos team."

Morgan felt lost, as if she was whirling in a maelstrom of fear and guilt. Faye and Gemma were her only surviving family so whatever it took, she would get them back but she also felt the first tendrils of intrigue as she considered the possibilities of the stones. She picked up one of the Moleskine journals, flicking through the first few pages. There were notes and diagrams in spidery handwriting. One of the initial pages showed a map of Europe and the Near East with red dots and lines drawn on it. Jake looked over her shoulder.

"That looks similar to the ARKANE map of where the Apostles went and where the stones might be, so it looks like you need some resources to back you up if you want to get the stones. We have contacts all over the world as well as facilities and transport so we can support you with whatever you need."

Morgan knew it was impossible to cover this amount of ground alone in the time she had. She saw the lifeline Jake offered, but she was still wary of him. ARKANE was an unknown entity. Protecting secrets was one way to see them, but perhaps their motives could also be darker.

"I'm thinking about it," she said. "Did you find out which Apostles our stones belonged to? I need to narrow down the places to look for the others."

"We think you have the stone of the Apostle John, the author of Revelation, and Faye has the stone of James Alphaeus."

"That accounts for two of them and ARKANE's stone is from Matthew Levi." She paused, then asked, "How come ARKANE had one of the stones all this time but didn't collect the rest of them?"

"Do you know how many Christian relics there are in the world?" Jake questioned.

Morgan couldn't help but laugh, despite the dire situation. "Enough of the true cross to fell a forest of trees, enough nails to build a house with and enough sacred stone to fill a quarry. I see what you mean."

"Exactly. It was just another unsubstantiated myth. The stones weren't important until the miracles of Varanasi and the discovery of the Resurgam comet."

"And until my sister and niece were kidnapped."

Jake nodded.

"Of course, and I'm sorry it got this far. But if you don't let us help you, there's no way you can fulfill his demands, certainly not in time for Pentecost. It's only nine days away."

"What does ARKANE have at stake here?" Morgan said, the notebook open in her hand.

"These are the kind of secrets ARKANE keeps. Whether

they have any real power or not, the stones are powerful talismans and they need to be protected. At least your sister is safe until Pentecost, so we have until then to try and figure this out."

Morgan hesitated. She was used to doing things her way, but looking at the rough map in the journal and knowing she had only a short amount of time to find Faye and Gemma, she knew she needed help. Pride would not stop her from rescuing them. She nodded.

"OK, we can work together on this and come to some agreement about the stones as we go. At least it buys me some time."

"I know it's not ideal but with your religious knowledge and ARKANE's research and resources we'll get the stones and your family back. I'll have the team work overnight on digitizing and cross-checking the diaries against our own research on the Apostles. Tomorrow we'll get started. Meanwhile, you need some rest."

Jake held out his hand. After a slight hesitation, she shook it, nodding her assent.

As soon as Morgan had left the Woodstock house, Jake went outside and dialed the ARKANE Director, Elias Marietti, on a secure line.

"I've convinced her that she needs us, Sir. I won't be able to get her stone right away, but I think she can lead us to the others. The team is being mobilized right now … You were right about Thanatos being after them … Yes, the sister will give hers up, I'll make sure of that … Thank you, Sir. I'll be there in the morning."

Hanging up, Jake looked back into the windows of the house. He could see David with his head in his hands, shoulders heaving in one of the upstairs rooms. It must be the little girl's room. Jake turned away. This wasn't the time to be sentimental. Collateral damage was inevitable, even in a purely religious war.

CHAPTER 5

Private airstrip, Surrey, England.
May 19, 5.34am

FAYE WOKE AS THE early morning light filtered through a tiny window and seeped under the doorframe. She raised her head tentatively and explosive pain made her head swim. She breathed in and out slowly through her nose as the nausea passed, her mouth still covered by a rolled cloth tied behind her head. Her first lucid thought was for Gemma, her baby. Where was she? Was she OK? Then she saw the tiny bundle curled up near the foot of the chair she was bound to. Gemma wasn't even tied up. They must have known she wouldn't leave her mother once she revived from the drugs. The little girl's face looked pale and creased but she was breathing normally and didn't seem to be injured. Faye desperately wanted to take her in her arms, hold her close, but she couldn't move.

She took a mental inventory of her own body, checking for injury and pain. Her legs were tied to the chair, her arms behind her back, but the drugs were wearing off and it seemed she was bruised but more or less uninjured. She thought back to the night before. She had been listening to a talk show and didn't hear them come in. A feeling of being watched had made her turn suddenly, but then she had been grabbed and pushed to the floor, a needle jabbed in her neck. She had only managed to briefly scream before she lost consciousness. Her thoughts flashed to David and she prayed that he was OK, that they hadn't hurt him. They had said nothing about what they wanted before they attacked. What could she possibly have that they would kidnap for? She began to pray silently. God would protect them through whatever trials they would face, but they needed to escape from here somehow.

Faye craned her neck to look around the small room. It was a large storage closet with high ceilings and a tiny window near the roof. The walls were metal, like a warehouse. Shelves stretched above them containing all sorts of tools. Maybe they could be used as weapons? If only she could get to them. Gemma whimpered and her eyes fluttered open. She looked around groggily, then faded back into sleep. Faye was grateful that she was sleeping, unaware of her surroundings. Perhaps this would just be a bad dream for her, one that would be over soon because it had to be a mistake.

Outside she could hear the roar of planes taking off, so they must be at an airport. Faye realized that could mean they were being taken out of the country. This galvanized her resolve and she began pulling at the ties holding her hands and feet, wriggling in an attempt to get them loose. Raw skin began to bleed at her wrists. Tears pricked her eyes. Her frustration rose as she realized she was tied too tightly.

The door slammed open.

"Awake, are you?" a man said from the doorway, a cup of steaming coffee in his hand, the smell making her realize she was hungry and thirsty. He was stocky and unshaven, his eyes baggy from a night without sleep. Faye could see past him into a hangar where a number of small planes were parked. There were two other men standing there, looking with interest in her direction. They made no attempt to hide their identities. She looked away, refusing to acknowledge them. He stepped over to her, chuckling.

"I don't think you'll be ignoring me for too long."

He was stroking her cheek now, his voice low. Putting his coffee down, he held her face towards him with one hand, and slowly ran a finger down her neck and onto her breast, watching her tears as he cupped it, then squeezed hard, making her wince.

"I think you'll be a good girl for me, otherwise your daughter might be next."

He let her go, laughing. He swung his leg right back as if to kick the little bundle of Gemma at her feet. Faye used all her effort to lunge forward in the chair towards her child, to protect her from this monster but she only managed to topple sideways onto the floor, smacking her head. The man laughed again and she heard the amusement of the other men outside the door, a camaraderie of humiliation.

He bent down to pull her up but his attention was distracted by his mobile phone ringing. He left her on the floor, answering it as he pulled the door almost shut behind him. She could still hear his words through the crack.

"Yeah, they're OK, the plane is due to take off in two hours. We'll be with you tomorrow, boss. No problems this end."

Faye realized then that there was no mistake; somehow they were the target of a kidnapping. She still didn't know why, but her thoughts went to Morgan, the sister who kept so much hidden of her past. David would only know to call the police and leave it to them, but she knew Morgan would act. She was incapable of staying still, of leaving it to other people. Faye thought of her as a caged animal that Oxford was trying to groom into something they recognized as a domestic academic. But Morgan was indefinable and couldn't be put into any box. Faye knew she would do anything for Gemma; the little girl represented hope that their family could start again, build another life around the future instead of the past.

Faye tried to shift, her body arching into painful spasms by the position she had fallen in. Gemma stirred and looked at her, still on the edge of consciousness. Faye smiled with her eyes and made soft loving noises to calm her. The little girl crawled closer and cuddled into Faye. Knowing they were both alive for now was enough, so Faye prayed into the beginning of a new day. For the strength to protect her daughter, and for the sister who would come for them.

Not long afterwards, one of the men came back, and although Faye struggled, he drugged them again. Their limp bodies were wrapped and loaded onto a cargo plane, hidden behind boxes of sports shoes and equipment. The plane took off over London heading for America, land of opportunity.

CHAPTER 6

Tucson, Arizona, USA.
May 19, 9.17am

JOSEPH EVERETT WALKED INTO St Bartholomew's
private psychiatric hospital where his twin brother, Michael,
had lived for the past fifteen years. He came to the hospital
at least every two days when he was not away on business,
and sometimes twice a day if Michael was in a bad way. The
hospital was a pleasant sterile façade laid over a maelstrom
of human misery. Jolly wall paintings belied the mental pain
behind every door. The warden at the front desk acknowledged him but said nothing as he passed. Staff here knew
of his frequent visits. Joseph left his keys and other sharp
objects at the security gate and proceeded through the main
corridors to the day room, pushing open the double doors.
He was grimly content as he considered the plan he had put
in place and how soon victory would come now that he had
leverage.

Joseph experienced the hospital as a toxic soup of fear,
confusion and jangled noise hidden beneath the drugs and
behavior modification necessary to maintain a superficial
calm. But it was the best hospital in Arizona, so he had no
choice but to keep Michael here. The staff were babysitters
to disturbed individuals who dwelt on the edges of what is

called sanity, though Joseph personally doubted that anyone was really sane all the time. He knew that people moved along a continuum of normality in many dimensions. Some days we could all be committed, he thought, with a glance at himself reflected in a bay window.

Joseph found Michael in the same seat he was always placed in. Every day he woke and the nurses took him to a window seat in the day room. He would sit all day, legs hugged to his chest, staring out at the world. He never looked at his brother, never seemed to hear any words spoken to him, yet he was placid and would take his meds, lie down when told and sleep. He was just empty, a shell of a person. Joseph touched him sometimes, smoothing the hair from his brother's forehead, but there was never any response. They were twins of a sickly opposite. Both were lean, but Joseph's muscles were well defined, he walked tall and strong. Michael was wasted and weak with cheekbones that stuck out through his pale skin and lips tinged with blue. Joseph spoke with vigor and moved with grace but his brother was silent and gaunt, folded into his space and staring into another world.

"How is he today?" Joseph spoke to the nurse on duty in the day room. They went through this ritual every time, and her reply never changed. But today she started at his approach.

"I need to get the doctor to speak to you, sir."

She went out of the room and returned with Dr Campbell. He looked serious and held a thick folder. He indicated a private room where they could talk. Joseph felt sweat prickle under his arms. The men remained standing.

"Mr Everett, we need to discuss how to best manage the next steps for Michael."

"Why? What's changed?"

"Nothing's changed. That's the point. He's been wasting away for months now, and he's getting too thin and sick for the main facility here. We have to move him to the intensive care ward, and soon he'll need intravenous feeding."

Joseph shook his head emphatically.

"No. He's fine here. He's going to get better, I know it."

Dr Campbell opened the file and pointed at the latest test results.

"It's all here. You have to face facts. We can make his body comfortable and keep him alive, but he is reaching a threshold. He will become catatonic soon."

Joseph's eyes were wide, his nostrils flaring in anger.

"How dare you. I've given the hospital millions in gifts. There must be more you can do for him."

The Doctor shook his head.

"I'm sorry. On my orders, he'll be transferred next week to the special ward and then there's a process to transfer him to the hospice when it becomes appropriate. The end is coming, Joseph. You have been the best and most devoted of brothers, but you can't do anything else now but help him die with dignity."

The doctor stretched out his hand to say goodbye. It wasn't acknowledged so the Doctor left the room. Joseph looked down at the patterns on the carpet, the inoffensive grey and pink swirls designed to mute the sounds of suffering this room witnessed every day. He pushed his fist against his temple as if to crush the negative thoughts. There was still one chance, but he couldn't tell the doctor that. Pentecost was not far away and with the power of the stones, he could still save his brother from this wasting death. Varanasi had demonstrated that miracles could flow from the power of the stones, now he just had to understand how to harness them. Joseph stood and pulled his Armani suit jacket straighter around him. Setting his shoulders square and his face to a mask, he went back to the main ward to see his brother.

Joseph pulled up a chair next to Michael and began to talk to him in a regular ritual he had performed for years.

Sometimes he reminisced about their childhood, but generally he talked about what was on his mind, another day in the life of a rich businessman, politician and pillar of the community in Tucson, Arizona. There were the usual immigration issues, the attempts to jump-start the housing market and protestors outside his office concerned about water in the desert region. He had posed as an academic, a researcher, to get close to Morgan Sierra, but academia was far from his real life.

Michael had become a diary of sorts, a soul into which he poured his own heart so that when he left, he felt lighter, emptier. It didn't matter that the words seemed to wash over his brother, who never spoke or even moved. Joseph was devoted to his brother; anyone at the facility would say he was the most caring and regular visitor to the ward. Michael did not want for anything, but then he didn't require much. He was fed the best food and had access to top of the line medications and psychiatrists, but it seemed that nothing could be done to make him better. Today Joseph leaned in close so the nurses couldn't overhear him and spoke quietly.

"I'm going to take you on a trip soon Michael. I've found a way to help you, I just need a little more time. But don't worry, it won't be long now."

He gently stroked his brother's thin hair and looked out into the garden where each twin saw worlds that no one else was aware of.

Joseph never stayed long at the hospital and was soon on the road again in his SUV, heading back to his home office. Working from his house in The Foothills outside Tucson allowed him the privacy he needed for his businesses and other projects. He had people who managed his offices in town and he had cleared his schedule for the next few weeks in order to focus on Pentecost. He felt some anxiety as there were too many variables right now and the situation was not entirely under his control. He was worried about the Thanatos group who were also pursuing the stones. Their evident determination, superior resources and firepower meant he had to bring ARKANE and the academic Morgan Sierra into the mix. He had been loath to do it but the frankly unexpected miracles of Varanasi meant he could no longer keep the quest secret from those who watched such events. He didn't know much about Thanatos except that they would go after the stones whatever the cost. He expected them to follow Morgan's trail first, but they would be after him eventually. He grinned then, his perfect orthodontic teeth flashing in the sun. He would release the power of the stones at Pentecost when the comet was closest to earth and he didn't care if they took them after that, as long as Michael was healed first.

As he drove, Joseph thought about what had brought him to this moment, how the past had shaped this quest and transformed his brother into a living ghost. The twins had been late additions to a miserable marriage and the target of their mother's fury with the world. Their father had been mostly absent, consumed with his research and the acquisition of knowledge and he cared nothing for raising children. They didn't know what he did with his time, only that when he was at the house, he shut himself away in his study. He often travelled, bringing back strange objects he kept locked away from their prying eyes and sticky hands. The twins were hardly seen and definitely not heard; their mother made sure of that for she was the one who roamed their nightmares. When they were young, she had made them wash all the time, calling them dirty and filthy. She made them scrub with pumice stones until their young skin was raw, chapped and bleeding, even on their private parts. They were stains she wanted to erase from her crumbling world.

Michael was the older twin by minutes and played the protective role, deflecting their mother's attention from Joseph. For this, she would beat him with sharp metal tools from the kitchen then shut them both under the stairs in the dark. Michael would hold Joseph until his terrified sobbing stopped. He often slept in his brother's arms there for there was safety was in being together. Apart they would die, but together they were strong. Perhaps I still believe that, thought Joseph.

They had growth spurts in their early teens and Joseph started to become more resilient and able to fend for himself. At 13, Michael had stopped speaking, communicating only with his hands or writing on scraps of paper. Joseph found he could understand his brother just as well, they had a kind of sign language but it was the control over his own body that their mother couldn't bear. In a rage, she had held Michael's hand onto the hob of the cooker to make him scream. He hadn't made a sound and she only stopped when the stench of burning flesh brought Joseph running to help.

At 15, Michael tried to cut off his penis with a knife in the kitchen in front of their mother. She had laughed and urged him on. Joseph had wrested the knife away from his brother but the cut was deep. As he bled, she had just stood there watching as if she would finish the job herself. Joseph called 911 then and told them everything. Social services had taken them away. Michael entered his first psych ward, and never emerged, his condition worsening every year. As Joseph had grown into a wealthy businessman, he had moved Michael into better facilities and always stayed close to the ward so he could visit all the time. Despite his riches, he sometimes felt he was still trapped in that closet with his brother. He needed Michael.

Shaking his head to clear the memories, Joseph turned

into the drive of his property, the gates swinging open silently at the touch of the remote. He drove into the underground car park and pulled in next to the other two cars, his own Bugatti Veyron and his wife's BMW Z4. This meant that she was home, but she would keep to her wing of the house. Joseph had charmed and married the Arizona socialite early in his business career, tempting her with his extravagant lifestyle in order to fulfill the public role demanded of him. He gave her everything she thought she wanted in return for her discretion, her presence at official functions and his privacy. She had learned early on not to ask any more of him, having spent a week in hospital for her audacity. The scars from the beating had marked her, but he had been careful to ensure she could still wear low-cut dresses and short skirts. It was important to maintain a good image at the many community functions they attended. He gave a great deal to the charities and projects of the state, his public life one of power, money and charitable giving. Yet Joseph's smile was ultimately a mask over the demons of his private life.

Getting out of the car, he walked through the house to the large open plan study that was his real home within the grand property. It adjoined a sparse private bedroom and tiny kitchenette separated from the rest of the house. Joseph even cleaned it himself, keeping it off limits from everyone. It was landscaped into the hillside of the property, camouflaged by the mesquite and juniper trees. When the couple held business receptions at the house, no one even knew it was there. Unlocking the door with the digital keypad, Joseph stepped inside and checked the security camera for intrusions. Nothing. He hung up his jacket and grabbed a diet soda. Pulling another of his father's diaries from the shelf, he began to read.

CHAPTER 7

ARKANE Headquarters. London, England.
May 19, 9.15am

JAKE TIMBER WALKED THE short distance from Embankment tube station to one of the hidden entrances of ARKANE. It was a nondescript doorway on Duncannon Street next to the Halfway to Heaven pub, a surprisingly appropriate name given what lay beneath. Camouflaged behind famous sculptures and carefully painted, the location of the various entrances was known to only a few. Most visitors would approach the official offices of the ARKANE Institute at the corner of the Strand and St Martin's Place where there were several floors on the top levels of the building and a semblance of diligent research was demonstrated. The windows could be seen from Trafalgar Square, flanked by Corinthian columns with a balcony topped by a flagpole, the Union Jack flying proudly in the breeze. A second tier of columns sat on the sixth level up from the ground, and it was here the Director of the Institute had his office suite. The public face of ARKANE had to be somewhere appropriate and imposing, but Jake knew it was a smokescreen for what really went on here.

He remembered when Marietti had first introduced him to the place and explained the history. Started as a purely

Christian defense, the Arcane Religious Knowledge And Numinous Experience, or ARKANE, Institute had developed into the world's most advanced, secret research center for investigating supernatural mysteries across all religions. It had an official face which ran publications and seminars and had experts speak from around the world, but it also had this secret wing that only a few in the top echelons of government knew about. It was called in to investigate when events went beyond the physical, when the police or other agencies needed experts in this unusual field. Their remit was circumscribed by a secret Act of Parliament that meant ARKANE worked above the law of the lands they operated in, hidden by the shadows between what could be proved and that which no one would admit to. In a modern world where ancient faith was now beginning to play an increasingly political role, they were often behind the scenes at the crux of international flash-points.

ARKANE were also called in whenever there was a situation that could be called supernatural. The people who worked in the small teams across the globe understood that there are other entities loose in this world, not human, not alien. There is an evil that humans conjure and use against each other even as it stalks their souls. There are words of power that can be used as weapons and a host of unseen things that were better off being denied. Myths that have spanned millennia are based on strands of truth and sometimes the evidence was hidden down here, in the vaults under London that belonged to ARKANE.

Jake put his eye to the retinal scanner and entered his password into the secure keypad on the elevator entrance. He entered and the elevator descended to the main level of offices below the throngs of tourists heading to Piccadilly Circus. The ARKANE Headquarters was built underneath the crypt of St-Martin-in-the-Fields church and extended right under Trafalgar Square in the heart of London.

In its current form Trafalgar Square was designed and completed by Sir Charles Barry in 1845. Barry had been a supporter of ARKANE and included the building of its subterranean tunnels and rooms in his design. The rooms were plotted on maps, stored amongst archives that marked the stolen treasures of kings, and protected as secrets of the realm. With the square constantly watched by cameras and people always present, it was also a secure location for precious artifacts. There was even a tunnel leading straight to No. 10 Downing Street, the British Prime Minister's residence. In the days when he cared about religious affairs, it was often used for secret meetings and even as a way out away from the reporters permanently camped outside the office. But the entrance had been locked and sealed after the Second World War and now the Prime Minister was in the dark about the occult knowledge they sought and studied.

Jake walked along the central corridor towards the main research rooms, his thoughts preoccupied with questions about the stones. He was also disturbed about having to work with Morgan Sierra. He was used to working alone or with a team who did as he said, and he had certainly never had to factor in an unpredictable, if highly capable, outsider. In modern times, funded by handsome grants from secret sponsors and the sale of certain precious artifacts, ARKANE's underground base had been redesigned to be an ultra-modern workplace. Flat screens and laptops sat in all the rooms, centrally placed as the walls were covered with bookshelves. The physical library was spread across the whole place in this way, except for those books that needed special environments or were too precious to be on display. These were held in pressure and temperature controlled vaults but ARKANE was no longer just a fusty library of old books.

As Jake walked, he looked into the rooms through glass paneled doors. Various teams were working in each, some in lab coats testing strange devices and others, white gloved, poring over manuscripts. He was a field operative but most at the base were researchers, eagerly working down here with their secrets. There was no natural light in the underground section but the lighting had been subtly tuned so it was bright but not fluorescent. On some of the walls were intricate trompe l'oeil paintings, so detailed they looked real. Windows looked out onto the Mediterranean sea or the Pyramids, one was a gabled room view onto the Eiffel Tower, and another a glade with birds and flowers. The rooms had different scents and sounds, surf and sea-spray or birdsong with sage and lavender. Jake knew it had been designed for peak creativity, making the place feel more idyllic than a deep, dark cavern underground where enigmas lurked in corners.

Martin Klein's office was one of the tiniest rooms in the ARKANE layout but it was a rare privilege to have an office to himself. He was officially Head Librarian but was considered more like the Brain of the Institute. He was highly intelligent, perceiving patterns where others could see nothing. He created worlds on the walls of his office in colored markers, drawing fantastical creatures and plants, other-worldly scenes of beauty while he pondered the problems of the Institute. Every now and then, the whole office would be painted white and he would begin again on the fresh canvas. His mathematical and data processing ability was considered genius level, but he did not quite understand the subtleties of human interaction. His compulsions may have set him apart in the office, but his ability to figure out how disparate knowledge fitted together was phenomenal and had earned him the affectionate nickname, Spooky.

Jake knocked on the door of Martin's office, and made sure the young man was aware he was there before he spoke,

"Hey, Spooky, what you working on?"

Martin spun around in the desk chair and jumped up, bobbing towards Jake and then retreating back to his desk. He was a tall man with a shock of blond hair, too long for an academic. He couldn't bear to be touched by a barber, so he roughly chopped it himself with scissors now and then, when hunks of it began falling down over his eyes. His glasses had thin wire rims, the lightest he could stand to have on his skin.

"Jake, welcome back. What do you need?" he said briskly.

There was no small talk with Martin: he moved in a linear fashion across the face of the world, he needed a problem to solve and didn't waste time. Jake liked him and felt a kinship with his loner status. The other ARKANE workers didn't socialize much with Jake because he worked mainly outside the office, on secret missions for the Director, while they did the real research beneath the teeming city.

"It's about the stones of the Apostles and relates to that death in Varanasi you were looking at a few weeks back. I need to know what else you've found, and I'll need your backup from here while we try to retrieve the other stones."

Martin sat down at the desk again, tapped out a staccato rhythm on the keyboard and pointed out the data on four monitors arrayed in front of him.

"After Varanasi, I set the ARKANE search engine into gear on the stones and the Apostles to try and triangulate mentions of them in historical record and myth. These are just some of the results I'm compiling for you with the topography of the regions mentioned. It narrows down the potential search possibilities at least. I'll have it finished before you leave."

The search engine was powerful, unique to ARKANE and had been programmed by Martin himself as one of his first jobs when he was recruited from Cambridge with his Doctorate in Computer Science and Archaeology. Director

Marietti had charged him with making sense out of the chaos of data so he had built super character recognition scanners and software, tying texts to multiple translations. He triangulated ancient legends with online maps and images, enabling patterns to emerge from the riot of information. With access to scanned data from all the libraries in the world, his empire was a digital powerhouse of knowledge, untouchable and unfathomable by most people. He drove the system like a well-oiled machine, knowing when to coax and when to use heavy handed programming tactics to get the information he needed. He was always adding more linkages, more ways to find related data, and continuously improving the algorithms. Jake examined the screens, seeing how far the ancient missionaries had roamed in their sacred quest. They had indeed reached the ends of the known earth at the time and there were some new locations that weren't included in the notebooks they had been given.

"That's a great start. What about the location of Everett?"

"We have his house under surveillance in Arizona but there's no sign of Dr Sierra's family. He has a complicated system of shell companies which the forensic accountants are sifting through. It may be that he's holding them in a place owned by one of them. Marietti has ordered surveillance only though."

Jake understood the stones were the primary objective but he felt an edge of unease that ARKANE was less concerned with the lives of Faye and Gemma Price. Even if the location was found, he knew Marietti wouldn't authorize their rescue unless the stones had been taken out of circulation. They also needed the leverage to get Morgan Sierra to work with them. What did Marietti see in her?

"I need to find out some other information as well. Can I use the pod?"

Martin grinned at him. "Sure, go ahead. I just added

some new features. I think you'll like them."

Jake stepped over to a device that looked like a tanning booth squashed between Martin's desk and the back wall. It was a prototype user interface for the vast libraries of digital knowledge that ARKANE held. The environment put people inside a virtual library where they could physically interact with the information. Martin had created it based on the Radcliffe Camera of the Bodleian Library in Oxford, but it was actually an old fashioned skin on a highly technical relational database. The user could roam the shelves, pulling various objects out and creating virtual pin boards or files of information. The system would suggest other artifacts or documents in the form of a friendly virtual librarian.

Jake entered the pod, and pulled the door shut behind him. As the device initialized he was transported to the open space of the Radcliffe Camera, surrounded by stacks of books and a high ceiling that stretched into the dome above. Even the quality of light was softer here, rays of sunlight streaming in from the arched windows. The librarian walked out from behind the stacks. She was the archetype of fantasy, complete with brunette bun and buttoned-up beige cardigan. Jake noticed that her cardigan had a button undone showing just a little more cleavage, no doubt one of Martin's 'improvements.' He addressed her directly.

"I need information on Morgan Sierra, paranormal psychologist and lecturer at Oxford University. What do you have on her?"

As the librarian accessed the databases, her image flickered. Then she smiled, passing him an old fashioned file that opened up to a full view screen in front of him. He scrolled through the information, flicking through Morgan's past, displayed in images, documents, even audio and video clips. ARKANE had access to all official records but also shared information with other secret services around the world. He stopped at her record from the Israeli Defense Force. He knew she had served, as all young men and women there are conscripted for military service, but there was more detailed information on her life back then.

Jake felt a twinge of guilt at looking through her life in this way, but he needed to know what he was dealing with. He saw that Morgan had been funded in her psychology studies by the Defense Force and had specialized in religious fundamentalism. She had headed up a team to try and understand as well as change the hearts and minds of those who hated Israel. It would have been a thankless task. There were also notes about her mental health and physical fitness. It seemed she could look after herself, being proficient in Krav Maga, an Israeli martial art. There were photos of her even competing in national competitions.

Jake opened the file on the death of Morgan's husband, Elian, who was killed in active service. It seemed she had been there when he died. Then he swore under his breath to read about her parents. Both were deceased, but her father had been murdered by a suicide bomber on the number 12 bus in downtown Beersheba, Israel. He opened the images. There were devastating shots of body parts strewn amongst metal shards and shopping bags. One picture showed a sack of oranges in bright color as a severed arm reached for them in the foreground. After the incident, Morgan had changed her name back to her father's Sierra and left Israel for life as an academic. Jake wondered whether the memories of that violence still haunted her, as the death of his own family tormented his endless nights and did it make her an unstable partner? Jake swiped the file into his storage area for later retrieval. A ping sounded and a message flashed in the corner of the screen from Martin. 'Marietti wants to see you. NOW.'

CHAPTER 8

Blackfriars. Oxford, England.
May 19, 11.17am

FATHER BEN COSTANZA KNELT in the dim light
of Blackfriars chapel, his white head bent in prayer as his
fingers counted the wooden rosary beads tied at his waist,
although his fingers moved more slowly now that arthritis
had sapped his dexterity. The church was simple for a Catholic place of worship with white stone walls lit in the day by
wide windows. There was no stained glass, only clear panels
with decorative stonework. Ben watched as motes of dust
floated in the light from the windows, streaming down to
the altar of russet speckled marble. At night, candles in large
silver candlesticks lit the corners of the church. There were
wooden choir stalls and hard, straight backed chairs for the
congregation, a modest place for a pure faith.

Years of devotion had made Ben's knees strong, but the
joints still protested as he sat back into the pew. He sighed.
In his head, he was still a young man but time had definitely
taken a toll on his body. He had enjoyed this chapel for
nearly forty years now, his passion for teaching and speaking
earning him a permanent place at the Dominican College
where they taught the ancient disciplines of theology and
philosophy as well as history, social science and ethics.

Ben was a tutor for the Angelicum, the Baccalaureate in Sacred Theology granted by the Pontifical University of St Thomas in Rome. He also lectured on inter-religious dialogue and had been heavily involved in the visit of the Dalai Lama to Blackfriars in 2008. He felt that the monastery should be a sanctuary in the bustle of the Oxford city and loved to tell people how it had survived for nearly a thousand years. The Blackfriars, Dominican monks, had established a priory in Oxford in 1221 when the Regent Master of the University joined the Order. There had been a working priory in the University up until 1538, when the monasteries were destroyed in the reformation of Henry VIII and the monks were scattered. Four hundred years later the current Blackfriars priory was set up on busy St Giles, a main road into the center of Oxford, between the Ashmolean Museum and Little Clarendon Street.

Ben loved the central location of the College in the city, an area home to the University offices, ice cream parlors and bars frequented by students living in this end of town. Amongst these modern distractions, the Blackfriars were a working priory, dedicated to a common life of prayer, study and preaching. Their daily mass was open to the public and a small congregation had formed around the little community, as well as students who came in for weekly tutorials. Ben was content here.

He crossed himself and left the church, glancing at his watch. He hurried across the quad, as he was expecting Morgan for their weekly catch-up. He smiled in anticipation, eager to hear about the gossip in the theological community. Morgan's particular speciality meant she was often in the center of the latest storm of controversy. He enjoyed hearing about it but his age gave him a perspective that many others didn't have. He knew the theological contentions they raged over had been debated for millennia and by far better scholars to no satisfactory conclusion. In God's wisdom, he allowed men and women of faith to have diverse views on fundamental points but in Ben's opinion, they didn't matter anyway. Faith was of the heart and the head was a distraction, but he still enjoyed the gossip about who was feuding with whom. His time with Morgan also gave him an insight into a University that was moving away from old men like him. As she had found her way into college life, and begun to build her own psychology practice, they had met weekly for coffee and surreptitious sticky buns in his tiny office at Blackfriars.

As he rounded the corner, he saw Morgan was already standing outside his study, her brow furrowed with concern. She looked exhausted and she rubbed the stone around her neck like a charm. Ben worried about her like a father, acutely aware that he could never replace what she had lost, but given his monastic life, she was as close as he could get to having a family. When she saw him, a brief smile flickered over her face and he ushered her inside, concerned. Shutting the door, Ben listened as she told him what had happened with Faye, about the stones of the Apostles and the need to swiftly find the remaining items before Pentecost Sunday when the comet would be in ascendance.

"What do you think, Ben? Are these stones real? Have you heard of them before? My father gave me mine and Faye has one, but that doesn't mean they belonged to the Apostles. It just seems crazy," she said, rubbing her tired eyes.

"The stones are clearly a matter of faith for the people who want them, therefore it doesn't matter what we think." Ben spoke in a soft voice, trying to to calm her. "Faith can indeed move mountains but it can also destroy lives."

Morgan paced his office, only managing a few steps in the small space before turning the other way. Father Ben sat back, pondering his bookshelf, the ancient tomes perhaps containing some wisdom they could use now. He wrestled with the many thoughts that teemed in his head. There were many dangers in this quest, but he couldn't send her off without trying everything. He had been a friend of her parents, meeting them on an archaeological dig. He hadn't agreed with how they had managed the divorce but he had promised Marianne he would always help her daughters. There were aspects of those times he wished he could forget, that continued to haunt his nightmares but now Ben knew he must help Morgan.

He looked up at a quote inscribed on his bookshelf from one of the Master Generals of the Order, 'Divine wisdom is like a spring that comes down from heaven through a pipeline of books.' Somewhere there was always a book that would help. He made his decision. Reaching up to the heavy bookshelves, Ben pulled down an antique tome. He opened it at a map of the ancient world at the time of Christ.

"Little is known of many of the Apostles after the book of Acts. They went their separate ways after Pentecost, and Christian tradition only gives hints of where they went after leaving Jerusalem. But it would seem best to focus on where the Apostles died, or where their primary place of worship is now. In that way, we might find clues as to whether the Keepers are still alive, or where the stones are hidden."

"You mean follow the corpses?"

"It's a place to start and there are some here in Europe. If Faye is in danger, you have no choice but to undertake this quest, even though I fear it could be for nothing. I guess you haven't involved the police?"

"There isn't time, and anyway I have the help of a group who specialize in retrieving religious artifacts, the ARKANE Institute. You must have heard of them?"

Ben's heart pounded in his chest as he heard the name. The secrets they kept were the demons that crept under the battlements of prayer he tried to strengthen each night.

"Ben, are you OK?"

He had gone white with fear as he realized how far in

she already was. He grasped her hand and leaned forward, his voice husky with concern.

"There are things you should know about ARKANE, people you need to be very careful of."

She frowned. "But I need them to help me get Faye back."

"At what cost? I've knowledge of this group, Morgan, the secrets they seek throughout the world. I worked with their men once, a long time ago, after the war. They have information that can bring down governments and change the world order. There are shadows behind their shining public face. You must be careful of them. They're not doing this for your benefit. You're nothing to them."

Morgan laid a hand on his arm.

"Of course, Ben, but they have the resources I need to get Faye and Gemma back and then I won't be working with them anymore."

He laid a hand over hers and said in earnest.

"If they're interested in these stones, then perhaps they are more than they seem. ARKANE only become involved when they know something is powerful and there *are* miracles on this earth, some indeed from the divine but others from the deceiver."

Morgan leant forwards in her chair.

"Tell me what you know about them. Why are you so ..."

Her question was cut off by the sound of breaking glass as an object came hurtling through the window behind Ben's head, and the sound of gunfire erupted in the quadrangle beneath them.

CHAPTER 9

MORGAN SAW THE GRENADE as it landed. Her years of military training kicked in and she yanked Father Ben out of the tiny office into the stone corridor just before it exploded. The force knocked them both to the ground, the old man coughing and wheezing. The thick college walls contained most of the blast but Morgan realized it may have been a ploy to flush them out.

"Are you OK Ben? We've got to go."

Ben looked up groggily, then back at his office door. Smoke poured out as fragments of paper and ash floated on the toxic breeze. They could hear increased gunfire in the quad, people screaming and trying to escape. Then the echo of footsteps could be heard on the staircase below, running up towards them.

"It must be about the stones," Morgan said. "We have to get away before they find us. Is there another way out?"

"Over there." Ben pointed towards the end of the corridor. "It's a back staircase the abbot constructed in the time when mistresses were tolerated. Few know it's here."

He seemed to pull himself together then and Morgan found herself rushing to catch up with him as the old man hurried down the passage. He pulled back one of the tapestries on the wall to reveal a narrow doorway and fumbled at his waist for a key.

"I've used it a few times over the years. The last abbot gave me the key as my office is so close to it. Here we go. Bother, it's sticky. Give me a minute."

"We don't have a minute, Ben. Hurry."

Morgan had no weapon on her, so she stood facing the stairwell, listening to the running feet coming ever closer. She moved into a Krav Maga fighting stance, slowed her breathing and began to focus completely on the energy to fight. She would not go easily, even in the face of firepower.

"It's open. Let's go."

Ben's voice broke her concentration. She turned and edged through the tiny doorway after him, pulling the tapestry down and the door almost closed just as feet hammered up the stairs. She dared not pull it shut completely as the creaking would give them away. So they waited, hardly breathing. They could hear voices outside the door muffled by the heavy tapestry.

"They're not here. There must be another exit. Search the other rooms."

A pause, then they could hear the frantic voice of a petrified monk as he was dragged from his hiding place down the hall. Ben's hand found Morgan's in the dark and he squeezed it, neither daring to move. She knew that they would hurt the man and she felt torn between her need to escape with Ben but also not to let this monk suffer for her sake. The monk began to pray aloud.

"Where are they?" the voice said.

There was a thud as something connected with the monk's body and he coughed with a cry of pain. The fleshy thuds began again. Ben was gripping her hand tighter now, seemingly urging her not to move. But Morgan couldn't listen to it any longer, she needed to get the men's attention.

"Get ready to run," she whispered.

She pushed against the door, sending the tapestry billowing into the corridor, clearly showing the hiding place and then she pulled it shut again, slamming it hard behind them.

"That door will hold them for a few minutes" Ben said. "It's so thick they can't blast through it easily."

Morgan held out her cell phone to light the small stairwell and they raced down the two flights to the bottom. Ben was doing well, but she knew he wouldn't be able to keep up once they were out of the building. She needed a plan to hide him so she could escape alone.

"Where does this come out?"

"Behind the Ashmolean Museum," he panted. "There's a service entry at the back."

"OK, I need you to get inside the museum and stay somewhere public. Make sure you're safe. They're after me, so I'll make sure I'm followed and not you."

They reached the bottom of the stairs as they heard the top door slam open and feet begin to descend. Morgan heard the first man radio for backup, so she knew there would be others coming. One of the first rules of Krav Maga was that running away was always more preferable to fighting. Sometimes she had railed against the truism, but this was indeed a battle she needed to run from, not try to fight. Pushing open the door, she pulled Ben out into the bright day, propelling the tired old man across the gravel to the back entrance of the Ashmolean.

"Go, I'll find you later."

He briefly touched her face. "Be careful."

Then he scurried into the museum, a haven of academics, tourists and security guards. She hugged the side of the building and turned to look back into Blackfriars quad. There were a couple of bodies lying on the grass, and two men were standing there with guns. The sirens of the Oxford police could be heard in the distance and would soon arrive. She knew the men had already been there too long. She could avoid them for now but she had to stay away from the police as well as there were too many questions and there was no time to waste with bureaucracy. This was her turf, she knew the labyrinth of the college back entrances.

Keeping low, she ran around the back of Blackfriars, through the thick trees and into St Cross College, which adjoined it to the north. She had escaped for now, but the men from Thanatos would soon be after her again. Morgan thought back to Ben's words about ARKANE and wondered if she was making a deal with the Devil in order to save her sister.

Father Ben eventually returned to his office, after running the gauntlet of the police and the questions of his superiors in the Order. He had clutched his chest and wheezed at them, indicating that he needed to rest. Age was always a convenient excuse, as people expected him to be weak and unable to cope but his body was a shell for a mind sharper than most around him. Ben had hidden his abilities well over the years, relaxing into this Order of life, camouflaged by habit and ritual.

As he stepped into the room, he clutched the doorframe in horror. The room was torn apart, both from the grenade which had shredded most of the books, but also from human hands that had ripped through his belongings, clearly looking for something. But it was the image nailed to the bookcase that made him gasp in recognition. It was a pale horse's head, drawn in thick black lines and colored chalky white. A flash of memory and he was back in the ancient ruins of Ephesus half a lifetime ago, an archaeology student watching as a man on the edge of insanity sketched this very symbol. A man who must surely be dead but whose past was entwined with ARKANE and whose heart was black with murder.

"Thanatos," he whispered. "Be careful Morgan."

CHAPTER 10

ARKANE Headquarters, London, England.
May 19, 11.30am

JAKE USED THE ELEVATOR from the vaults below up the eight floors to the penthouse of the ARKANE Institute and stood silently in the doorway to the grand office. Dr Elias Marietti sat at his desk gazing out the bay window, the grey London light giving his face an unhealthy pallor. Even at the beginning of summer, the sunlight had an ashen pall from the pollution of the great city. The study light was on and papers were strewn across the large mahogany desk. Marietti had told him the desk had been the property of George Frederic Watts, an English painter in Victorian times, who had seen visions of God but rejected religion in his own life. The Director had seen the irony in that. One of Watts' paintings also hung on the office wall, a loan from the Tate Gallery: 'She shall be called woman,' a powerful vision of the creation of Eve, a life force blown from above into a figure surrounded by nature and cloud. Jake knew that Marietti lived a solitary life, so he surrounded himself with culture as an intellectual escape.

Jake coughed to get his attention. Marietti turned in his chair but didn't get up. He waved to the facing chair and skipped the small talk.

"This is an important mission, Jake. The celestial events associated with the Resurgam comet are accelerating and we cannot have those stones loose at the height of the comet's trajectory. I'm also concerned by the timing of the advent of Thanatos."

"Martin wasn't able to provide much information about the organization," Jake said, "but I've heard some ugly rumors about what they're capable of."

Marietti sighed, leaning back in his chair. Jake could almost see the weight of responsibility on his shoulders. He also saw the veiled look in Marietti's eyes as the Director spoke, as if he hid some deeper secrets.

"Thanatos was formed after the Second World War, a splinter group searching for powerful occult objects based on the research of the Nazis. They used perversions of ancient prophecy to proclaim the end of days. I thought we had defeated them then, but clearly they went underground. Their return now means events will accelerate from here for Thanatos has no regard for the lives of individuals, only a blind pursuit of what they define as religious truth."

He paused. Jake knew there was more Marietti wasn't telling him.

"So what about the stones of the Apostles?" he asked. "Does that mean they really do have power of their own if Thanatos want them so badly?"

Marietti looked grim, his brow deeply furrowed.

"After Varanasi we collaborated with the Vatican to verify the miracles. From the preliminary investigations, it looks like they were real. The stones are made of a certain kind of radioactive material with magnetic and other properties not seen in any other rocks known on earth. We don't know how they are used or how Varanasi happened, but they certainly have some kind of power. You have to ensure they don't reach the hands of these fanatics because even without the miracles, they are a potent symbol that will unite fundamentalist groups."

Marietti passed a photo across his desk.

"While Thanatos are the primary threat, we also have Joseph Everett, a businessman and rising star in Arizona politics. His father was a freelance biblical researcher and stole one of the stones. It seems Joseph is carrying on the tradition and aims to collect them all."

Jake took the photo.

"Kidnapping Morgan's family seems like a desperate attempt to speed up the process, but why does he want the stones?" Jake asked.

Marietti handed him another photo.

"We think this is his motivation. It's his brother Michael, a mentally and physically ill twin held in a local psychiatric hospital. Joseph visits almost every day and after the power demonstrated at Varanasi, we think he believes the stones will help heal his brother."

"Do you think he's working with Thanatos?" Jake asked, studying the photos.

"No, Everett seems to be entirely focused on his brother but Thanatos want the stones for a larger purpose and we're only seeing a small part of their plans. I think they will take his stones too before this ends."

Marietti looked away, his dark eyes black in the dim light, bushy eyebrows overshadowing a craggy face that had seen so much. He was silent for a moment. Jake knew this man had paid a high price for the position he now held and shared little but he didn't want to know the secrets that Marietti kept hidden. The Director stood and walked around his desk. Jake pushed back his chair, realizing the interview was over.

"Your focus must be on retrieving those stones, Jake. They haven't been in the same place since Pentecost over two millennia ago. Alone the stones are powerful: together with the comet they could be catastrophic."

Marietti put his hand on Jake's shoulder and Jake felt the weight of responsibility and trust this man had in him.

"I need them back here, but I'm too old for this now. It's time for you to step up, Jake, a new generation of ARKANE. We're coming into an age where the spiritual and supernatural are embraced again. These are dangerous times to have any artifact revealed to the world that gives credence to a particular faith. So you must bring them back here … at any price. No individual is worth more than this. Remember that."

Jake left the office and walked out onto The Strand, one of the busiest hubs of London traffic and tourism. He merged into the crowd and was carried along back towards Embankment tube station. As he walked, he considered how he was going to work with Morgan Sierra. He felt a strong attraction to her, both physical and through a sense of kinship for their disjointed lives, but his loyalties ultimately lay with ARKANE.

He remembered when he had been recruited by Marietti while in Africa, overseeing aid in Sudan. His British special military team had been ordered to stand by and hold as the National Islamic Front had slaughtered Catholics, including children. It was a political decision, and there was nothing they could do but wait it out. Marietti had been sent from the Vatican as a representative of the Holy See during the hideous war that raged senselessly for years. Late one night they had both been awake and stood on a verandah together in the dark listening to screams in the distance. Jake had cursed God that night, feeling their blood on his hands, and Marietti had explained to him how it was not God but man who twisted faith into something evil. Religion had torn humanity apart for millennia and it would never stop but there was a way to be part of the solution.

That night Marietti had told Jake of ARKANE, a covert group solving spiritual mysteries and supernatural enigmas, attempting to understand a world beyond the physical but not tied to one religion. ARKANE sought to understand the myths behind religious artifacts in order to harness their power and keep them safe from the extremist fringes. After Jake had completed his tour of duty in Africa, Marietti had contacted him again and recruited him but it seemed a long time ago now. He had seen so much since that day.

Just as he arrived at the entrance of the underground train station, his cell phone rang. He answered it on the first ring.

"Jake, it's Morgan. They're still after me. I was attacked at Blackfriars. I think it was Thanatos again, but with some serious firepower this time."

"Are you OK?" he asked, amazed that they would attempt something so serious in broad daylight.

"I'm fine now, but clearly they're not going to stop until they have my stone. We need to get out of here and start the search, and I know where we need to start looking."

CHAPTER 11

Tucson, Arizona, USA.
May 19 4.35pm

JOSEPH EVERETT SAT BACK in the armchair his father had loved. The leather still creaked with the same tone it had when the old man got up to reach for another book. He and Michael had listened to it over and over when, as children, they had sat with ears pressed to the ever closed study door. Joseph had recreated the study here at his own house, sure that the secret to his father's quest lay within the pages of one of these books and he was determined to find it.

The large desk he sat behind was teak, inlaid with rosy marble round the edges. There was an accountant's lamp, green hooded with a pull down switch that sat on the corner of the desk next to the old professor's fountain pens. His father had collected them, spent hours cleaning the tiny parts and loved to write with them. Joseph idly fingered the red Montegrappa that he had been beaten for touching as a child. That pen had pride of place on his father's desk, whereas he and Michael had been discarded and ignored. Joseph examined the pen closely, the texture of the barrel, the intricate nib carving. It was beautiful.

But today was different. Today he was one step closer to his goal, one step closer to beating his father to the stones he had sought in his lifetime. He bent down, placed the ruby pen on the floor, and firmly crushed it underfoot. He ground the pieces into the carpet, purple ink staining the cream color, spreading out like a bloodstain. Joseph smiled and thought back to when this search had begun.

Five years before, when his father had learnt he was dying of lung cancer, he had called Joseph to his bedside. The bedspread was stained where his father clutched it while coughing up blood and bile. The air smelt of vomit and death crept around the walls, waiting for the inevitable end. His father was weak and could hardly talk, but Joseph hated the man and didn't care if he died. His father had taken the stone from around his scrawny neck and given it to Joseph. He had whispered, his speech halting.

"This is a Pentecost stone ... powerful ... protect it from those who ... it belongs to you now." The dying man had broken off in a coughing fit, then spoke again, his words even fainter. "There are more stones ... increase in power together ... complete the circle ... Death increases their power, Joseph, remember that."

He had slipped into a coma soon after, and Joseph had held the stone, feeling the warmth from his father's body leave it. He didn't know what the words meant then. It was just a piece of rock, but it was the only thing his father had ever given him. The next day he rifled through his father's study and began to read his diaries and papers. One of the journals had revealed the hypothesis that the stones held a power of God that could be harnessed and made stronger by the twelve being together. Joseph had copied the passage from the book of Acts about the healing miracles, speaking in tongues, and the power to convert people. All he could think about was Michael. Two were stronger together. Could these stones restore his brother?

Joseph opened another of his father's diaries, as he did every morning before his business day. Each was dated in the front and contained only a month or two of notes. There were hundreds of journals stacked into the large bookcases that covered the walls in his study, all brought from the old house, filed in chronological order as his father had been a meticulous man. Joseph searched every day for information on how to energize the stones when they were together in one place.

It was in these pages that Joseph had found vital knowledge about the estimated dating of the comet elliptical and how it would come again on Pentecost this year. It had given him a timeframe to work to, but he hadn't thought it would take so long to achieve his goal and now time was short. As he read, he also delved into the other research and the life his father had led. It seemed he had hardly noticed his children, or his wife as they were never mentioned. The books were concerned with discovery and research about the religious relics he had sought throughout the world. They were filled with scraps of cuttings and articles he was proud of, most of which were in obscure and fringe publications. These were not diaries in the confessional vein, but more the chronology of a mind over years of immersion in the subjects of arcana.

This morning, Joseph was re-reading a notebook that mused on the power of the twelve and whether it was enhanced when the stones were together. There was mention of the physicist Wolfgang Pauli and whether the stones could even change matter itself. There were lists of people in history who might have owned the stones, based on documentation of their spiritual and physical gifts including great artists as well as scientists and political figures throughout history. Joseph noted the mutterings of a driven, raving man amongst the occasional clarity of the scholar but he learned more about his father from these books than he had ever done when the man was alive.

His father had written that the stones had been cut from

the rock of Christ's tomb after the resurrection, plain at first, but over time each had been shaped and carved with words of power. The twelve had wanted to remember that unique time and to bind themselves together in faith, so the stones had been hung on strips of leather, silver chain or metal rings to be carried on missions to the ends of the known world.

There were clues to the locations in the notebooks his father had made over the years but nothing concrete, so he had given Morgan Sierra the notebooks with the best information as he knew she would find what he sought given the imminent threat to her sister and the child. Even if he couldn't get all the stones in one place to recreate the power of Pentecost, maybe he could somehow increase the power of the stones he did have with a sacrifice. The diary he was reading contained some of the experiments his father had carried out after noting that the power of the stones could be increased by the energy transfer of death. This section was dog-eared and smudged from multiple readings.

He searched for those pages again today, for a reassurance that his plan would work. He read of a recovered scrap of a Gnostic gospel containing tales of healing that occurred with a stone after the martyr's death of an Apostle. There was a note about life force and what might possibly empower the stones further. Originally it seemed the resurrection of Jesus had given the stones their power, a residual force of life overcoming death. The stones were intimately connected with the balance between life and death, a latent power to be used for good or evil. Certainly the nun's death at Varanasi had resulted in miracles.

Joseph pulled out one of the loose leaves from the book he was reading. It was a page from a diary in Latin script with a translation beside it. From the Middle Ages, it described a brother in the church murdering another for one of the stones. At the moment of death, the stone was charged and miracles occurred, like those in the book of

Acts - healing, speaking in tongues and mass conversions to the cause. It was as if the life force of one could be the energy that moved into others with the stone as a conduit. Joseph had seized upon this idea and he thought back to when he had decided to test the theory.

After his father's death, his mother had sat in the kitchen, dressed in funeral black, the author of their misery squatting like a toad over their lives. The hem of her skirt was too high and the bulging blue veins in her thick legs revolted him. She slurped from a cup of tea and he flinched. He hated the sound of her drinking, the sound of her living.

"Now you're the man of the house, Joseph, I expect you to earn money to support me and your brother. You owe me that," she had said.

That night he had slipped the cord of the stone around his neck, gone to her room and held a pillow over her face. When she started awake, unable to breathe, he held her down, resting his body weight on top of her until the struggling stopped. Then he held the pillow there for another hour to make sure it was done. He had wept then, for the end of whatever it was people called family. Now it was just him and Michael against the world, but then perhaps it had always been this way.

Joseph had brought Michael to the funeral, sedated in a wheelchair because he became anxious when they took him out of the facility. He had gently hung the stone round his brother's neck then but nothing happened, nothing changed. He was angry then and confused. Perhaps God had not seen his sacrifice or he had his back turned in heaven as his earthly father had on earth. Or perhaps in Varanasi it was the death of the Keeper which had caused the miracles that night, he mused. Maybe that was the missing link.

Joseph sat back in the chair and stared out of the window

to the roseate Catalina Mountains. Michael was the half of him that had almost died to protect him in his childhood. Joseph owed him life and soon he would summon it.

CHAPTER 12

Brize Norton Airfield, England.
May 20, 7.08am

"So why Spain?" Jake asked, once they were seated in the 737, waiting for take-off. The plane was set up as a mobile ARKANE base, with a meeting room and galley up front and a central workspace with computers in the mid-section. Weapons, equipment and bunks were to the rear. A couple of crew were readying the plane and Jake had mentioned a team available on standby if they needed backup. Morgan could see that ARKANE was taking this search seriously and she appreciated the extensive support. In a show of good faith, she decided to share the information she had learned even though she still had suspicions about their involvement.

"Before the attack at Blackfriars, Ben and I discussed the more ancient legends about where the Apostles went after Pentecost. It seems logical to think that the stones would be near the bodies themselves, either with a Keeper or preserved with the relics of the saints."

"That makes sense," Jake said, "and it ties with our research as well."

"We should go after the more obvious Apostles first, so I narrowed them down. We know that I have the stone of

John, so Patmos, Greece is off the list and we think that Faye has James Alphaeus' stone."

Jake nodded.

"ARKANE was given Matthew Levi's and our researchers think it was Nathaniel's taken in Varanasi and the stone of Matthias that was stolen in Jerusalem."

"So that makes five," Morgan added, "and I'm pretty sure that Everett already has the stone of Thomas. His father's diaries describe the Maltese and Goan myths around where the Doubting apostle ended up."

"OK, so we know six are accounted for. What about the other six?"

"Given our time frames, Spain seems the best place to start. It's a short flight and we can get started quickly. The bones of St James are supposedly stored at the Cathedral of Santiago de Compostela, in the north west. There are so many myths about what happened to the Apostles after they left Jerusalem, but James' story is pretty stable across the many extant documents, so we should try there first. Perhaps Everett will trade if we can show some early success."

Morgan's voice trailed off as Jake's eyes slid away from hers and he busied himself in readiness for take-off. He clearly didn't share her hopes for a quick resolution. In the last 24 hours, she had been smothering her fear in the intellectual rigor of research but now a gaping wound opened, and she felt a jolt of terror for Faye and Gemma. Grabbing her smartphone, she scrolled to the pictures of her family. One of her with Gemma's little arms tight around her neck pricked her eyes with tears. She pretending to wipe something from her eye, not wanting Jake to see her vulnerability. Elian and her father had been ripped from her life too soon, and she would not lose her sister and niece this way.

Once they were airborne, Jake pulled out various maps from his bag as well as the Moleskine diaries.

"I thought about doing the Camino de Santiago myself a few years ago," he said, as he opened them up on the table between them. Morgan glanced up at him, surprised by his words.

"To pay for what sins? What could an ARKANE agent possibly have on his conscience?"

The Camino was a thousand year old pilgrimage route through southern France and northern Spain. Morgan knew that the 780 kilometers were traditionally walked on foot as a spiritual journey, culminating at the cathedral of St James in Santiago de Compostela where the pilgrim received forgiveness for their sins. It was the very church they were heading for.

"I haven't always been so squeaky clean," Jake smiled broadly. Morgan noticed the scar above his eyebrow crinkling. He opened the map of Santiago de Compostela, and located the main square. His fingers were long, like a piano player's, less calloused than she had expected but there were also old scars on his knuckles, evidence of a harder side.

"It's only an hour or so until we arrive and we won't have long at the Cathedral." Jake said. "We need to know what we're looking for. We have to think like the people who've protected the stones for all these years."

"There might not even be physical Keepers for all the stones," Morgan said. "It's much easier to track down people than as it is to find a stone that has been buried for millennia, so it's possible that some were just hidden."

Morgan was trying to be upbeat about their prospects. One moment she found herself excited about the research and the next bowled over by the enormity of their task, but she wouldn't contemplate failure. It was easier to comprehend her own pain and death than those she loved.

She opened one of the journals from the package. It was

a finely drawn, handcrafted book, with spidery labels and ancient names marked alongside modern cities. The world had changed since those days but the steps of holy men could still be traced, although some had multiple journeys marked and an unclear place of death.

"These diaries are amazingly detailed. Everett's father was aware of some of the other Keepers and started to track where their stones might be. He had so much information. It's odd that he didn't manage to find the stones after all that research."

"Maybe he just didn't have the right team," Jake flashed a grin. She couldn't help but smile back. They had a long journey ahead of them and she appreciated his attempt at friendliness. They studied the street maps looking for the best route in and out of the Cathedral square.

"Don't you think it's strange that the Apostles scattered and never regrouped after Pentecost?" Jake said. "They had such an intense shared experience and yet it seems they never saw each other again. They couldn't have known their message would spread so successfully throughout the ancient world, even though it meant persecution and martyrdom for most of them and their followers."

"They had a mission, I suppose," replied Morgan. "Maybe Pentecost gave them certainty of the authority they held, or perhaps the power scared them and they scattered, knowing it had to be taken to the far corners of the world?"

Morgan went quiet as she considered some of the pictures in the journal. There was a page filled with flames and agonized faces in the midst of dancing fire. The drawings were made up of thin lines with detail of realistic pain, as if drawn from life by a close observer.

"Whatever these stones can do, it's not all healing and marvelous acts of good. The man who drew these pictures clearly knew the dark side of fire. Perhaps the power of the Pentecost stones is not something to be taken lightly."

CHAPTER 13

Santiago de Compostela, Spain.
May 20, 11.10am

THE ARKANE PLANE LANDED outside the city of Santiago de Compostela at a private airport.

"I'm just going to radio in for backup from the Spanish team," Jake said, reaching for the equipment. Morgan stopped him, placing her hand over his.

"There's no need for anyone to come with us," Morgan said smiling, persuasive. "Don't you think we'll attract more attention in a bigger group? Why don't we just go in as pilgrims to touch the foot of St James and have a look around?"

Her voice was light in tone, but her posture said she was ready for an argument. Morgan was determined not to let Jake run this mission. It was her sister's life at stake and she was still suspicious of what ARKANE wanted out of this. Their help was too readily given, too good to be true. A pause and then Jake nodded. Morgan left her hand on his for just a beat longer.

"OK, we'll try it your way for now," he said. "I'm happy to start with the softly, softly approach but we'll call in the troops if necessary since we're going in unarmed because of the tourist police. We don't have much time to get this done."

They took a taxi to the center of town and walked out into the Plaza de la Quintana where the Cathedral loomed over the bustling square. Spires stood against the city skyline, an ancient bastion of faith in a heaving modern city. From the square itself, two towers rose up high into the blue sky.

"The towers represent James' parents, Zebedee and Maria Salome," Morgan explained as they walked towards the cathedral entrance across the square, dotted with pilgrims as it was a popular time of year to walk the Camino.

"I've always wanted my own personal tour guide," Jake grinned back at her. Morgan relaxed. His words seemed like a peace offering and she was already enjoying his easy manner. Working together might even be a pleasure. "So what else do you know about this place?" he asked.

"I love what Santiago de Compostela represents. Like you, it's actually one of my dreams to walk the Camino." Morgan looked up at the towers. "I didn't think I would make it here by plane and taxi though. I had hoped to limp in like the rest of the pilgrims."

Jake laughed, "I'm sure you'll manage to hobble through this square one day."

"It's on my list," she said, continuing the story as they walked across the square. "Legend tells that James brought the gospel to Spain and, although he was martyred in Jerusalem, his remains were brought back here. The tomb was abandoned in the third century but was rediscovered in the ninth by a hermit who saw strange lights in the sky above it. A chapel was built to commemorate the miracle of finding the saint's bones under the stars and over the years the church was embellished to become the great cathedral it is today, as befitting its importance to the Catholic faith. The bones of James are presumed to have rested here for thousands of years."

"So this should be a good place to start looking for the stone. If it was kept with his bones, that is."

"If they even are his bones," Morgan replied. "The Church did an excellent trade in relics, sold as forgiveness for sin to those desperate for a better life after death. Ancient bones of the saints are hardly rare."

Jake laughed. "The Middle Ages sounded pretty bad. I guess their lives were so miserable on this earth, it's no wonder they spent their money on indulgences."

By now they were standing by the stairs leading up to the entrance of the Cathedral. Morgan indicated the statues of David and Solomon, wise Kings of ancient Israel. She pointed out the scallop shell carved into the flagstones, the symbol of St James also worn on the staff of the pilgrim.

"How did he come to be represented by the scallop shell anyway?" Jake asked. "Seems odd for a Middle Eastern Jew. Aren't shellfish considered unclean?"

As they progressed into the holy place, Morgan replied quietly, "You're right, it is odd. The legend says that when the body was being transported back to Spain from Jerusalem, a knight fell into the water and emerged covered in shells. But that sounds like a poor cover-up for the more likely version - that the scallop shell was a symbol of fertility carried by hopeful couples and this pagan symbol was taken by the church and incorporated into the legend of St James. The Christians were great at integrating pagan ideas to build their empire. It's why the gospel was accepted across such diverse cultures and spread so widely."

Jake touched her arm, guiding her into the church.

"I guess we have to start somewhere. Let's see what we can find."

Morgan felt the pressure of his fingers and was acutely aware of how close he was but she didn't pull away and they continued deeper into the church.

"Put yourself in the shoes of the Keeper," she whispered. "James was beheaded, and the corpse eventually brought back here. As a disciple of James' would you have kept the stone secret all these years, or buried it with the body?"

Jake replied close to her ear, his breath tickling a little, making the hairs stand up on her arms.

"We'd better find his body then."

The cathedral wasn't too crowded for a week day, although the usual line of pilgrims snaked through the nave. Morgan pointed past them towards the Portico da Gloria in the western façade.

"That's where the statue of James is. We should go and touch his foot like the other pilgrims, and see what else is there."

They walked towards the Romanesque Portico. Christ the Judge and Redeemer stood in the middle, surrounded by statues of the Apostles and Old Testament figures with their names on books or parchment. The statue of James was surrounded by pilgrims, some forming a line to touch his left foot where a groove had been worn in the stone over the years.

Morgan looked around her at the glory of the Catholic Church displayed in grandeur, funded by the thousands of pilgrims who visited. Yet she knew it wasn't the final destination that mattered on the Camino, it was the journey itself. Putting on a backpack each day and heading into the early morning mists of the track, one foot in front of the other for days on end. It was a time of contemplation and healing. People didn't walk the Camino for physical challenge alone; it was a penance or a way to seek answers. She thought of why she herself considered it, in remembrance of what her life had been or what it could have become with Elian. There was still time for healing her own pain. She wondered why Jake wanted to do it. She didn't know much about the ARKANE agent but then she didn't expect this tentative partnership to last long enough to find out.

This type of church was a strange end to a humble walk in nature for hundreds of miles. After living at a level of basic subsistence for weeks, pilgrims emerged from the track to this opulence. Could God be found here in the gold and marble extravagance, or on the Way in the shadow of stone walls and the taste of newly baked bread after a long day's walk? Morgan thought that faith could better be found in the relief of taking off walking boots, the stretching of calf muscles and the sweet respite of sleep, not the communion of saints and the drowning of incense. Despite the imposing magnificence of the place, she felt there was a palpable sense of emotion, of an overwhelming belief in something, even if that something was not the God venerated in the church. Maybe it was a collective hysteria bred by pilgrims high on lack of sleep, exhaustion and relief, but there was a sense of the end, an accomplishment beyond the feeling in a normal church. She knew that many people found a spirituality on the Way that was denied them in the city. Even if you didn't find God, it was said that you could find peace on the Camino and right now, Morgan wished for just a little of that feeling.

They reached the statue of St James, and stopped as pilgrims would, looking it up and down. Morgan ran her fingers along the statue, touching St James' foot but there was nowhere for the stone to be hidden here. Suddenly there was shouting towards the cloister. People turned their heads to look in the direction of the noise. Jake glanced around apprehensively and Morgan knew he was regretting leaving the backup team behind.

"You concentrate on finding the bones," he said. "I'll go and see what the fuss is about. I'll meet you back at the plane if we can't leave together."

He slipped off towards the clamor.

Morgan headed towards the main altar, looking around her for any indication of where the stone of St James might be. Near the altar, she found a way down into the crypt where the relic bones of the saint were kept. It was a plain staircase, quite incongruous surrounded by the extravagance of sculpture and fresco. At the bottom of the crypt stairs was a small room with a locked iron gate. She held one of the bars and peered into the gloom. She could make out a silver and gold reliquary on an altar a few meters beyond the gate. The crypt was badly lit and clearly not designed to be part of the tourist attraction of the cathedral. She tried to put herself in the place of the Keepers, passing down secrets across the generations. Did they know the power they protected? Did she even believe in it herself? Only one way to find out here. Morgan tried pushing on the bars, but the lock was solid. Then a voice made her jump,

"Why do you want to go into the crypt, young lady?"

Morgan turned as an old priest shuffled forward out of the darkness behind her, his hand shaking as he indicated the locked door. She smiled in greeting.

"Buenos dias Father, I'm a scholar from Oxford University researching the bones of St James. Do you know how I could gain access to the crypt?"

The old man hobbled forward with a cane. His breath wheezed with chest infection. Morgan moved to help him to a marble bench by the crypt door.

"We don't get many people wanting to look at the crypt any more. I'm the Custodian. What are you particularly interested in?"

He patted the seat next to him. Morgan felt odd talking to this stranger but she was running out of time and there was a long way to go in the next few days. Her father had always believed in honesty. He trusted people implicitly, believing, when it came down to it, that people sought to do good in the world. It hadn't saved his life, but she knew he would still stand by those values. She made her decision.

"I'm looking for a stone," she said, sitting down on the bench next to him. "It was with St James when he died and may be here in the church." The old man went pale and clutched at his chest, the wheezing growing worse. "Are you alright?"

"Who are you really, child?" he asked, taking Morgan's hand and squeezing it tightly.

"Truly, I'm just a researcher. My name is Morgan Sierra and I work at Oxford University."

"You must know more than you're telling me. I need to know about the stone you seek."

Footsteps on the stairs down into the crypt made them both fall silent. Their conversation was not one to be shared in public. As Morgan saw the boots and then black jeans of the man descending, she tensed, aware that she was trapped down here with no backup. The man ducked down to enter the small crypt. It was suddenly crowded in the tiny space. Morgan bent her head, hoping the man was just a tourist and that he would pass them by. Putting her hands behind her back, she felt around the back of the bench for anything that could be used as a weapon, just in case. She was regretting the decision to come unarmed. The priest called out,

"Can I help you, my son?"

"Yes, I think you can," the man said as he turned towards them. In that instant Morgan saw the pale horse tattoo on his left arm.

CHAPTER 14

Cathedral of Santiago de Compostela, Spain.
May 20, 12.32pm

LEAVING MORGAN BY THE pillar of St James, Jake walked towards the cloister, his steps quickening as the noise escalated. The cathedral was hardly silent, but raised voices were attracting attention even amongst a multitude of pilgrims. The cloister was a large quadrangle that led to the cathedral relics and the Library. Its stone tessellated floor was surrounded by buttressed arches and opened out to the azure Spanish sky. Jake stood behind one of the arched pillars and watched as three men argued with a gesticulating priest. He recognized them as ex-military operatives like himself from their stance and the faint shapes under their clothes indicated that they were armed. One had the pale horse tattooed on his arm. They were from Thanatos. He would have to create a diversion long enough to allow Morgan time to find the stone, and then they would both get out of here.

The largest man was holding the priest's arm and pointing into the church, clearly demanding that he show them the bones of St James. They weren't going to waste time looking for the stone discreetly, they were going to use brute force. Pilgrims and other priests were moving closer, but the threat of the three men was enough to keep them at a safe distance. Pushing the priest in front of them, the men started to head towards the church entrance and Jake's position. He still wore the original stone that he had shown Morgan. He quickly weighed up his choices, then unhooked the stone from around his neck. He stepped out in front of the men, who were now only a few meters away.

"Father, I found it!" he shouted as if talking directly to the priest, holding the stone in front of him on its leather string. The mercenaries started running towards him, pushing the priest to the ground. Jake sprinted away from them into the main body of the church. The three men, weapons drawn, followed close behind.

Jake ducked low behind a group of pilgrims as they entered through the main door. They were huddled together, an emotional group intending to finish their journey at the statue of St James. Jake stayed with them, head bowed yet watching as the men scanned the room, their weapons concealed again. They couldn't risk having their guns out in a such a crowded place. It would be mayhem within seconds and the tourist police were nearby in the square below. Jake moved with the group towards the main altar, aware that Morgan was somewhere close and that he didn't want to lead them to her. He needed to create a diversion. Looking towards the main altar, he saw a heavy rope hanging down and knew just what he could do to bring everyone's attention onto him.

He had read that the cathedral held one of the most famous Botafumeiro or Incensory in Christendom. It was the largest censer in the world, weighing over 170 pounds. On holy days and high mass, the Botafumeiro was filled with incense and swung over the crowd of pilgrims who crushed into the cathedral for a blessing. The heavy smoke from the incense settled over the gathered faithful, a heavenly scent to some, and a choking, cloying stink to others. The smoke curled its way up, taking prayers to God, bridging the gap between the spiritual and physical worlds. Jake also knew that one of its purposes was to mask the stench of pilgrims who had rushed to the church after days on the trail without washing. The heavy rope that linked the pulley system for the giant thurible was tethered near the main altar. It went right up into the dome above the main crossing of the church, the highest place to swing the incense over the faithful.

One of the men spotted Jake and shouted. He saw them rushing towards him, hands on concealed weapons and they spread out to trap him near the altar. Jake sped towards the rope for the Botafumeiro, drawing a knife from his leg holster. He grabbed the attachment end of the rope, wrapped it around his waist and leg. He slashed the stable line that held it in place and the pulley system hoisted his weight high into the church. One of the men reached for his arm but the rope whizzed Jake away up into the dome. Nearby pilgrims watched in wonder as he was taken into the air high above the altar. Priests started to run towards the sight, shouting at him and waving their hands. They were appalled at the sacrilege, calling urgently for security.

Jake laughed at the sight of them all rushing to stop him, for by then he was flying in the dome, swinging above them. It was indeed a marvelous view from up here. With the cross of the church below him and the flash of cameras lighting the scene, he rocked his body back and forth causing the pulley to swing as it would do with the incense. The three men faded back into the crowd, obviously waiting for security to bring him down. At least their attention was now on him and not on looking for the stone. They thought he had it up there with him. The only question remaining was, how would he get back down?

CHAPTER 15

Crypt of the Cathedral of Santiago de Compostela, Spain.
May 20, 12.41pm

MORGAN SAW THE MAN'S hand move inside his jacket and knew she couldn't let him fire a gun in here. Her Krav Maga close combat training kicked in, and her anger exploded. She launched herself at him, springing up and jabbing an elbow into his gut. As he doubled over, she rammed her knee into his face. He didn't go down easily and as his eyes widened in surprise at her attack, he grabbed to catch her as he pulled a knife from his boot with the other hand. There was little room in the crypt but Morgan ducked under his arm, just as the old man rushed in to separate them, unaware of the danger he was in. The attacker's knife connected with the priest's body and he sagged with a faint exhalation of surprise as crimson blossomed on his white cassock. Time slowed for Morgan in that moment. She had to finish this now. Grabbing a heavy Bible from the bench, she swung it into the attacker's face, smashing his nose, driving him backwards as he gasped in surprise. She kicked his wrist and the knife dropped to the floor, leaving a skid-mark of blood. Seeing a silver candlestick on a ledge just behind him, she ducked under his clumsy punch and whammed her elbow up under his chin. As his neck snapped back, she jumped onto the bench, grasped the candlestick and swung it hard, connecting with the side of his head in a dull thump. He collapsed to the floor, and she followed him down, weapon held high to strike him again. A moan from the old priest stopped her. He whispered, "No more, please."

Morgan paused, then nodded, aware that she was in a holy place and the stone was her first priority. She felt for a pulse in the attacker's neck. It was weak, but he was still alive. Quickly she felt in his jacket and took his gun, tucking it into the back of her jeans. She kicked his bloody knife into the crypt behind the locked gate. Then she pulled the man's belt off, used it to tie his hands and finally stuffed one of the ornamental altar pieces into his mouth as a gag.

Moving close to the priest, Morgan knelt and put pressure onto his wound, trying to stem the bleeding. It wasn't deep, as his voluminous robes had caught the force of the blow but he was still in pain.

"I have to get you help, but that man was also looking for the stone of the Apostle James. You said before that I must know more. You're right, I have a stone myself, from John, the beloved disciple."

She reached into her shirt and pulled out the stone that hung around her neck. The old man reached up and gently touched it, his eyes bright in wonder and reverence despite the pain he was in.

"La Piedra de Dios." He spoke in a whisper. "The stones are a secret carried by only a few through millennia but I heard rumors of a reckoning. There's a prophecy that speaks of a new Pentecost in the end times."

"I don't know if this is that time, Father, but I have to find the stone and I need to get you some help. Let me call someone."

He shook his head. "Not yet. If others come, you won't be able to take the stone from the crypt."

Morgan's eyes widened.

"It's here, then?"

The old man looked away from her into the darkness of the crypt.

"I'm clearly no longer able to protect the stone," he said. "But will you protect it for the church, Morgan Sierra?"

She hesitated, and then spoke honestly. "I'm not a Christian, Father, but my sister's life is at stake and I need the stones to get her back."

He sighed.

"You're a Keeper and the stones know their masters. It's time for this one to be seen again."

He pointed at the gold and silver reliquary behind the locked gate, his hand shaking.

"It's in there. I've never seen it myself but the relics were authenticated in 1884 by Pope Leo XIII. At that time, my great great grandfather was a silver worker. He fashioned the reliquary and was given the stone to hide by the Pope himself. They were trying to protect the stones by ensuring they stayed apart."

"Why was it so urgent to hide the stones?" Morgan asked.

"Pope Leo had a vision that year which shook him deeply." The priest crossed himself, his eyes haunted. "He heard the voices of God and the Devil while praying at his private altar. Satan boasted that given 100 years he could destroy the Church and gain absolute power over the faithful. It seems that God would allow Satan to do his worst as he did with the prophet Job. But Pope Leo was determined to bolster the Church's power and ensure that the Devil didn't claw a foothold. Hiding the Pentecost stone was just one of the things he did to protect the Church from those who would use its power for evil."

"So where did they hide the stone? Did your father tell you?"

The priest nodded.

"It's molded into the top of the reliquary. Here, take this and you can see for yourself."

He produced a key from his vestments and gave it to her, waving her towards the locked gate and the ornate box inside. Morgan unlocked the gate, pushing the creaking door inwards. The reliquary was a large engraved silver chest, resting on top of a mahogany table in the center of the crypt. An altar stood before it with large candlesticks and a crucifix. She inched her way behind the altar.

"Look at the top," the old man called faintly from behind her. "There are two raised silver discs. The stone is hidden under one of them."

"But which one?" Morgan ran her fingers over the silver detail, marveling that the stone could be here. "And how the hell do I get it out?"

"My father told me of a mechanism to release the stone. On the sides of the box are scallop shells. Count three in on the left side." Morgan followed his directions. "Follow the seam to the figure underneath. That's the servant of James, the first Keeper. He holds the key to the stone. That's all my father told me, passed down from his father before him."

Morgan looked closely. The figure seemed to be the same as the other molded statues on the side of the reliquary. She bent closer and saw that his staff didn't seem to be part of the molding. It was a separate piece of metal. She carefully pried it out of the hands of the servant, a sliver of metal finely tooled, like a needle with a hooked end shaped like a scallop shell. She felt over the raised dials on the top of the box, acutely aware that it might contain one of the most holy relics in Christendom, the bones of the Apostle James. Her fingers found a tiny hole in the dial on the left side and she pressed the metal shard into the little space. It slid in snugly but nothing happened. She tried lifting it like a lever and the silver dial opened smoothly to reveal a plain grey stone in the space beneath.

"It's here," she said with reverence. She still couldn't believe the stones contained innate power, just that they were wanted by a madman, but here was a priest who swore there was something to the myth. She gently lifted the stone out of its hiding place and closed the lid with care. Removing the tiny silver lever, she returned it to the servant's figure and went back out. The old priest held out his hand.

"Please let me see it," he said. "I've spent years making sure it stayed hidden. Now I release it to you for protection."

Morgan knelt by his side and laid it on his palm. It was just a plain stone, dark grey with rough edges, nothing out of the ordinary. Where her own had been hidden in plain sight, decorated as jewelry, this one seemed to be as clean as when it was hacked from the tomb of Christ himself. The old man closed his hand around the precious object, his eyes closed in prayer. Morgan watched as he seemed to lighten and relax as he prayed. Then she heard shouting above them in the cathedral nave. A hacking cough jolted through the old man and he clutched at his wound, blood staining the stone. He gave it back to her.

"You must go now. Take it far away. The other priests will find me soon enough and I'll explain this mess away. After all this time, it's good to know the stones will be together again. Now go and be careful."

He pointed Morgan towards the exit staircase, one hand on his chest, the other waving her away.

"Thank you. I'll keep it safe."

Then she turned and walked up the stairs, leaving the old priest in the darkness below.

When she reached the main nave of the cathedral she could see what all the noise was about. Jake was suspended in the dome of the church, swinging on a thick rope and laughing maniacally, playing the part of a crazy pilgrim to a perfect end. After her experience in the crypt she could only suspect he had a run in with other men from Thanatos and had found a unique way to handle the situation. Looking up at him from the gathered crowd, she realized that he was making her smile despite the terrible situation she found herself in. She reluctantly considered that he was a good partner to have around, whatever the motives of ARKANE. She needed to signal to him that she had found James' stone, but how to get his attention in this crazy circus? She had to do something even more outrageous to attract Jake's attention as she left.

Morgan looked around and saw the Holy Door of the Pardon, now unguarded as all the security guards were trying to bring Jake down from the Dome. They would retrieve him soon, so she needed to get his attention while he was still high up. She knew that the Holy Door was only meant to be opened in the Holy Years, when the Saint's Day of St James fell on a Sunday. This was not a holy year so Morgan knew that opening this door would attract attention. More people were flocking into the main church to see the spectacle and the security team was surrounded so they wouldn't have time to reach her before she was away.

Making her decision, Morgan walked quickly towards the Holy Door. Clearly the ancient lock was just for show. She pulled the gun she had taken from the attacker and shot it away. The sharp bang and resounding screams in the church drew attention away from Jake and towards her. She knew he would have seen her. Morgan yanked the door open and ran out into the Plaza de la Quintana behind the cathedral. Knowing security and the police would soon be after her, she disappeared into the back streets of Santiago de Compostela leaving Jake to fend for himself.

CHAPTER 16

Tucson, Arizona, USA
May 20, 10.08pm

JOSE RAMIREZ PULLED THE blanket closer around him as he curled into the doorway, trying to make himself invisible. He had walked most of the day, always moving, to avoid the police who seemed to be on every corner. He had tried to cultivate an air of going somewhere, of being on an errand. He didn't want to seem journey-less. Arizona was cracking down on illegal immigrants, but how did America expect them to stop coming when there was opportunity here, even if you had to fight to get it? Jose had spent his last coins on a meal earlier and considered how he would make it through tomorrow. Maybe his cousin would help out, if he could only make it that far north. But at least the Tucson streets were warm enough all year round to make waking up tomorrow a likely event. Jose started to feel sleep easing him away from the hard ground, when a vehicle pulled up near him, engine idling. He lay motionless, hoping it was not the police or immigration come to take him away. If he stayed very still, perhaps they wouldn't even see him.

A car door slammed and footsteps came towards him. No chance of escaping notice then, he thought. He sat straight up, preferring to see who it was, to give himself a chance if he needed to run. A man stood in front of him dressed in black fitted clothes. He didn't look like a cop. A van marked 'Tucson State Shelter' was parked on the road behind him.

"Do you need somewhere to stay?" the man asked. "We have a shelter and food for the night. You shouldn't be on the streets."

"I'm OK here, man. I'm moving on tomorrow. Thanks for the offer."

"There may be work tomorrow if you come with us." The man was insistent. "We have some construction going on at the shelter. You could help out and earn some cash. You need some money right now?"

Jose considered his options. The money would definitely come in handy. He ignored his misgivings and nodded. Then he picked up his blanket and meager bag of possessions and walked towards the van. The man opened the back and waved him inside.

Jose realized his mistake as soon as the door shut behind him. Another man was hidden within, who grabbed him as soon as he stepped inside. Slammed down on the floor, he felt a needle being pushed into his neck. He struggled wildly, shouting as the van drove off until the drugs silenced him. There was no one to hear him on the street outside, and security cameras would only show a homeless man being helped to shelter for the night. No one would report him missing. No one even knew he was there.

Jose woke up to the dull thunk of wood being chopped. It was a sound he knew well from his childhood in Mexico where he would cut wood for the cooking fire with his father. His head was fuzzy but he could feel his hands tied behind him and his feet secured tightly. He opened his eyes and realized he was strapped to a wooden post, stacked firewood around his legs. A gag was wrapped around his mouth, the stink of smoke and some other rank smell on the material. A man was watching him. A tall slim figure, expensively dressed, who caressed a stone that lay in the palm of his hand.

"The Lord's fire purifies as well as destroys." The man said with a smooth tone, as if he were a professor giving a lecture to interested students, not to a terrified homeless man tied to a post. "Fire has been part of ritual sacrifice through many geographies and to many gods. It was the death assigned to martyrs of the Christian faith, and was a favored instrument of mercy for the Dominicans in the auto da fe of the Spanish Inquisition. You are in esteemed company, my friend."

The drugs had completely worn off now and Jose began to struggle as another man began piling up smaller logs and kindling around his legs, stacking it close.

'Please,' Jose tried to speak and plead with his eyes. 'Why?' was the question on his lips. The firewood was piled high enough now, and the man leaned in to look at him more closely. He reached forward and put the stone over Jose's head so it hung against his chest. Jose could feel the weight of it, coolness against his flesh, and yet he knew it would soon be searing pain.

"This stone is a blessing for you. You should be honored that I have chosen you to die in this way, wearing the stone of the Apostles, symbol of the brotherhood in Christ."

He stepped back and signaled to the man behind him, who brought out a can of gasoline. He sloshed it over Jose and the pile of wood beneath him. Jose struggled again in his bonds, seeing his death upon him and terrified of the pain to come. He screamed against his gag, the throttled noise stifled by material that was now drenched in gasoline. He shut his eyes in fear, feeling the soaked clothes he stood in and whimpering, praying wildly for some miracle to save him. Then Jose heard the click of a lighter, and the man lit a taper.

"So long, my friend. Let the fire take you through."

The light dipped, small flames crackled and began to take hold. The initial warmth grew quickly to sparks which caught on the gasoline, exploding into tongues of flame, engulfing Jose. His legs began to burn and he howled into the gag as the agony spread, obliterating his consciousness. He died with a last prayer on his blackened lips. It was only a few minutes before the skin on the man's body had burnt through and flames consumed his flesh.

Joseph Everett stood watching, engrossed in the patterns of the fire, a wet cloth over his mouth and nose to block the stench of gasoline and cooking flesh. He watched for the moment the man died, his spirit transfigured into flame, a meditation of life into death. He gazed as the glowing stone burnt into the man's flesh, bright gold lit by the dancing fire. This was how the spiritual masters felt when their souls were refined, he thought with triumph. This was the moment of glory.

The fire was just embers and ashes when he removed the stone. He cracked it from the burnt chest cavity and pulled it over the corpse's head. Joseph didn't touch it, but wrapped it in a pure white linen cloth, feeling the last of the warmth it contained. Then he headed out in the dawn, back towards the city and the hospital, leaving his men to clean up the mess. Perhaps this time …

CHAPTER 17

Santiago de Compostela, Spain
May 20, 2.45PM

JAKE ARRIVED BACK AT the airport in a Spanish police vehicle and bounded up the steps into the plane. Morgan lay back reading one of the Moleskine journals on the reclining seats.

"Coffee?" Morgan lifted the fresh mug at him nonchalantly. "Just made, still fresh in the pot."

Jake grinned at her.

"Glad you were so worried about me. Nice diversion with the Holy Door. You should have seen the faces of the priests as you left, with me still swinging in the dome. All their worst nightmares come true."

"I think the pilgrims will suffer with enhanced security from now on," she replied with a smile, sitting forward on her chair. Jake sat down next to her.

"The police mentioned there was a stabbing in the crypt. Are you okay?"

"One of the Thanatos guys made it down there but he didn't win this prize." Morgan pulled the stone from her pocket and handed it to Jake. "This one is somehow more authentic than the ones we have already. It's hardly been touched. There's no decoration or carving like the others."

Jake examined it.

"Do you think we should be feeling something now we have three stones in one place? Should we be speaking in tongues or something?"

"You believe that about as much as I do," Morgan replied with a smile. She took the stone back and tucked it away deep in her jacket pocket. "But I still need to get the others. Whatever they can do, we need to hurry for Faye and Gemma's sake."

"I know," Jake sat down at the table, putting his hand over hers briefly. She waited just a second before she pulled her hand away and the moment was broken. He noticed a curl of dark hair hanging down across her face and she brushed it back behind her ear, her skin luminous from the Spanish sun shining through the plane window.

Jake had known she would get back from the church with no problems. When he had seen the Holy Door open and Morgan dash out, he had slid back down the rope and let the police take him away, knowing she was safe. They made a good team, and what he had heard about the fight in the crypt made him even more sure of the fact. He had only heard second hand about what happened, but clearly she could look after herself and that confidence made her strangely unapproachable. He hadn't met a woman like her in a long time. Someone he didn't have to look after. He snapped out of it.

"I need to speak to Marietti and report back. Maybe we can get some help on our next location."

"Go ahead," Morgan glanced up, a frown on her face as she studied the journal. She was cross-referencing it with the information Ben had given her. Jake walked into the small pilot's area and put in a call to Marietti.

"Do you have the stone of James?" the Director said, curt and business-like.

"Yes, sir. Morgan found it but we were tracked and a

team from Thanatos were there to intercept. They may still be following us, so we need to move on quickly."

"We've had intel that there's a bounty out on you two so it's likely you'll be followed all the way. You must stop those stones falling into the wrong hands, whatever it takes. Talk to Martin now, he has your next destination."

Jake was patched through to Martin Klein in the basement of ARKANE. He walked back into the main cabin and switched to speakerphone, gesturing for Morgan to listen in.

"Hey Spooky, what have you got for us?"

The line crackled a little, but Martin's enthusiasm could be clearly heard.

"The stone of Thaddeus; I think it's in northern Iran."

Morgan looked quizzical and leaned forward to speak.

"Hi Martin, it's Morgan. What's the specific link back to the Apostles? I know there was an early Church in Persia but why would there be a stone there?"

Martin outlined his research.

"You're right, Christianity was established early in Persia, now Iran. Some of the people who heard the Apostles speak on Pentecost were Persians, and it's written that they took the Gospel back with them and started the Church. The Apostle Thaddeus, also known as Jude, is venerated as one of the founders and patron saints of the Church there. Despite its modern reputation for intolerance and fundamentalist Islam, Persia was at the forefront of culture for millennia."

Morgan nodded. "I see what you mean. Christians have been persecuted there but ancient churches still remain. Iran has some phenomenal archaeological treasures, but it's not exactly a tourist destination these days. Go on."

"Well, the Armenian Apostolic Church is one of the oldest Christian communities in the world. Armenia was also the first country to adopt Christianity as its official religion in 301 AD, tracing its origins to the Apostles. The

Armenian Church followed its own path, officially splitting with Rome and Constantinople in 554 after rejecting the position of the Church at Chalcedon."

Jake was looking a little lost at the finer points of Christian history, so Morgan explained, "Chalcedon was a turning point in early Church history with the differences in belief causing a schism between east and west."

Martin continued.

"The Armenians and Eastern orthodox believe in one incarnate nature of Christ, uniting human and divine, whereas the Roman Church believed in a dual nature: human and divine as separate. The Armenians still have claim to a part of ancient Jerusalem and one of their Patriarchs resides there. The Persians also have a long history in the Bible, with Cyrus the Great, Cambyses and Darius all mentioned. It's also near the rumored location of biblical Eden itself."

Morgan nodded. "We don't have any other solid leads right now so it's worth a try."

"OK Martin," Jake said. "Can you email that over and we'll review it en route?"

"Sure, it's a long flight. You'll need some reading material. And be careful, Jake. Thaddeus is the patron saint of lost causes and desperate situations. Just make sure you don't need his help out there. Good luck."

He hung up. Jake looked at Morgan.

"Guess it's Iran next, then. I'll sort out the clearance."

After checking all the data with the flight crew, Jake went back into the cabin to find Morgan curled up asleep in her recliner chair. Her face was creased with concern and Jake knew she worried about her family. For a moment he was struck by jealousy. He had no family to worry about, and none to care about what happened to him. Had he really allowed himself to become so isolated? Or had his lifestyle at ARKANE nipped any relationships in the bud. He shook his head. There was never any time to change things in between the increasing frequency of missions. It seemed the world erupted with global threats on a weekly basis, but they had about seven hours before they arrived in Iran, so there was time to rest now. Jake pulled down one of the flight blankets and draped it around Morgan. She stirred a little and then settled back in, her face more relaxed. He sat back in his own chair, watching her breathe, a frown creasing his forehead as he puzzled how to deal with the challenge ahead.

CHAPTER 18

Tabriz, Iran.
May 21, 10.02am.

MORGAN FOLLOWED JAKE THROUGH the main bazaar of Tabriz, a full length burqa hiding her body as well as concealing weapons beneath. Jake walked briskly in front, without looking back at her, as a man should in this part of the world. She keenly observed the bazaar around them through her veil. It was high domed with red brick ceilings studded with star-shaped skylights that let in shafts of light. The barreled arches were vaulted like a cathedral but it was clearly a place of commerce and business. There were shops selling carpets and sweet tea, men in suits and fez hats playing chess, fabric shops and sacks overflowing with grain and flour, spices, dates and walnuts, apricots and almonds.

Morgan felt that the high ceilings gave it a light feeling, akin to the European covered markets of Brussels and London. Upmarket shops were built into the bazaar walls, with wooden paneled doors and goods spilling out on to the footpath hinting at the treasures inside. Morgan knew that she could have lingered here under different circumstances, fingers trailing over silk, the scent of jasmine and cinnamon hanging in the air. But there was no time for that now.

The muezzin's call to prayer echoed through the bazaar

as they walked through. The faithful threw down their mats and prayed with the imam. Jake hesitated briefly but others scurried past, ignoring the devotion, so they continued on, deeper into the souk. Men smoked sheesha pipes in the cafes, drinking mint tea. Women talked in anonymous groups nearby, hidden in full length black. Piles of soap were heaped up next to oil paintings, sweet shops jostled with clothing hanging from doorways, gold glittered in the jewelry shops while the hot sun poured down through the skylights. Morgan noticed that some of the arches were decorated with Koranic verses in deep indigo, a holy color overlaid with glorious pearly Arabic script, and gold patterns set back in the niches.

It was Morgan's first experience of Iran, and certainly not the way she had expected to see it. Tabriz was a mottled azure city, colorful and busy with architecture from millennia ago to skyscrapers of the industrial age. She had learnt from Martin's notes that it was the fourth largest city in Iran, situated in the north western corner of the country, near the borders of Turkey, Armenia, and Azerbaijan. An archaeological paradise few were able to visit because centuries of invasion, war and neglect had left the ruins unable to be explored.

They were heading for the church of St Mary, considered to be the second oldest church in the world after Bethlehem in Israel. Built in the twelfth century, it was the seat of the Archbishop of the Armenian Church. It was even mentioned by Marco Polo in his travels, as Martin's notes had informed them. As they entered the tiny square in front of the church, Morgan noticed the high bell tower with its ancient bronze bell and a rough hewn rope hanging down, ready for ringing. It was quiet today, only being rung on high festivals. The whole atmosphere was one of remaining quiet and unnoticed, a silent witness to an ancient faith practiced in an overwhelmingly Muslim country.

The church had been built over an Armenian holy place, some of the rocks as old as the faith itself. Morgan and Jake approached the porticoed door to the church and stooped to enter the small door set in large wooden panels. A heavy scent of incense overwhelmed them as they blinked in the dark interior of the church, eyes adjusting to the dim light but the cool air was welcoming after the harsh heat outside. At first glance, the church was simple and clean with wooden seats facing a basic altar but looking more closely, Morgan could see frescoes of ecclesiastical figures on the walls.

"Stay here, I'll talk to the priest," Jake whispered. He moved down the aisle towards a robed figure tending the altar near the front of the church. Morgan took the chance to kneel for a moment. Through the veil shielding her face, she looked around the church for some symbol of the Apostles. It was a long shot, coming here, she thought. They really had no idea where the stone might be, but the Armenian Church was one of the most ancient and the apostolic succession was indeed precious to the faith here. She knew that Armenian Christians had been persecuted as early as in the first century AD so the faith had caught hold quickly so it was possible a stone could be here. Morgan could see that there were side altars and a staircase on the eastern side of the church, but it would be too obvious to investigate them closely on her own. There were no women in here, only a few men, so she stood out by her very presence.

Jake returned and bent down next to her.

"There's a shrine to the Apostle Thaddeus at the side of the church. Follow me. I said we wanted to pray there."

He walked away and she followed closely, her head down in a modest pose as they entered the shrine. The side chapel was decorated with graphic images from the gospels, as well as the deaths of the saints depicted in fine detail. Morgan noticed a panel showing Simon the Zealot being sawn in half with a long saw while crowds of people looked on, jeering.

His face was bright and shining; a halo lit his features. He showed no pain, though blood spurted from his side. Opposite was St Peter's crucifixion in Rome, upside down at his own request because he didn't deserve to die like his Savior. The scenes glorified and paid homage to death, or perhaps to the triumph of faith over a physical end. Illuminating the chapel was a large stained glass window intricately decorated with symbols of the saints. Morgan quickly scanned the side panels, looking for any sign of Thaddeus, while Jake went to the altar and knelt in case the priest was watching. She found the figure of the Apostle on the western side, recognizable by the club he carried.

"Jake, look at this," she whispered. "There are flames around his head but it's as if he's above all this suffering. He's even wearing a stone." Morgan could see the necklace seemed to be raised above the rest of the painting. "Do you think it's actually in there? Under the paint?"

Jake came over quickly.

"It might be but we don't have much time in here, so you'd better work fast."

Morgan nodded.

"You stand by the doorway and keep watch if anyone comes near. I'll see what's under this paint."

With Jake guarding the doorway, Morgan hoisted up her burqa and revealed a tool belt underneath along with a couple of hand guns. She took out a tiny metal file and started to saw around the bump in the panel, careful to cut closely so as not to disturb too much of the fresco. The disturbing image of Simon's bloody sawn torso just to her left made her shudder. What people suffered for faith. Would she be able to go that far for her family if it came down to it? Jake's low whistle broke her concentration and she looked behind to see him frantically motioning her to stop and come over. Looking around the corner of the door, they saw a group of men in military uniform entering.

"I recognize the leader from the cathedral in Spain," Jake whispered. "They must have tracked us here."

"Then we must take the stone. We can't leave it here. You need to hold them off."

She handed him one of the pistols she had concealed. Back at the fresco, she started to cut more quickly, less worried about preserving the painting and more concerned with her own life. Five men were heading down the aisle to the priest, weapons drawn.

"Hurry," Jake whispered.

He began to slowly close the heavy door to the chapel, just as the leader spoke to the priest who pointed in their direction for this was no sanctuary for armed men or Westerners. The leader swung around to see the door shutting and immediately shouted to his men. They took cover, fanning out around the church, weapons pointed at the closing door.

"You'd better be ready soon," Jake said. "We're about to have company." He stood next to the door, back pressed against the wall of the chapel. "Lucky these old places have such thick walls. It will buy us some time."

Morgan desperately poked the file under the stone, trying to lever it out.

"I've just about got it. Give me one more minute." Flakes of paint lodged in her fingernails as she scratched at the broken surface.

"I don't think we have another minute," Jake said, as the firing started, bullets ricocheting off the ancient door and walls. "They'll blow up this door soon."

"I've got it," Morgan said, as she prized the stone loose from the neck of Thaddeus the Apostle. It was covered with bits of paint but she could still make out the carvings. It was the same rock as her own stone. "Let's get out of here."

She tucked the stone deep into her tool belt, securing it under her robe. Jake grinned and pointed up at the dramatic stained glass window.

"There's no way out of this chapel, except through that."

"You know we're going to hell for blowing up a church." Morgan replied, a wry smile on her face. "Just make sure you only shoot out a few panels."

"We can get through the biggest one there," Jake said, pointing upwards. "It looks like the gates of Hell. How appropriate."

The door started to rattle as the team of men slammed into it, using one of the pews as a battering ram. Morgan was certain they would move onto explosives next.

Jake indicated the window with his gun.

"As soon as we're out, we need to split up and meet back at the plane. Are you good with that?"

"It's easier for me to get lost in the crowd. I'm more worried about you."

Jake laughed. Morgan noticed that the crinkles around his eyes made his corkscrew scar dance.

"Time to go."

"I think you're enjoying this just a little too much," Morgan said, as Jake raised his gun and shot several times at the stained glass window's bottom panel. Jumping up onto the altar, he used a candlestick to smash the final shards of glass and helped Morgan up through the hole. She used her robe as a cushion against the broken glass and dropped the short distance onto the ground outside. The commotion in the church had caused a crowd to gather, but they were mainly looking curiously at the pair as Jake jumped down beside her.

"See you at the plane," Morgan's smile was masked but her eyes were shining. Despite all the problems they were facing, she had to admit there was an up side. It had been too long since she had felt this alive. Perhaps she had discarded the adrenalin rush of combat in haste when she had left the military. An explosion burst behind them, and they ran off in opposite directions into the crowd. It wouldn't be long before the men started to track them through the souk.

Morgan ran a little way and then slowed, ducking into an alleyway to pull the burqa over herself properly. She emerged and entered a fabric shop where she blended in with the other women shopping. She breathed deeply in relief knowing that the men pursuing her could not risk stopping any women on the streets to search them. This was a strict Muslim city and they would be punished for harassment. Soon she was confident the danger had passed and she went slowly back to the plane, hoping Jake wasn't in too much trouble.

CHAPTER 19

JAKE SLIPPED INTO THE crowd but people were turning and staring at him, some pointed and soon several of the men were charging after him. The bazaar seemed the best place for him to hide so he kept turning corner after corner, doubling back towards the church. He heard shouting behind him and ducked into a barber's shop that clung to the side of the souk.

A man was being shaved and several cut-throat razors lay on a side table. Jake pulled out a pile of US dollar notes and shoved them at the barber, picking up a razor and ducking out the back of the shop. The barber shrugged and pocketed the cash. It was not his business what this man wanted with a razor in the narrow streets of the market. Jake waited outside the back door of the barber's shop, knowing that they would come after him. He was tense and ready, stilling his breathing and focusing on what he must do next.

He heard voices in the shop, angry shouting. The barber must have pointed out the back as the noise grew closer. There were two men at least. They must have split up, but he was still outnumbered. Jake tensed, ready to strike. At least he had surprise in his favor.

One man came out, then a second, both striding away from him into the alley behind the shop. They clearly didn't expect him to be waiting for them. He grabbed the second man from behind and sliced across his throat with the razor. The man didn't even have time to scream. Blood spurted over Jake's arm and as the body dropped he shoved it into the back of the first man, ripping the gun from his hand and firing it into his body. It was done in less than thirty seconds.

Jake's breath came heavily and fast. He slowed it purposefully, calming the adrenaline rush. He had not killed in a while, but his pent up anger and knowledge of what these men would have done to him and Morgan had left him no choice. There was too much at stake here to let them live, and he knew they would not have stopped for him. The frantic shouting of the barber was enough to get him moving again.

He ran down the alley away from the bodies and back towards the plane. Marietti would have some cleaning up to do, as his prints would be on the razor and people had seen his face. Luckily ARKANE had connections that made these issues go away. They also provided a priest for confession if team members needed it. Jake didn't. He had made his peace with death a long time ago, when he had identified the bodies of his butchered family in Walkerville, near Johannesburg. South Africa was a mess of politics and religion wasn't the only thing that could spark attempted genocide. After he had revenged their deaths with a silent bloody rampage, he'd needed an outlet for his violence. His mother's British passport enabled him to join the British military and he soon rose through the ranks until the fateful night he had encountered Marietti. So Jake didn't shy from killing if the mission demanded it, and he didn't need to talk about it afterwards. Life was brutal and there were no prizes except to stay alive.

CHAPTER 20

Tucson, Arizona, USA
May 21, 11.09am

JOSEPH EVERETT WAS READING Eusebius' 'On the Martyrs' in his study. He punctuated the passages by pacing back and forth as he considered his plan. After the death of the homeless man, he had taken the stone to Michael and put it around his brother's neck. He thought he had seen a glimmer of fire in the dead eyes but there was no change. He was disappointed and desperate for an answer. Now he was scouring these ancient texts for clues as to how the deaths of the saints might transform the stones to instruments of healing and power.

As he read, he noted the inventive ways they had of killing people in those early centuries. In the face of such horrific death people became even more fanatic for their faith. Emotion stirred up by the murder of martyrs seemed to be what sustained the growth of the Church. Perhaps blood and violence were the price to pay for vibrant faith? He knew that people valued something more when the price was high. For those willing to give up their lives for their beliefs, it must have been a heady time. He stopped pacing as the implication of his thoughts hit him. Maybe he needed to remind Morgan just what was at stake here, how high the cost could be if she didn't bring him the stones. He speed dialed a number on his phone.

"Take the woman out to the desert but leave the child."

He made another call to his property manager.

"Start the fire in the kiln, I'll be needing it later. We're driving out now. See you in a few hours."

Joseph's fascination with flames went back for many years, a pyromania that fed his soul. It was creation in destruction, leaving a path for new life in the wake of old. The sense of power was intoxicating, that a tiny spark could grow to consume whole cities and it was the elemental spirit of fire that he craved. The fires of Hell were nothing to a pure soul and the Christian iconography had those pure in heart walk through the fires unharmed. He loved the story in the book of Daniel where the faithful walk in the furnace with the angels and then emerge, triumphant and unscathed. He had devoured the details of mass cremation of the bodies at Auschwitz; the Nazis had been experts on disposal of physical evidence and so he had learned how fire could be used to hide dark deeds. Joseph had started with arson as a young man but the risk of prosecution soon became too great as his business and political ambitions grew, so he had found sublimation for his pyromania in pottery and kilns. It was a socially acceptable way in which he could indulge his visceral need for flame, his own addiction. The physical act of feeding the fire, the colors that danced in the kiln, were an alchemy that he ached for, a fiery transformation of matter to his desire. Over the years, he had found that the kiln could be used for other purposes than just firing pots.

Joseph headed out in his four wheel drive to the desert scrubland south west of Tucson. The kiln was on his desert property giving him the privacy to indulge himself out here. It was far away from the city and desolate enough that no one would even want to trespass here. The land was technically owned by one of his subsidiary businesses, buried in shell companies so it couldn't be traced back to him.

As he drove, Joseph thought of Michael in the hospital, listless in his bed. Then he shook his head as if to clear the thoughts - he shouldn't focus on the past, but on the future. The search for the stones energized him now, as if a part of his mind clung to a primitive belief, desperate that the power of God in the stones would heal them both. Joseph smiled, his mirrored sunglasses flashing in the harsh Arizona sun. He had faith in business and money but increasingly in an ancient power. Not a personal Jesus but a primal energy that lifted the dead from the ground, brought fire and wind to earth on Pentecost and burned the early Church into the consciousness of millennia. He would call this power back to earth soon enough.

Out in the desert, Joseph pulled up to the basic hut that was a few hundred meters from the kiln. Another car waited by the hut where two of his men sat in the air conditioned interior with the woman, Faye. She was tied, her hands behind her back and a gag over her mouth. The men got out as Joseph approached.

"Take the rest of the wood to the kiln and stoke it up," he said. "I need it burning at its hottest today. I have a special firing to do."

The men moved away and Joseph opened the door where Faye sat restrained. She was shaking but her eyes were defiant.

"Oh, my dear, what you will experience today," Joseph said, reaching towards her. She turned her head away, the only motion she could manage in her constrained state. He moved his hand swiftly into her hair and pulled it savagely back, exposing her throat. Leaning close, he whispered, "And your sister is going to watch."

Laughing, he let go and walked away from the car, leaving her to sit in the heat while he joined the men by the kiln. It was the size of a large cupboard with shelves for pots, but with room for a person in the middle of the space to make it easier to stack the shelves. There was a thick glass window in the door so the pots could be watched. It took hours to build the temperature high enough for firing but at that point, the flames would burn blue and bright. It was almost ready now.

Joseph set up a video camera at the front of the kiln, turned it on and then motioned for one of the men to bring Faye. She struggled and kicked, screaming into her gag. The man ended up throwing her over his shoulder and carried her, kicking all the way. They finally got her tied to a chair, facing the door of the kiln. Tears ran down her cheeks. She was shaking with terror.

Joseph bent down to her.

"This is what happens if your sister doesn't bring the stones to me by Pentecost."

He pulled his gun and whipped around quickly, using it to smash the face of the man who had carried her over. The man was knocked to his knees, briefly stunned and he shook his head, trying to clear it as blood poured from his nose. Joseph laughed and turned to kick the man, his boot connecting with a thud and the man fell back, his face confused.

"What …?" he tried to ask what was going on but Joseph was on him, his heavy desert boots audibly breaking the man's ribs as he rolled over to protect himself. Faye could see a mania in Joseph now as he called to the other man.

"You, help me."

Together they opened the door of the kiln and threw the

overpowered man in. The flames roared as they sucked in the oxygen from the air and a surge of dry heat washed over Faye as she watched in horror. The man's brief screams were terrible as the heat immediately caught his body. Through the window she could see that he seemed to dance in the blue fire before falling to his knees. Finally he curled up on the floor as the flames consumed him.

Faye had shut her eyes, but Joseph forced her face towards the blaze. He spoke into the camera, his voice low and mesmerizing, hypnotized by the sight.

"Watch how he burns, Faye. There are demons in the flames, you can see their shapes dancing, and they draw you in. You want to caress them, to capture their essence between your fingers, but they will destroy you if you get too close."

He leaned in closer now, his breath hot on her face with the flames burning behind.

"Yet we are still drawn to it, enraptured by its beguiling dance and sensuous nature. We love to be naked with it, warmth dancing on our skin, candle wax dripping, burning but hurting in a deeply pleasurable way. Imagine what it would be like to feel the lick of that tiny tongue of flame along your skin, Faye. It looks so gentle, like it would tickle you. But that blue orange dancer is pain and death, its caress the last pleasure you would feel in this life."

With these words, he licked the side of her face. He held her chin steady, his tongue darting around her jaw line and swirling into her ear. Faye squirmed and tried to evade his wet tongue, the overwhelming heat from the kiln seeming to burn through her. He wound his fingers through her hair and held her in a tight grip again, the tears running down her face soaking the gag that choked her.

Joseph spoke louder, his words a challenge with the backdrop of the raging fire behind him.

"Fire is a cruel mistress, taking to itself as much as it would have before dying out when there is nothing left to consume. Fire is elemental, it is the key to life, but it also burns, destroying whatever it touches. Fire feeds the soul and spirit. The saints died by fire and the smoke from candle flames take the prayers of the faithful to heaven, crossing the boundary between earth and spirit."

Joseph stood straight, taking the stance of a preacher before his church. Faye cowered beneath his upraised arms. He knew what a powerful image this would make on the film he would send to Morgan and ARKANE and he reveled in the feeling of authority.

"Fire has ever been the basis of myth. Prometheus brought fire to humans from the Gods. He stole it from Zeus and with it transformed humanity from bestial needs to higher thought. Fire was such a precious and secret gift that he was punished for his crime by being tied to a rock while a great eagle ate his liver every day, only to have it grow back overnight and be eaten again the next day, for all Eternity. From fire mankind's highest purpose was born and is fed to greater heights."

Wheeling around, he pointed into the kiln itself, where the blackened body was burning still.

"Volcanoes brim with fire and Vulcan works there, shaping weapons for the gods from the flames. Fire goes down to the center of the earth, an ever shifting core of molten element that waits to overtake us with destruction. Then the phoenix rises from the flames, a mythical fire spirit with wings of flame gold and scarlet. It is a sign of resurrection, the being that rises again from destruction, a continuing cycle of rebirth from the ancient to ancient again."

He broke off and pointed dramatically at Faye sobbing with her eyes shut.

"The Pentecost stones will bring resurrection to my brother and the beginning of a renaissance in faith and miracles. Bring them to me or she will be my sacrifice to the gods of flame."

Joseph fell silent then and stared into the fiery kiln as the sound of Faye's sobbing and the roar of the flames filled the air. There were no angels in the fire today, only djinn of dirty smoke. He knew the glaze today would be stained with dark red, russet like the desert earth and the blood of men.

CHAPTER 21

St Peter's Basilica. Vatican City, Italy.
May 22, 8.40am

MORGAN AND JAKE STOOD on the Ponte de Castel
St Angelo, looking over the Tiber towards the cupola of St
Peter's. Neither had slept on the plane from Iran to Italy, not
after Marietti had sent them the video. Morgan's mind was
still filled with the images of the flames consuming that body,
petrified it had been Faye and then seeing her, terrified, tied
to a chair and gagged, the reflection of flames flickering in
her eyes as the madman Everett ranted at the screen. They
both held steaming cups of black coffee, deep dark circles
under their eyes. Now Morgan cradled her cellphone under
one ear, listening as David cried and then screamed at her,
venting his rage and helplessness. She turned away so Jake
couldn't hear their conversation, as her voice broke with the
anguish she felt.

"I'm trying David, I truly am. I'm so sorry. We'll get
them back. I promise."

After Tabriz, Morgan had thought that the four stones
they already had would be enough to start bargaining for the
lives of her sister and niece, but the video made it clear that
she needed to get all of them. There would be no bargaining. With no other leads, they had decided to refocus on the

places where the Apostles' bones were known to be kept. Rome, the parish of the Holy Father, home of the Catholic Church, was the obvious next step. The stone of St Peter would surely be kept near the Popes in the basilica named after the saint. It was just a question of narrowing down the potential locations. The myths of the stones emphasized one of the spiritual gifts was an enhanced creativity, a stunning ability to render the earthly as divine and surely this place was the pinnacle of artistic creative expression.

Morgan gazed up at the Papal fortress and the tomb of the Roman Emperor Hadrian towering above them. The castle was linked to the Vatican by the Passetto di Borgo, a covered, fortified tunnel but today they would not be secretly stealing in a back entrance. They would be walking straight in the front door. People came from all over the world to see Il Papa, and twice a week he performed an early Mass in the magnificent church. Lines to enter the Basilica only started around ten when day trippers made their way there, so to get a seat in a service before that time was easy enough, and this would be their way in.

Jake was speaking on his cell phone, making last minute plans for their pickup. If they were to take something from the Vatican, they would need a quick exit. Morgan stood beneath the replica of Bernini's Angel with the Crown of Thorns. It gazed down at her with blank eyes, holding one of the instruments of Christ's passion. Bernini was the final architect of St Peter's, his works were all over the cathedral. It was his vision that finished the dome after Bramante, Raphael, and Michelangelo and he was also known as a creative genius, perhaps touched by divine power so Bernini's fingerprint would be the one they sought in the basilica.

Martin Klein had been analyzing the potential location of the stone of St Peter, and it made sense for it to have been kept in Rome for millennia. Morgan knew that Peter was 'The Rock' of the Church and the iconography of stone was deeply bound into the Vatican, a persistent theme in the art and architecture of the ancient city within a city. Martin had proposed a theory that the Apostle's stone had been handed down by Keepers within the Vatican who were touched by the power of the stone, a blessing of creativity. He had traced the potential Keepers down to Bernini, the sculptor, artist and architect, but then the trail had disappeared. Their best chance was to follow Bernini's creations, and they were all over the Vatican, culminating in St Peter's Basilica itself.

They walked the short distance from the bridge up the Via della Conciliazione to the grand oval of Piazza San Pietro. Morgan looked up to the top of the colonnades surrounding the Piazza, to the saints who watched over the pilgrims. One hundred and forty saints sat atop the colonnades, men and women of faith throughout the ages, many martyred and standing here as testimony to the power of their God. Bernini had designed these colonnades along with the fountain in the forecourt, but it was the ancient red granite obelisk that dominated the piazza. It dated back to the fifth dynasty of ancient Egypt, brought to Rome by the Emperor Augustus, and was the only obelisk not to have toppled since ancient Roman times.

Jake and Morgan walked over to the tourist entrance, waited in line for a short time and passed easily through security at the gates. They walked through the colonnade, past the Swiss Guards in their red, yellow and blue striped tunics. Their primary job was to protect Il Papa and that's what Jake and Morgan were counting on today. Once the Pope was in the cathedral, all attention would be on making sure he was safe and they could act while backs were turned.

They filed into the church with the other worshippers, past the statue of Moses with the Ten Commandments, up the steps and into the imposing Basilica. There was a palpable sense of expectation in the air. Pilgrims to the

Basilica were praying and weeping at the culmination of their journey to this center of the Christian world. The scent of incense filled the air, dispersing in clouds towards the dome of Michelangelo and Morgan was vividly reminded of the cathedral in Santiago. A smile crossed Jake's face and she could see he was thinking about it too but there would be no attention-drawing stunts here. This time it was all about remaining unnoticed.

They walked into the main nave of the church, past the groups of people waiting for seats while others thronged the aisles trying to get into a good position to see the Pope when he entered. Morgan looked around her. The overwhelming color in the Basilica was gold, reflecting light from the high up windows. Even in the gloom, gold shone from the statues and decorations. From her study of ancient religion, she could see the influence of ancient Roman polytheism incorporated into the Catholic Church. The statues of previous Popes sat as gods on podiums with the faithful at their feet, praying for intercession. The cadavers of great Popes lay embalmed behind glass so the believers could look upon them and pray for their eternal souls. Morgan's favorite part of the Basilica was Michelangelo's *Pieta*, set in a niche by the door. The lips of the Virgin were soft, almost pliant, life-like even in marble. She barely looked the age of her dead son.

Just then, the choir begin to sing the Magnificat, filling the church with spiritual balm. It was the beginning of the pre-service, aimed at calming the crowd and instilling a sense of devotion before the Pope himself entered. Morgan loved the singing. It was a peace she often sought within the walls of Blackfriars although Father Ben seemed a long way away right now. She wanted to stop by one of the soaring columns and listen for just a minute, but Jake motioned for her to follow. They had two places to check for the stone and little time to do it in. Morgan looked at her watch. Eleven minutes until the Pope entered for Mass.

They made their way through the praying crowd to the tomb of Pope Pius X, his body lying behind glass near the front of the basilica in the Eastern arm of the cross. His body had been disinterred and was remarkably well preserved despite not being embalmed. It was said to be a miracle and other wonders had apparently occurred at the tomb so it was possible that this Pope had been a Keeper of the stone. Morgan and Jake knelt in front of the tomb and bent their heads to pray, looking through their fingers into the glass and bronze sarcophagus. Perhaps it was buried with him as miracles were said to have occurred here.

"There's something around his neck," Morgan whispered, glancing up at the Swiss Guard at his nearby post. "But I can't tell from here. How can we get closer?"

"You need to be more religious," he whispered back, before flinging himself at the sainted figure, prostrating himself in a fit of simulated enthusiastic prayer. He managed to press his face close to the glass before he was hauled back from it by the Swiss Guards on duty near the shrine.

"Scusi, scusi."

Jake apologized, his hands out in supplication. They let him go but watched warily as he knelt back down.

"It's an amulet of sorts but not the Pentecost stone. If it's in there with him, we'd need better access anyway. There's no way to break the glass. Let's try the Alexander monument."

Making the sign of the cross as they backed away, Jake and Morgan moved slowly across the church to Bernini's final masterpiece in St Peter's, the mausoleum of Pope Alexander VII. His statue sat in a niche on the western side, over a door to the outer church. Their focus was the huge bronze skeleton that supported the pink mottled marble, its arm uplifted, holding an hourglass. It was a homage to the end of time, certainly the end of Alexander's and perhaps Bernini's as well, as he died soon after it was finished. His family had worked in the church for many years, so he could have found and hidden the stone again. If he was a Keeper, Morgan wondered, what would he have done with it? They now had two minutes until the Pope entered.

"This is it, I'm sure. If Bernini had the stone, he would have left it here. The symbolism fits," Morgan whispered, as she stood near the statue, facing into the Basilica, as if watching for the Pope. "This will be our only chance. We have to take it."

Jake looked up at the hourglass held by the skeletal figure of death, whatever it contained was obscured by dust and time. It was also firmly attached to the skeleton's hand.

"Get ready to run. I'm going to try and break it."

A respectful hush fell on the cathedral and then the choir broke into song. All faces turned to the back of the church. The organ pealed and the sound of a thousand cameras clicked as the Pope walked into his parish, a rock star priest amongst a flock of fans. All eyes were upon him, including those of the Swiss Guard nearest them.

No one saw as Jake quickly climbed up onto the statue, wrapped a cloth around the hourglass and smashed it with his ultra-hard cell phone case, catching the splinters of glass in the cloth. The sound was masked by the adoration of the choir, but the Pope was swiftly nearing the front of the church and soon eyes would look forward again and they would be seen.

"There's nothing here," Jake said as he slid back down, the wrapped fragments in his hand. "It's empty. We need to go, right now."

They ducked out of the side door under the looming skeleton. Morgan felt a shiver of fear as she went under it, the face of Death staring at her as she passed. The failure to find the stone put her family one step closer to that monster.

They walked quickly away from the Basilica and out into the streets of Rome, stopping at a café to gather their thoughts.

"It was too much to hope that we would just find it there," Jake said. "But a full search of the Vatican archives is beyond our capability at this point. We may not be able to find all the stones, but we have to try for the other ones before it's too late."

Morgan held her head in her hands, eyes closed as she thought hard, desperate to find the answer to where the stone might be. She shook her head.

"I'm not giving up on this one yet. Just give me a little time."

Jake ordered them some pasta and coffee. There was nowhere to hurry to right now, as they needed to decide on their next destination. Morgan stared out the window at people passing, wondering how she could have been so wrong, chastising herself for wasting precious time. Where had they gone wrong in their research?

She watched Jake check email from Martin on his cell phone. He said something about Andrew and Amalfi but Morgan was still thinking about Peter. If any of the stones survived, then Peter's must have been the most protected, the most precious. Then she remembered something about the body of Pius. She had seen that coat of arms before.

Grabbing her own cell phone, she checked up on some facts about the Popes and Bernini.

"I've got it. This must be the right place. Look at this."

She turned the phone so Jake could see. It was a coat of arms, crossed keys with a lion and an anchor.

"What is that?" he asked.

"I think Martin was right about Pius X," Morgan replied. "This is his coat of arms and look, the lion of St Mark. Pius was Patriarch of Venice before he was Pope, and Mark was the evangelist who supposedly accompanied Peter on his travels. One of the gifts of the stones is communication and Mark's Gospel became the basis of Christian orthodoxy communicated across the world. He was like a beloved son of Peter, so it makes sense that he took the stone after the Apostle's death. The stone of St Peter must be in Venice."

CHAPTER 22

St Mark's Square, Venice, Italy.
May 22, 11.45pm.

PIAZZA SAN MARCO WAS dark as they approached by boat, the lagoon dancing with lights from the watery city, the smell of salty ocean on the light breeze. Morgan had been to Venice for the Biennale with Elian late one summer. Her memories of the place were colored with golden light reflecting on the water in the city of lovers. The air had been filled with music as string quartets played on the streets and the mood was champagne fizz and dancing. But the only strains of music she heard now were a lament for those lost days. She pushed those heavy thoughts away as the motorboat pulled alongside St Mark's Square wharf.

Gondolas bobbed in the water, gold trim glinting in the dark as water slapped against their sides in the quiet night. By day, the well worn paths from St Mark's to L'Accademia were packed, but now only a few people walked along the banks of the lagoon. Morgan and Jake hopped off the boat and headed across the square.

Morgan looked up at the imposing pink and grey granite columns that had stood guard over the square since the twelfth century. One column was topped by St Mark's winged lion gazing out to sea, symbol of the gospel writer himself. St Theodor, the first protector of Venice, perched on the other, with an ancient dragon-crocodile beneath his feet. The original pagan saint had been displaced by St Mark in the ninth century. Morgan smiled thinking that a gospel writer would always trump a lesser known saint. Between these two pillars in ancient times, criminals had been executed before baying crowds. She had read that, even now, Venetians will not walk between the pillars in case the bad luck followed them.

Legend told that the original Venetians were noblemen who fled from ancient Troy, and Morgan could see how the grandeur of days past was still aflame in the memory of this proud people. The twin columns cast shadows onto the square, reflections in the water that flowed out of the drain holes. Morgan knew that the lagoon city flooded more than sixty times a year now, this being one of those nights. She and Jake sloshed in rubber boots towards the Basilica, barely lit in the shadowed square. It was nearly midnight and they didn't have long to achieve their goal.

A whistle came from the shadow of the Doge's Palace and another man joined them. Jake and he exchanged a rough handshake, then he turned to Morgan.

"Welcome to Venice, I'm Mario."

"Mario's on our team based here," Jake said. "We have rooms in the secret chambers of the Doge's Palace."

"Why's ARKANE working here?" Morgan asked, curious to know despite the cold.

"This." Mario pointed down at the floodwaters that chilled their feet through the boots. "There are many who believe Venice won't last another generation. A larger than usual flood, a tidal wave, any freak weather event and this floating city will be washed into the sea. We have a project that is cataloging, studying, and in some cases removing, the religious art works from sites here. ARKANE is working under the auspices of religious study and research, but in the case of removal, we're putting expert forgeries in their place. The great paintings of Titian and Tintoretto as well as the Canova statues are all under threat. The two meter flood of 1966 devastated the city, so we need to protect what is here for when the waters come again. And they will come; it's just a matter of time. Our hope is to save the treasures of Venice while the locals continue to deny the change is coming. There is history here too vital to lose because stubborn people resist the might of nature."

He noticed Morgan shiver. "But it's cold out here. Let's get inside."

They waded through the ankle-deep water to the Basilica. Even in the muted light from the street lamps it was a riot of multicolored marble. Morgan knew that each pillar supporting the church was a different kind of stone, sourced from around the world to demonstrate the glory of the Venetian republic, La Serenissima. She looked up at the stunning mosaics. One of the panels showed St Mark's body as it was rescued from Egypt under siege in the ninth century. It had been smuggled to Venice under a pile of pork so the Muslims wouldn't search the cargo. She remembered that St Mark had supposedly washed up in the marshes of the Venetian lagoon after a storm and an angel had told him that his body would rest here eventually. Hundreds of years later, it came to pass.

Now, with the help of Martin's ARKANE database they had found that Pius had engaged repairs to the Basilica of St Mark's while he was Patriarch there in 1901. He could have hidden the stone then before relocating to the Vatican. Morgan dared hope that they would find it here, her desperation increasing with the imminent threat to her family. The skeptic in her doubted that the stones had any powers are all, but the weight of history and legend was beginning to press on her. If any of the stones had power, then St Peter's must surely be the most important. The Apostle anointed by Christ to become the rock of the church, the denier who became a champion of the gospel, who died in Nero's bloody vengeance for the great fire of Rome, crucified upside down, unworthy of the same death as his Savior.

Mario led them around the side of the building and in through a side door.

"I still have the keys from the last project we did here … and a private tour impresses the girls," he grinned. "The Basilica was built as a mausoleum and private chapel for the Doge, the elected ruler of Venice. It's attached to his Palace but we'll go in here to avoid the cameras on that side. So what are we looking for?"

Morgan could see that Mario was keen to help and eager to make a good impression. Clearly Jake had some influence within ARKANE.

"We're looking for a piece of stone," Morgan said. Mario laughed, the sound echoing in the cavernous dark.

"Have you seen the Basilica before?"

"It's been years since I was here for the Biennale and we didn't come inside but … wow!"

Mario shone his powerful flashlight into the dark and lit up patches of the walls, ceiling and floor.

"We have a lot of stone here," he said. "More than 8000 square meters of mosaic cover the walls, vaults and cupolas of St Mark's. Where do you want to start? Any information will help us narrow it down."

"OK," said Morgan. "We're looking for a rock that was part of the Pentecost story. Is there anything relating to that in the Basilica?"

Mario grinned at her.

"This is the right church for Pentecost. Come upstairs.

Be careful now. We need to go up to the balcony viewing platform."

Mario handed out headlamps which they put on, keeping their hands free to help them climb. The steps were ancient and worn. Huge gaps between them made it hard for pilgrims to mount but had made it easier to defend against invaders in ancient times. Morgan grasped the rail to pull herself up, her headlamp dimly lighting the way. They reached the viewing platform and Mario swung his powerful flashlight beam out over the abyss below them, and then towards the ceiling of the main dome.

"That's the Pentecost mural," he pointed upwards. "A glorious depiction of the Holy Spirit descending onto the twelve Apostles."

Morgan stared up at the scene. A huge circular mosaic of gold depicted twelve seated men, each with a stream of fire touching them, emanating from the throne of the Holy Spirit in the center. Four angels stood with wings outstretched, bright gold encircling them all.

"The detail's amazing. It's so bright even in this dim light."

Mario nodded.

"The mosaic work is incredibly detailed, all of it gold or precious stone. It's priceless."

Morgan pointed up at the mosaic. "Those red streams from their heads must be the tongues of fire. They all come from the central point. We need to examine the throne of God further." She used the powerful binoculars they had brought to examine the mosaic as Mario aimed the flashlight. "There's definitely something on the throne."

It looked like there was a small grey stone embedded there, a plain marker against the gold and jeweled ceiling.

Overshadowed by the number of bright stones, it could hardly be seen at all, but Morgan wondered whether it was actually the real jewel of the mosaic. Had Pius hidden the Apostle's stone in plain sight?

"What do you think?" Morgan passed the binoculars to Jake so that he could see it too. Her excitement was clear in her voice as she asked. "How can we get a closer look?"

"There's no way to get up there," Mario said. "The dome is directly over the main church nave, fifty meters above the ground."

Jake examined the buttress of the balcony, rubbing his chin in thought.

"There's no time for scaffolding," he said. "What other equipment do you have here?"

"There's the remote viewer we used to salvage some of intricate work on the church of Maria Salute. It's a mini helicopter so it'll be noisy."

Jake nodded. "We really have to get that stone tonight. If it's our only choice, we have to try."

"Sure, it's just next door in the Doge's Palace," Mario replied. "I'll be back in fifteen minutes. Sit tight, you two. Enjoy the view."

Mario headed back down into the darkness of the Basilica. They heard his footsteps retreat and the creak of the door shutting behind him. Now they had a moment to stop, Morgan felt the rush of the last few days catching up with her. The need for just a moment of respite was overwhelming.

"Can we turn off the lights and just be in the dark for a bit?" she asked. "It's so peaceful here."

"Of course."

She could hear the exhaustion in Jake's voice as well. This mission was taking it out of both of them. They turned off their flashlights and sat in silence, leaning against the ancient stone. The smell of incense was strong even at night, but the stink of the sewers was a dark tone beneath it, a pervasive problem of the flooding. In the quiet, Morgan felt an affinity with Jake, the first real tendrils of partnership. That was dangerous though. She was tired but that didn't mean she could let her guard down. She still didn't know enough about ARKANE but perhaps now was the time to find out.

"Is ARKANE retrieving artifacts alongside the Italian government?" she asked.

"Yes, although we're working primarily with the Vatican. Italy doesn't want to hear of Venice flooding or disappearing."

"Wasn't there talk of a flood barrier?"

"There have been plans for all kinds of ways to stop the waters, but nothing has been done and it floods all the time," Jake replied. "Venetians have to pump water from their houses and shops every morning as water rots away the foundations. We may be scuba diving in this gorgeous church in our lifetime."

Morgan imagined the eerie sensation of diving in here, the pillars looming from murky green water and the glint of gold from underwater flashlights.

"That would be amazing, but devastating," she said.

"There's nothing that can be done though for the ocean can't be stopped. It's been inevitable for centuries. Money has slowed down for urban renewal and people are leaving. Soon it will be a ghost town composed of memories. Even now it exists primarily for tourists because most of the young Venetians have left."

Morgan sighed. "It's such a shame. Venice feels like it should be an eternal city, but perhaps it's more of an idea than a real place. I must admit that the physical experience is a disappointment after the mental images built up over so long, although this Basilica is spectacular. It feels like a more spiritual place than St Peters for me, although perhaps that's because no one else is here."

In the darkness, Morgan felt Jake shift beside her. He was close but not quite touching. She could smell the clean scent of him and feel his body heat. She wanted to lean into him, to be held for just a moment in his strong arms, but there was danger there. She felt the connection between them, a spark of attraction that could explode in violence or passion. But in the dark, ghosts haunted them both, chilling their skin, pulling them away from the abyss of what could be. Morgan stopped herself, forcing her body to remain rigid, unbending even as he spoke from the dark.

"Do you believe in God, anyway? Are you doing this with any sense of belief about the stones or just for Faye and Gemma?"

His voice contained no trace of judgment, just curiosity. Morgan felt safe, concealed in the dark. It gave her courage to speak her real mind to a man she was beginning to trust.

"I believe in something beyond our experience, a realm above the physical that I can't see or touch, but that I feel sometimes in certain places. I don't believe in a savior who died for my sins, or a personal God who cares if I'm hurting. But I know there's an energy beyond us, a power of good and evil, a light that gives life and a darkness that can destroy us. I don't know. What do you think?"

Jake's voice was gentle, almost wistful.

"I used to be a Christian once, but what I've seen has destroyed that. Artifacts from ancient times and sacred words have blown my mind and changed my experience of the world and what people call God. I've decided that it's not about the religion you belong to, but the spirit of intent and of seeking your own truth."

Morgan was silent for a moment, debating whether to speak more. She felt a pressing desire to share her thoughts but was also wary of his opinion.

"I feel most spiritual and close to whatever God is when I scuba dive," she said quietly. "I'm so insignificant on the face of the world and yet so privileged to see life all around me. Nature shows the splendor in the universe, when so often what man creates comes nowhere near it." She paused. "Once I lay back on a dive alone and looked up through giant kelp to the surface. The sun was shining down through the deep green fronds, their pods waving in the surge. I saw God in that moment, in the tiny worlds living their life out under the oceans, with no thought of us."

The dark was a cloak to mask their honesty, their first real conversation held in the blackness of a magical place.

"What of the magnificent churches that we've been in over the last few days?" Jake asked. "Do you feel God here, or back in Rome or Santiago?"

"This is an amazing place, but the aim of cathedrals was always to make people feel in awe of their God. It was a sign of the power and riches of the Doge and the Venetian republic at a time when the grandeur of churches would demonstrate power and piety to all. Pilgrims would come, but is it awe of God, or man's creation? I prefer to find my spirituality in nature where man's hand is yet unseen."

"And what about the stones?" Jake asked. "What was Pentecost anyway? Is it a myth built on a grain of truth or a real power that we will put back together when the stones are reunited? If one stone can perform miracles like Varanasi, what will all twelve do in one place?"

"I can't see past Faye and Gemma now, Jake. We're in this for different reasons but I don't believe in a power that can change matter or perform miracles through pieces of rock. I'm a psychologist, and mass hysteria can explain the miracles in India. Even if there were miracles, that doesn't make them from God and it doesn't matter anyway. I need to do this to save my family. Can I count on you to help me to the end?"

Jake's silence was just a fraction too long but then they heard the door below open and footsteps echoed through the church as Mario returned.

They switched their head torches back on and blinked a little in the light. It brought them back to real life in the church and they avoided each other's eyes. It was as if the honest conversation in the dark had never happened. Mario reappeared on the balcony struggling with a metal suitcase containing the apparatus.

"We used this to inspect the dome of Maria Salute last year and repair cracks in the ceiling."

He put the case down and opened it to reveal a small remote controlled helicopter, with pincers and a tiny drill as well as a catch bag. Morgan could see the two men grinning at the mini-copter like little boys with a new toy.

"We used the attachments to plug holes and the catch bag to stop the mortar falling on Maria Salute but I think it'll do the trick. We need to hurry though. It's pretty loud. We can't get caught here. I'm not sure even Marietti would be able to placate the Patriarch of Venice over the desecration of the Basilica."

Fitting the equipment together, Mario and Jake made sure the rotors spun properly and started it up. The loud buzzing echoed, resounding around the dome. At first Mario used the controls to hover above the ledge and then directed it up to the Pentecost cupola. Jake spotlighted the stone with his stronger hand-held beam.

"There's a mini camera on the drill," Mario said. "It pokes upwards and around the rotors so there's no interference. Check out the image on the monitor, Morgan. It's grainy but you can clearly see the middle stone is different to the surrounds on the throne. That must be it."

Morgan knelt by the tiny monitor, anticipation building. Her professional curiosity was roused by what could be hidden here, and she felt immediately conflicted. How could she find enjoyment in what they did while Faye and Gemma were held hostage? She focused on the task at hand.

"Do you think anyone will notice it's gone?" she said. "After all, this could be the true relic of St Mark's, not the body of the evangelist."

"Don't worry Morgan." Mario reassured her. "You take this stone and I'll fashion a replica and replace it tomorrow night. No one will even know it's gone; the mosaic is too high up to see." Gently drilling around the side of the stone, Mario neatly positioned the catch bag underneath to catch the debris. "Almost there now. It's so small. I just have to lever it out ... OK, it's in the bag."

Mario guided the mini-copter back to their ledge and shut it down. Jake opened the catch bag, sifted through the fragments and scooped out the stone. He held it out. It was a rough dark circle, just smaller than his palm. The side that had been facing into the church was blank, almost worn, but the inner side was roughly carved, a circle within a square.

"Is that it?" Mario looked disappointed. "Is this all you're looking for?"

Jake turned it over in his hand, and looked at Morgan.

"What do you think? Can you verify it?"

"It looks like the same rock as the others," she said, "but it has to be the right one. Why else would a dull stone be mounted in the center of the golden Pentecost mural? It must have tremendous significance for the church."

But Morgan felt a sense of foreboding as she touched it. They now held five stones of the Apostles, but that wasn't enough. They had to find the others because time was running out.

CHAPTER 23

Desert property of Joseph Everett, Arizona.
May 22, 7.02pm

JOSEPH EVERETT WATCHED THROUGH the one-way mirror as Faye tucked Gemma into the small bed in the sparsely furnished room they were being held in. He listened as she finished telling her daughter a story.

"The princess was very brave and didn't cry, even though she was trapped in the magic castle."

"The prince is coming to save her, isn't he, Mummy?"

"Of course my darling, but the prince has to have adventures along the way, so he's a bit late."

"What 'ventures?"

"Sleep time now, GemGem. I'll tell you about the adventures tomorrow night."

Faye bent and kissed the little girl, stroking her hair. She turned the desk lamp away so Gemma's face was in shadow and she could sleep. Joseph felt himself admiring her. The woman was definitely resilient, or at least hid her fear well in front of the child. After the kiln she had been brought back here and Joseph had sat watching them. She had snatched Gemma into her arms and held her tightly, burying her head in the little girl's hair until she was pushed away by the protesting child. Then Faye's face had cleared and she pretended

that nothing had happened. It was as if she compartmental-
ized the experience and would not let her own terror affect
her daughter.

Joseph raised his hand to the glass and traced the shape
of Faye's face on it. She still sat on the bed looking down at
Gemma, holding her little hand. He felt a pang of longing
for this woman and a little girl to love. Could he have had
this life if his bitch of a mother had been different? What
if she had tucked her boys in and told them stories? All he
could remember were insults, taunts and the filthy cupboard
under the stairs, and now his own marriage was one of fear
and duty, bound by the public face he wanted the world to
know. But only Michael had really loved him, had told him
stories in the dark, stroking his hair as Faye was doing now.
What if he could take this woman for himself? Would she
love him?

He shook his head, wondering at his temporary weakness. He didn't know how to be with a woman like that.
She was nothing to him but a symbol of a life lost. Michael
didn't have a wife and child. He barely had breath left in
his body but his brother was his only family. Slamming his
hand against the glass, Joseph watched Faye start in surprise
and fear. She instinctively bent her body, protecting her
daughter as Gemma woke again and started crying. Joseph
stalked from the hidden room, focused on the end-game. It
was time to make plans for Pentecost.

CHAPTER 24

Doge's Palace, Venice, Italy
May 23, 2.33am

MARIO CAREFULLY PACKED THE pieces of the mini-copter back into the suitcase then the trio retraced their steps down the stairs and exited through a hidden doorway.

"This was once been used by the Doge for his personal visits to the church," Mario explained as he led Morgan and Jake behind the great marble pillars of rose and teal. "The secret rooms are hidden in floors built behind and above the open public rooms. These are simple wood, whereas the others are ornate and painted gold for impressions' sake. There are prison cells and even a torture chamber here."

Morgan shivered, memories of what she had suffered at the hands of those in power invading her thoughts. She pushed them away.

"Governments are all the same throughout the ages," she said, "nothing changes."

Mario shook his head.

"Actually, Venice was one of the most impressive early democracies. The government had a complicated election process that prevented the nepotism and despotism that plagued other parts of Europe at the time. It was truly a light in the medieval darkness of tyranny on the continent."

Morgan heard the pride in his voice, defense of his beloved city. She knew she had her own conflicting feelings about Jerusalem, a city she loved and despised, where truth was ever malleable and people's lives hung in the balance of the great religions. Perhaps Venice had been just as tangled.

Mario led them through the maze of tiny wooden spaces.

"This is the authentic Venice, the real halls of power. Casanova was imprisoned here, you know. He was one of the few who escaped. It is an amazing historical place, once the keeper of all the secrets of the republic."

They walked up the grand staircase to the first floor of the Doge's Palace, torchlight illuminating the colors of paintings covering the walls, the opulence of a once wealthy Venice. Mario stopped at a painted scene of a group of nobleman and opened a panel with a key. The hidden door swung open and they went inside the secret rooms of the Doge's government. The ceilings were low, half the size of the grand rooms they had come through, designed to fit two levels of offices to each of the public facing levels with tiny windows camouflaged into the outside walls, providing a little light to the dark space. Here the civil servants of the Venetian government had toiled away, the real power behind La Serenissima.

They finally reached a large open plan document room from which all the original Venetian paperwork had been removed. Wooden panels around the side walls were painted with the coats of arms of noblemen who had ruled Venice over the years. Morgan sank down into one of the chairs, still holding the stone they had retrieved. She wasn't letting it go. Even after their honest conversation in the dark of the Basilica, she couldn't trust Jake's motives for seeking the stones. But it had been a long day and she badly needed sleep. Mario pulled some blankets and a sleeping bag out from one of the cupboards.

"You can rest here for a few hours until morning if you like," he said. "As long as you're gone before the other workers come in. People here are late starters. They like to have their coffee first."

Morgan nodded, barely able to keep her eyes open now but she quickly texted David to keep him updated on their progress. Then she made a rough bed with some blankets and curled up, grateful for her ability to sleep quickly even under great stress.

JAKE STOOD IN FRONT of one of the windows, trying to get a cell phone signal. Finally he connected with Marietti and spoke low so as not to wake Morgan.

"We have the stone of St Peter. Morgan was right, it was here in Venice."

"Excellent. It's imperative that you also get the others before Thanatos is able to find you again."

"We haven't had any trouble here. Maybe they've lost our trail."

"Or maybe they're in front of you, Jake. They know ARKANE is involved, and what is at stake at Pentecost. We can't leave any out in the world."

"Where are we heading next?" Jake asked. "Did you have Martin narrow down the options?"

"Since you're in Italy, you'll be heading for Amalfi, where the relics of St Andrew are kept. There's evidence they were taken there after the Sack of Constantinople. The plane will take you down there tomorrow morning. We'll speak again after that."

The phone went silent as Marietti terminated the call.

Jake hung up and stared out the window at the dark lagoon lapping against the Doge's palace. He could see the Bridge of Sighs leading over to the ancient dungeons lit by the lights from the Ponte della Paglia. The sighs of the damned, he thought, as he turned to look at Morgan's sleeping form. Tonight he felt as if he walked among those ghosts of ancient Venice, trapped into living their bleak sentence every night.

CHAPTER 25

Salerno to Amalfi, Italy.
May 23, 9.16am

MORGAN SAT AT THE back of the boat, staring out across the azure ocean. They had risen early in Venice and flown to Salerno, where they hired a speedboat to take them along the coast to their next destination. The drive around the cliffs was spectacular, but the boat would be quicker and they were less likely to be followed. Amalfi was on the opposite coast of Italy to Venice, southeast of Naples. Morgan knew it had been a center of medieval power around the turn of the first millennium and, because of its beauty, had become a popular holiday spot for the British aristocracy in the 1920s. The town nestled at the bottom of the dramatic cliffs of Monte Cerreto and opened out into the Gulf of Salerno. It had once been an important port and maritime power, but now tourists visited mainly for the gorgeous coastline.

Morgan looked back on the last few days as a blur, running, hiding, creeping around in the darkness and desecrating churches. It was a relief to be out in the sunlight, the rich colors something she missed in the grey of England. Israel had this quality of light too, with a brilliant blue of the sky rarely seen in Oxford. She knew that this was a brief respite and closed her eyes behind dark sunglasses, lifting her head to the sun. She wore shorts and a t-shirt, but part of her wanted to strip down and swim in the bright ocean.

She remembered the last time she had swam, a day trip with Faye and Gemma to Brighton beach on a surprisingly sunny day in April. It was the archetypal British seaside town, with deck-chairs set out on the stony shore. Seagulls swooped low to snatch discarded fish and chips from newspapers and ice cream sellers hawked their sugary treats to the British public, who were desperate to soak up the rays of the infrequent sun. Knowing the vagaries of the weather forecast, they had taken sweaters and waterproofs as well as bathing suits and towels and made a nest on the beach.

Faye had taken the chance to relax with a book so Morgan had held Gemma's hand and led her down to the ocean. The little girl's face was a rapture of delight as the gentle waves had tickled her feet and they splashed together in the shallows. Morgan remembered her giggling, squealing at the cold as they darted in and out, Gemma demanding to be lifted and swung out so she could see further out to sea. At that moment Morgan understood simple pleasure. She forgot Elian and what she had lost in Israel, focusing only on what she had now found with her family. Gemma had shown her joy and the memory of her childish laughter echoed in her mind. She would not give that up. Morgan was grateful for the dark sunglasses she wore as she blinked away the tears that were starting to well.

Jake interrupted her thoughts as he sat down beside her, holding his smart phone with more information from Martin back at the ARKANE office.

"St Andrew certainly got around," he said. "Did you know he's the patron saint of Ukraine, Scotland, Russia, Romania and Greece as well as here in Amalfi, and other cities in Portugal and Malta?"

"So why does Martin think the stone is here specifically?"

she replied, gazing out at the view to center herself back in the present. This was indeed a beautiful place; no wonder the aristocrats of Europe had come here for years. Sports cars and yachts were the hallmark of the area, yet as they sped across the ocean it seemed timeless. Towering cliffs, unchanged for millennia, overshadowed white houses with red roofs interspersed with green olive groves.

"Martin said that the cathedral of Amalfi is dedicated to St Andrew. The Apostle and his relics were transported here in 1208 following the sack of Constantinople, although Andrew's head only finally joined the rest of his body in 2008. If the Keepers followed the bones of the Apostles, there must be something here."

They disembarked at the Porta Marina in Amalfi. The powerboat looked tiny next to the mega yachts and other luxury craft in the wide bay. Morgan looked up at the terraced hillsides that stretched above them, glimpsing hidden palazzos and boutique villas nestled into the headland. Their guide gave them a map and pointed up into the town.

"The cathedral of St Andrew is just up the hill, in the center of the old district."

Jake and Morgan headed out of the marina and into the town, pushing through the hordes of tourists who thronged the marina walls. The hotels on the waterfront were brilliant white with racing green shutters, many with buttresses and towers built on top for the town could only grow upwards here as the cliffs pushed it into the sea. There were old style iron lamp posts and iconic Vespas parked on the street.

Morgan smiled at the scene, "This is such a different Italy, Jake. It's so beautiful. If we weren't in such a hurry, I'd love to stay a while. I know Faye would love it here too."

Morgan thought of Faye's amazing cooking, so different

from her own functional relationship with food. Her sister's melanzane parmigiana could definitely hold its own even in this Italian heartland.

"Hold that thought," Jake replied. "You'll be able to come back with Faye, I know you will."

They entered the pedestrian section of the town and walked up narrow streets, past tourist shops and cafes to reach the cathedral.

"It seems we're on a tour of some of the best cathedrals in Europe," Jake said smiling, as he led the way into the piazza. "And here's another."

They stopped at the fountain to look up at the cathedral and the ancient bell tower which rose above it. Cafes and pasticcerria dotted the square, with red tablecloths and carafes of wine on tables where happy tourists basked in the sun. Morgan sneaked a glance at couples holding hands in the romantic place and she felt a twinge of jealousy, a pang of longing. It seemed that no happiness lasted long in this world, but the ephemeral nature made it all the more precious.

A long staircase led up to the front entrance of the church with shops tucked underneath, for every spare inch was a business opportunity here. The cathedral had a black and white façade, striped and decorated with arched lattice windows. The decoration reminded Morgan of the Mezquita at Cordoba in Spain, an amalgamation of Jewish, Muslim and Christian decoration. She sat on the fountain edge looking up at it.

"Maybe we should just go to America, to where Everett is holding my sister. Can't you get Martin to research where he is, instead of where the Apostles' relics are? Surely you can do some kind of analysis on the video or the voice we've heard, or his picture. I feel like we're chasing the wind with these stones and I need to find my family."

Jake turned to face her, his back to the church. She held

up a hand to shield her face from the sun as she looked up at him.

"I need to tell you something," he began. Suddenly there was shouting and the vrooming sound of a motorbike engine. They turned to see a denim clad rider on a bright red sports bike speeding out of the cathedral and down the steps. He was wearing a helmet so they couldn't see his face clearly.

People on the stairs screamed, throwing themselves out of the way as the rider bumped his way down. He shot off the last steps, skidded a little and then headed off into the labyrinth of the Amalfi passageways, shouts of tourists indicating where he had gone. The whole area was packed with people walking, so he wouldn't be able to get anywhere fast until he escaped the narrow streets.

"One of Thanatos' men," Jake shouted. "It must be."

Looking around, they spotted Vespa scooters at the side of the square. Jake ran to get one started. Morgan saw her chance and pushed a passing tourist off another motorbike that had stopped in the erupting chaos. She jumped on and headed off after the speeding bike, leaving the rider in the dust as people rushed over to help. The carabinieri would be there soon, so Jake hurriedly jumpstarted one of the other bikes and headed after her.

Morgan raced the motorbike after the man, her senses heightened as she plunged into the narrow streets. She could hear screams of people ahead and tried to speed up to catch him. Tourists bottle-necked the streets so they couldn't go too fast, but he was clearing the way in front of him, so she was gaining. She didn't know how far he could go up the hill before running out of town and the Vespa was struggling in the winding streets but it looked like the steep hillsides kept the main roads to a minimum.

She caught a glimpse of the biker's denim jacket through the crowds and tried to push through faster, revving the little Vespa to clear the way in front of her. He would make a mistake at some point, then she'd be on him. The streets were narrow here, tall buildings several floors high with stone archways over the top joining the buildings. The man was heading away from the main tourist track into the back streets of Amalfi overlooked by cast iron streetlights, balconies with mini palms and looming mountains behind. Away from the tourist areas, the walls were still Mediterranean white but dirty with graffiti. Oblivious as to whether Jake was following, Morgan was determined to catch the man on the bike and she didn't care who he was. He had something she needed.

The wind whipped some hanging laundry in front of her and she thrust it away as she turned another corner. She hadn't been on a motorbike for a few years now, but she'd ridden with Elian in the desert, even street racing in Tel Aviv. As she zoomed along, she realized she had missed the adrenalin rush of the bike and the chase. It seemed she couldn't entirely bury her old self with academia.

Morgan turned a corner and saw a dead end ahead of her. They had reached the end of the town streets, the other man clearly wasn't a local either and they were both lost. He had turned his bike and was revving it as he prepared to come back at her. She braked and stopped by the corner. He held a gun but didn't have a clear shot yet but he would when he came back out of the tight corner.

She waited for him, racing her engine, and then gunned out as he tried to pass in front of her. She braced herself for impact and then crashed straight into the side of his bike, knocking him into a wall, his body crushed under the heavy machine, gun ripped from his hand. Morgan jumped off her bike, ignoring the slight whiplash from the impact. She grabbed his gun and pointed it down at him. He was mostly unhurt, but trapped by the weight of the bike and he cursed her in Italian as he pulled of the helmet. He was tanned dark from the Mediterranean sun with long thick hair tied back with a leather string. Morgan thought that perhaps Thanatos were using local Mafioso now. She flipped the safety off and held the gun under his chin, speaking slowly but firmly as she pressed the muzzle hard into his skin.

"Give me the stone."

"There's no stone, I couldn't find it." He spoke English with a rough Italian accent. "I have nothing. Get off me!"

Morgan's voice was low and calm, the threat apparent.

"I don't believe you. Where is it?"

Sirens began to sound as the carabinieri drew closer. Jake came round the corner on a scooter. He skidded to a halt near them and began to get off the bike.

"We don't have much time, Morgan. Does he have it?"

She glared round, gun still held against the man's neck.

"Back off, Timber. This one's mine."

Jake backed away at the possession in her voice, like a bear defending her kill. She moved the barrel of the gun to the man's exposed knee, thrust forward by his position half under the bike.

"I need that stone. Give it to me or your knee goes."

He sneered at her, "You don't have time for this."

Without so much as a change in expression, she shot point blank into his knee. The man howled in agony, clutching at the shattered bone, blood oozing through his fingers. Jake rushed forward, but she swung the gun on him.

"I mean it, Jake."

He put his hands up in surrender and retreated. She bent low to the man's ear.

"I will take your manhood next and leave you to bleed to death. Don't doubt my words. Where's the stone?"

"Puttana," he spat. "If you take it, they'll kill me."

He was pleading now but his hand moved to his chest. Keeping the gun on him Morgan pulled the zip of his jacket down and reached in for the stone, wrapped in a white handkerchief. She pulled it out and turned to go.

"Don't leave me, please. They'll find me."

Turning back to the trapped man, she saw the pale horse tattoo on his arm holding tightly to the knee she had shot. Blood dripped down onto the pristine paint of his motorcycle. Her eyes narrowed.

"That means nothing to me."

The sound of running feet could be heard now as the police closed in on their position and Jake hurriedly pulled Morgan away. They climbed the wall at the dead end of the street and ran back down the hill to the marina. Exhausted, they dropped into the boat and the skipper cast off, heading back to Salerno.

The ARKANE plane was waiting for them at Salerno and they boarded, having hardly said a word on the journey back. Morgan's violence sat between them, uncomfortably acknowledged but not discussed. She knew she had crossed a line by turning the gun on Jake, but she had been in a haze of anger. For a moment the man had embodied the terror that held Faye and Gemma and she had wanted to hurt him. Part of her had willed him to defy her so she could have put a bullet in his head instead of his knee. This was the side of her she had been trying to forget, for violence only spiraled into more violence, but was it so deeply embedded in her that she couldn't let it go? And could she justify it for the end result? After all, they had the next stone.

Jake sat across from her, reading quietly as the crew prepared for take-off, even though they were unsure of the next destination. She knew that neither of them were team players and she had pushed his help away back in Amalfi. It felt as if the tentative relationship that had begun to grow in the Venice night had been blown apart by her actions. She felt the need to reach out to him again, to patch up what was unsaid and unacknowledged. This was no time for division.

"We don't have the stone of Philip yet," she said, leaning forward. "He was the most organized of the Apostles, the steward of the group." She pointed at the notes she had made with Ben, scanning them with a finger as she told the tale.

"It seems that he may have preached in Ethiopia and North Africa, but he ended up dying in Jerusalem either of old age or perhaps beheaded as a martyr. He also wrote a gospel that was later suppressed by the Church as heresy as it apparently demonstrated the more esoteric side of Jesus' teaching. The relics of St Philip were supposedly taken to Germany by the mother of Constantine. They are held in the Abbey Church of Trier, built in the twelfth century but still an active monastery."

"So the stone could be in Trier?" Jake said. Morgan was grateful that he had taken her conversation opening because although she felt bad she still didn't feel she had anything to apologize for.

"Perhaps, but only if it was kept together with the bones. We've seen a number of different places the stones of the Apostles have been kept, so we can't assume this one is in Trier and we don't have time to get it wrong again. Philip was mostly active in Jerusalem. The other stones left there with the Apostles, but maybe this one remained. I think we have to go to Israel."

"That's crazy," Jake looked incredulous. "Jerusalem is packed with relics of all kinds and it's a security nightmare. How would we possibly find the Keeper of this stone in such a short timeframe?"

Morgan sat back.

"I know Jerusalem, Jake. Ben and I discussed this and Philip preached to the Ethiopians for much of his career. He wrote his gospel in Ethiopia, so we should start with the descendants of his church. The Ethiopian Coptic church is one of the most ancient and is even rumored to protect the Ark of the Covenant."

"What? Like Indiana Jones?"

Morgan laughed.

"There's a legend that it was taken to Ethiopia by Menelek, the son of Solomon and the Queen of Sheba. They still claim to have it. Whatever the truth, the Ethiopian Coptics are good at keeping ancient secrets. It makes sense that if there were a Keeper for his stone, then they would know who it might be."

"So do they have a church in Jerusalem then? A special place for Ethiopian Coptics?"

"They sure do. Only at the most holy Christian church in the world, the Church of the Holy Sepulchre. They live on the roof, and that's our next destination."

Extract from New York Post, May 24: Comet not seen since the time of Christ enters Earth's orbit.

The Resurgam comet will light up the night sky during the next week as the body of celestial matter enters the earth's atmosphere, streaming a colored tail of dust and gas. The comet was named with the Latin Resurgam meaning 'I shall rise again' because it hasn't been seen since 33AD, the time of Jesus Christ. In ancient times, comets were considered to be bad omens and indeed some have claimed that the violent weather events currently wreaking havoc in the South East are related to the comet's approach.

Celestial influence has been seen recently with Elenin, a comet that passed close to the earth in 2011. During the period it aligned with the Earth and the Sun, earthquakes wracked the planet producing the Japanese 9.0 quake,

Christchurch in New Zealand and before that, Chile. There is a concern that the Resurgam comet will have a similar impact, bringing widespread natural disturbances. There are claims from conspiracy theorists that the government is covering up the possibility of cataclysmic occurrences but repeated statements from NASA downplay the potential impact.

"There is some evidence that the sun is becoming more active and earth-changing events are becoming more intense and frequent," NASA scientist Dr Marie Isherwood said at a press conference this morning. "But it is pure fiction to suggest that comets have any impact on the earth's climate. They just don't have enough mass to generate such a gravitational pull."

However, religious groups say the comet is evidence supporting the Biblical references to the end times. Pastor Jesse Warren of San Bernandino said, "The gospel of St Mark says that in the end times there will be earthquakes and famines. The earth will be darkened, and the moon will not give its light; the stars will fall from the sky, and the heavenly bodies will be shaken. These are the beginnings of birth-pains, for the new world will be born in this turmoil."

The book of Revelation further describes these end times. "There was a great earthquake. The sun turned black like sackcloth made of goat hair, the whole moon turned blood red, and the stars in the sky fell to earth, as late figs drop from a fig-tree when shaken by a strong wind. The sky receded like a scroll, rolling up, and every mountain and island was removed from its place."

Wherever you stand on the debate, the best views of the comet will be in the desert areas of the Northern Hemisphere, away from city lights. Sightings can be logged on the NASA website that will be tracking the comet's movements across the skies.

CHAPTER 26

Church of the Holy Sepulchre, Jerusalem, Israel.
May 24, 8.45am

JAKE AND MORGAN CAME out of a narrow passage-way and entered the courtyard in front of the Church of the Holy Sepulchre, an ancient building crushed into the dense heart of the Old City. The church seemed to be within the walls of the souk, stuffed amongst the traders and hawkers of the market, brimming with religious baubles and trinkets. Tourists milled around eating felafel and sweet harissa cakes. They exchanged shekels for Palestinian glass, Jerusalem t-shirts and statues of the Virgin Mary. Morgan thought that perhaps this was appropriate, for surely Jesus would have held his ministry amongst these people, the merchants, the hagglers, the real people of the city.

Walking these streets was a bittersweet joy for Morgan as she felt the sun on her skin while the smells of the souk permeated the air about her. Despite its conflict, Jerusalem was her home and England would never arouse this passion in her, but there were also ghosts here. Out of the corner of her eye, she saw Elian in the doorways of the teahouses, his broad smile welcoming, and she caught a glimpse of her father bent over a manuscript in the antique booksellers. This country had dashed her heart on the ancient rocks that were the foundations of the city. It thrived on a fast-moving river of bloodshed and violence and when she left, she had been sinking into its depths. But as the sunlight dappled the cobbled stones of the old city, just for a moment, she regretted leaving. It had beaten her then but Morgan knew her relationship with the city of God wasn't over yet, and yet this could only be a fleeting visit. There wasn't time to see her old friends or visit her father's grave and she couldn't even show Jake the secret spots of the city she loved. Instead she weaved between the tourist groups towards the entrance of the Holy Sepulchre.

The church was a short walk from the Western Wall, the only part of the Jewish Temple left standing and sacred to the Jews. Behind that stood the Temple Mount topped by the golden Dome of the Rock mosque, sacred to Muslims. This was the heart of the three greatest religions on earth and yet, just outside the Old City walls, it wasn't far to the shopping malls of Ben Yehuda street, a temple to consumerism.

As usual, the small square in front of the Holy Sepulchre was packed full of tour groups, with guides holding umbrellas high, shouting to be heard. This was Christianity Grand Central and millions of the faithful came on pilgrimage here annually. Morgan led the way through the crowd, glancing back now and then to make sure Jake was still close.

They entered the church in a haze of incense, a cloying sensory overload that made Morgan cough. She had been into the Holy Sepulchre many times as part of her psychology of religion degree. She had compared it to the clean, plain synagogue her Father had worshipped in, and wondered how the Christians could stand the smell for it made her feel heady and nauseous. She was briefly blinded until her eyes adjusted to the darkness, lit only by strings of candles and lamps. They joined the throng who gathered to touch the stone where Jesus' body lay after the Crucifixion. People pushed and shoved each other, a far remove from what would be expected in such a holy place. There was no spiritual peace to be found here and it was loud and unbearably hot. Sticky hands pawed idols, cameras flashed and public displays of overt religiosity erupted everywhere. Pickpockets prowled the crowds, finding easy pickings from the rich Westerners who flocked from America and Europe on pilgrimage.

"This way. We need to make our way to the Ethiopian Coptic section," Morgan said as they walked past Calvary. The faces of the believers gathered there were lit with candles that burnt briefly for those they prayed for. Here they believed Christ suffered and died, and pilgrims lined up to put their hands down to touch the rock itself through a gold rimmed portal in the floor. The icons and paintings on the walls crowded in with their bloody images of the scourging and crucifixion of Jesus, denoted in horrific detail.

Pilgrims knelt, kissing the ground and praying out loud. The whole place dripped with excess adoration, weeping women and pious priests. They all crowded towards where the body of Jesus had lain, the rock where he was crucified and the sepulcher where he was buried and rose from the dead. It was a study in human behavior to watch people worshipping, a competition in piety before their God. Morgan led Jake past the Stone of Anointing, hung with ornate candleholders like canopic jars suspended over the praying pilgrims.

At last they were in the center of the church where Christian denominations were thrust uncomfortably together. It may have been the center of Christianity, but Morgan knew that within the church the different branches hated each other. The throne of the Jerusalem Patriarch of the Orthodox Church buttressed against the Shrine of the Armenians and the marble urn in the middle of the church, marking the Omphalos, the center of the Christian world. This was a highly political building, a mish-mash of theology and architecture composed of Roman Catholics, Eastern Orthodox, the breakaway Armenian church and the Ethiopian Coptics. United in believing that Jesus died and rose again, most other aspects of faith were still debated between them. Grievances between the groups caused blows to be exchanged in the one of the holiest places in Christendom.

The first century tomb was adjacent to the Syrian chapel in the east end of the church, behind the Holy Sepulchre. Back there was also a tiny Coptic chapel, just big enough for one monk to maintain constant vigilance and prayer.

"This isn't even the real tomb of Jesus," Morgan said. "Just the place that Helena, wife of the Emperor Constantine, decided would be the tomb in 300AD. The shrine was built then and continues to be a place of faith, but it's really based on political lies."

Jake looked surprised. He'd been to Israel before but his role in ARKANE was generally on the action side rather than research. "How come this isn't the real place? Surely they could have got that right?"

"Jesus wasn't famous when he died," Morgan explained. "He was just another criminal to the Romans, another failed Messianic pretender to the Jews, so the place wasn't marked. It's wrong because it's inside the walled city for a start, and crucifixions would not have occurred here. They were held outside the gates, where the unclean bodies were left to rot on the crosses and stoning could occur in the quarries below."

"So where's the real crucifixion site?" asked Jake, genuinely interested.

"The most likely place for Golgotha is now the main bus station in Jerusalem."

"Seriously? That's hardly an appropriate place for the spiritual center of the Church."

"I don't know." Morgan gestured at the crowds. "This is a crazy place and perhaps a dirty bus terminal is fitting as a transit center for the crossroads of humanity. If you look up to the white cliffs above the station, you can still see the holes of the eyes in the rock walls. The place of the skull eroded and chiseled by two thousand years of weathering."

"So why is all this here?" questioned Jake, pointing around them to the excess material spirituality.

Morgan shrugged. "Tradition I suppose, and a turf battle over this ground that has raged for generations. But there is a place outside the walls, a garden that some believe is Gethsemane where Jesus spent his last night crying out to God."

"Why's that a more likely location?" Jake asked.

"I don't know if it is," Morgan said, "but the olive trees there are thousands of years old and it's still a place of meditation and peace. There's also a rock-hewn tomb that is rumored to have been owned by Nicodemus the priest, with a stone rolled over its entrance. It could be the right place."

"You sound like you almost believe it yourself." Jake said.

"Of course not, but I'm fascinated with what others believe and why. These sites could all be false, but does it matter where the real place lies? Faith is in the heart."

Jake paused, looking through the crowds of people.

"Jerusalem is one crazy place," he said, "like a religious theme park. I'm sure many of these people are devotees but most seem like tourists, experience junkies snapping pictures and loading up with tacky icons. Plus, I can't see anything to do with Pentecost here. It's not like the Basilica in Venice."

Morgan nodded.

"The legend of Pentecost isn't strong here. It's celebrated as one of the festivals of the church but this place is all about Christ. His death and resurrection are venerated, not the Acts of the Apostles that came afterwards."

"So where do we look next?" Jake asked.

"There's no apostolic iconography here but I still think the Keeper can be found through the ancient tribe that lived and worked with the Apostle Philip in Ethiopia. This was their constant vigil and, after all, the Pentecost stone was meant to have been cut from the stone where Jesus rose from the dead. So, maybe it returned to the source. You wait here. I won't be long."

She strode off into the crowd.

The Chapel of the Holy Sepulchre, where Jesus supposedly rose from the dead, was only big enough for a few people, so a constant line stood outside and the scalloped entrance was so low that pilgrims had to stoop to enter. Morgan walked past the faithful and went alone into the Coptic sanctuary behind the shrine. Largely ignored by the praying hordes, a single Coptic monk sat there with his Bible open, staring at it in meditative silence. He didn't look up as she entered and Morgan thought the monks must be sick of being curiosities to the pilgrim-tourists who had been coming here daily for hundreds of years. She knelt by the altar, almost at his feet because the chapel was so small.

"Abba," she said, using the term of respect for a father of the church. He looked at her, a question in his eyes. Reaching into her pocket, she brought out the plain, rough-hewn stone of St James and held it before him. He gasped and then spoke swiftly in Geez, the Ethiopian language, exclaiming something and pointing to the door. Morgan tried to make sense of it.

"I need to speak to the head of the Coptics here. Is that possible?"

He pointed again, seeming to indicate that he could not leave his post but encouraging her to go and speak with his people. The stone must be here. Back outside, Jake was staring at the lines of pilgrims. She pulled him away.

"Come on, we need to get onto the roof. He definitely recognized the stone. Let's get out of here and into the fresh air."

They found the way up to the roof from the courtyard of the Greek Orthodox Patriarchate, and climbed the roughly hewn stone steps into the home of the Ethiopian Coptic Church in Jerusalem, an incongruous village of monastic cells known as Deir el Sultan. A strong faith sustained the little community despite the poor conditions and meager resources. Morgan looked around her. Huts with low doorways were built above the chapel of St Helena, one of the oldest parts of the church where the monks and a few nuns kept their stake alive in the holy place, as close as they could get to the heart of Christendom. She knew that there was a small chapel dedicated to the Archangel Michael up there which might hold information about the stone.

An old nun sat on a metal backed chair in a patch of sunlight, leaning against the side of one of the rotund shrines. She seemed to just be sitting, perhaps in prayer but certainly enjoying the sun. Simple pleasures were still to be relished even this close to God. She pointed above and behind them, clearly accustomed to directing pilgrims to the chapel for prayer or holy tourism. Morgan and Jake turned to see rickety stairs that led up to the Coptic chapel, badly in need of repair. The Ethiopian Church, although ancient, had never been wealthy like the Roman Catholics. They were mostly a forgotten people to the rest of the Christian world.

They walked up and entered the little shrine. Although the chapel was poor, it was rich in colorful paintings from the story of Solomon and Sheba, central to the Ethiopian traditions. The bright red of the Patriarch's chair, the deep brown of the lattice of the holy screen and the paintings on the wall achieved a more celebratory atmosphere than the Sepulchre below them. Fresh air also blew through the space, making it inviting and a welcome break from the incense overload they had escaped. A monk knelt by the altar, a vital middle-aged man, ebony skin highlighted by his bright saffron robes. He rose to meet them, greeting them with a smile of welcome.

"We're closed for private prayer at this time, but can I help you?"

His voice was deep and sonorous, a touch of an accent to his clearly educated English. Morgan pulled out the stone of James.

"We're looking for another stone similar to this. It belonged to the Apostle Philip and we think it might be hidden by the Ethiopian Church."

The monk reached behind them and closed the doors to the chapel, locking them in place. He ushered them further in towards the altar.

"There have been rumors that the time has come for the stones to be revealed again. I've heard from my brothers of deaths among the Keepers and now you are here."

His eyes betrayed his suspicions.

"There have been deaths but not at our hands," Morgan explained. "But there are men coming who want the stones and will continue to kill for them. If we take the stone, we can lead them away from you."

The monk sat down. "Why should I trust you?"

Morgan opened her shirt at the neck to reveal her own stone.

"I am a Keeper, a holder of the stone as you are."

The man sighed, his body sagging as the tension left him.

"Our stone has been passed down from monk to monk for generations. It was brought back here a few hundred years ago, and it has remained since in this shrine. I am the present day Keeper but if you take it now, we will lose this final relic of the Apostles."

Morgan lent in towards him, her voice gentle.

"But if we don't take it now, it will be stolen from you by force and some of your people may be hurt. We're being followed by men who will not rest until they have all the stones. I promise that we'll protect it with the others."

As she spoke the words, Morgan felt a twinge of unease. Her promise rang false when she considered she was planning to give the stones to Everett, but part of her wanted to find a way to save her family as well as preventing the sacred talismans from being used for evil.

She felt the monk's gaze on her, his eyes seeing her true motivation, but then he nodded.

"There was a prophecy passed down with the stone, that in the end times the twelve would be together again, as they were at Pentecost. A band of men bonded by the death and resurrection of our Lord dispersed to all the ends of the known world. The only remembrance of their brotherhood was the stones. Philip, who preached among us, gave it to the first Patriarch when he left to return to Jerusalem. Perhaps it is fitting that you take it now, and reunite the twelve again. I do not want to bring violence to this place and my faith is in the unseen, not a piece of rock."

Jake had been quietly observing them, taking in the paintings on the walls, but now he spoke.

"What do you believe about the stones Father? Do they really have power?"

"If the legend is true, then this stone is from the tomb where Jesus Christ rose from the dead. The resurrection is the miracle I live my life by but miracles happen every day, my son, and God does not need rocks to perform them. But the power of myth is strong and there are those who seek earthly power. Such talismans can wield authority, so take our piece and protect it with the others."

He rose and went to the altar behind the lattice, patterns of the sun through the skylight forming a shining nimbus around him. He pulled out a tiny leather satchel from beneath the altar and handed it to Morgan.

"This is the stone of Philip. I give it to you as a Keeper of the stones of the twelve. Protect it, and go with God."

Morgan took it with reverence and they left him standing there in the ancient Coptic church, a proud religion in the heart of sacred Jerusalem. As they walked away through the twisted streets of the Old City, Morgan said, "I'm torn, Jake. I feel as if these stones have been entrusted to me as a Keeper to protect them and keep them safe. But then I have to give them up to save Faye in only a few days' time. How can I do both?"

Jake turned, his eyes shaded by the dark sunglasses he wore against the bright sun. "Maybe the choice will be made for you."

CHAPTER 27

Tel Aviv, Israel. May 24, 1.30pm

BACK ON THE PLANE, Morgan sat with the laptop roaming the ARKANE search engine. She was hunting for the myths of Simon the Zealot, the last Apostle who held a Pentecost stone. Jake had told her that the ARKANE search engine was a powerful tool linked to the secret archives of the world's knowledge. ARKANE was trying to digitize the remaining hidden scriptures of the world so they could be indexed and analyzed. They even had a clandestine team in the Vatican who were cataloguing the secret archives there. This team photographed texts with hidden cameras and the images were archived at the London base. Morgan was absorbed in knowledge suppressed for millennia, hidden as dangerous and seditious and she wanted to lose herself in this esoteric labyrinth. Every document she found was some new temptation to read and become immersed in. For an addict of learning, this was a powerful drug and she felt the pull of desire to dive deeper.

Martin Klein had written algorithms to tag items with keywords for easier relational search. He was also working on a huge map of all the different faiths and traditions, linking common elements and trying to track the spread of ideas across the world. Jake had told Morgan that Director Marietti had a vision of establishing some kind of evolutionary religious psychology, a grand scale spread of ideas demonstrating how similar the faiths were instead of how divisive. ARKANE had published a number of papers from the study in mainstream journals. Unfortunately, most of the knowledge they had access to had been gained by less than legal means, so much of the ground breaking work could not yet be published. But the ARKANE network was growing, with scholars interested from all fields so this database was surely the best place in the world to search for a missing relic.

Morgan sat back in her chair, rubbing the base of her neck and rolling her shoulders. They had been at it for hours now, trying to track the path of Simon the Zealot across the early world of the early first century. They couldn't leave Tel Aviv until they knew the next destination. Time was running out to find the final stone before Pentecost, but still they sat in a hangar waiting.

"No wonder Everett's father couldn't work out where the stone might be," Morgan said with annoyance. "This guy went everywhere. His notebooks trace the same possibilities we've found, but there's nothing conclusive on where Simon might have ended up."

Jake looked up from his laptop, where he was reading Martin's findings on the physical properties of the stones. He had extrapolated the effect of the stones when they were together based on the miracles of Varanasi and modeled the impact if they were somehow activated together.

"So what have you found so far?"

"There are so many accounts but Simon the Zealot was definitely a great traveler. He is said to have gone into Egypt and across North Africa to Carthage, then on to Britain before heading back East and being martyred in Persia. He was killed by being sawn in half, hence the saw he is often shown with in hagiography. One of his arms ended up as a relic in a church in Cologne, Germany but there are possible sites for his body as far away as England, Egypt or Tunisia in North Africa, and even back in Iran. How do we even know where to start?"

Jake leaned over to look at the map on the screen.

"We left this one for last because it's the most difficult to find. We knew that," he said with encouragement. "Just try to narrow down the options."

"But we don't have time to just sit around here." Morgan said. "I have to check in with David soon, and he'll go crazy if we don't know where we're headed next."

She jumped up, nervous energy making her pace the length of the highly equipped cabin.

"I need Ben's help," she said. "The Blackfriars have access to so much history and tradition and maybe ARKANE doesn't have everything in the database. Ben will be able to research at the same time as us and hopefully turn up some new information. He's a walking encyclopedia of the early Church, so he might be able to shed some new light on the options."

Jake hesitated as he knew Marietti had some history with Father Ben. He had warned Jake to stay away from him as much as possible and keep him in the dark about their journey. But the first priority of the mission was to find the stones, so he nodded.

"There's Skype installed on the laptop. Go ahead."

Morgan turned to the monitor, put on her headphones and skyped Ben. Technology was welcomed at Blackfriars and Ben was often in his study. He was there when she called and Morgan smiled to see his old face on the tiny screen. He embraced new technologies as much as he loved the crumbling old books of the Bodleian Library. His face was delighted at first but then creased into a frown.

"Morgan, where have you been? I've been so worried about you. The police are still investigating the murders here, calling them a terrorist attack on a religious institution. I've kept your name out of it so far, but those men are still after you."

"I'm fine, Ben," Morgan smiled. "Really. I'm sorry to have been out of touch. It's been a whirlwind few days. We've found several more of the stones but I can't tell you much right now. There's no time. We only have a few days left and I need your help with a problem I can't seem to solve."

"Of course, what do you need?"

"I need to know about Simon the Zealot, where he went or may have ended up, and anything you can find on his relics." Ben nodded in the little video screen, "and I need it soon."

He looked directly into the camera.

"I understand the haste, Morgan. You'll be desperately worried about Faye and Gemma."

"It's not just that. Our deadline is the feast of Pentecost itself when the comet will be at its zenith. Everett wants to re-enact the fiery event and call down the power of the stones."

Ben raised one shaggy eyebrow.

"Pentecost is a grand myth, Morgan. It is a metaphor for the might of the Holy Spirit empowering the church through the Apostolic tradition. Why does he think the power of the stones is actual truth?"

Morgan glanced over at Jake, aware that her own doubts were crumbling under the weight of the evidence showing the possibility of a latent power.

"Something real happened at Varanasi," she continued. "But whatever the truth really is, I need to take the remaining stones to him by Pentecost in order to have Faye and Gemma returned safely and I have to go along with what he wants for now. But this last stone seems to be the hardest one to find."

"Of course," Ben said. "I'll head to the library now. There is knowledge here that even ARKANE doesn't know about.

I'll get back to you with what I find as soon as I can. "

CHAPTER 28

Blackfriars, Oxford, England.
May 24 11.53AM

BEN LOGGED OFF AND gazed out of his window down onto the Blackfriars quad. There were young lay students there, as well as some of the monks in their habits and several policemen. They all seemed at a loss to understand what had happened here just a few days ago. Ben had played the forgetful old monk card and they had bought it, assuming him to be an innocent bystander caught in the cross-fire. No one else had seen Morgan, so her name was kept out of the news. Maybe he had Marietti to thank for that. At the thought of that man, Ben's face darkened, but remembering what Morgan needed stopped him from descending into ancient memory and despair. He couldn't let the past prevent her from saving Faye, but he was deeply suspicious of what ARKANE wanted and worried about how far Thanatos might go to get the stones. ARKANE dabbled at the edge of the supernatural, where shadows darkened at the edge of the light but sometimes they strayed too far into the grey.

Ben had several tutorials lined up that day with bright students, all eager to study the Church and find a way for the future of faith in these dark times. Ben sighed. The same arguments raged now as they did millennia ago but these students would still debate the meaning of the trinity, the paradox of suffering and the coming end times. There were no new thoughts under the sun, but Ben continued to live for the joy of studying here. Blackfriars was his true home, where he could immerse himself in learning and teaching as well as fulfilling a lifetime vow made to a dying friend.

Heading down into the Blackfriars library, he sat at one of the solid wooden desks so characteristic of ascetic Oxford. The chairs were hard to encourage students to get up and leave, or to choose to suffer physical pain while enriching their minds, a monastic attitude honed from centuries of learning. The windows of the library looked out onto St Giles, a busy road in the heart of the city with leafy green trees and students riding by on bikes piled high with books. The libraries in Oxford were still lending books; technology didn't seem to change the need to physically handle these old tomes, but the project to digitize the entire Bodleian was nearly finished. The University was changing, albeit slowly in a fast-paced society and Ben knew the outside world looked at monks strangely, wondering why they made the choices they did. Part of it was the speed, for he had chosen the simple life of contemplation over the urge to be more, acquire more and yet remain unsatisfied.

He gazed out through ornamental stained glass panels, their colorful beauty filtering the light in shades of vermilion and aquamarine. Each panel depicted the heraldic emblem of an important friar in the history of the Blackfriars back to the 14th century. This was a center of tradition, an oasis of research that both exhausted and invigorated. Here was knowledge and devotion for God, the hours eaten up by the studying of ancient truth and the adoration of the divine.

Ben spent his free time in the many libraries of Oxford, as well as the Ashmolean Museum, a magnificent treasure trove of antiquity. He lived for new things to learn and study, no longer concerned with the physical. He had given that up as his penance and his service to the order. The only other obligation in his life was the protection of the twins and his promise to their mother. This promise now drove him to the books, hoping he could find what would help Morgan.

Ben's experience lent him wisdom but the overflowing bookshelves behind him were his reference library. He retained almost photographic memories of which book held what information and where the book was in his own library or that of the school itself. The Blackfriars library had tomes that were physically large and chained in place to stop the students taking them away or damaging them, so they had to be read standing at special lecterns placed for that purpose only. He stood at one of the lecterns and pulled down the library's copy of the 'Legenda Aurea', the Golden Legend, a collection of the lives of saints compiled in the thirteenth century. It was a popular ecclesiastical book and one of the first to be published in the English language by William Caxton. The original gospels, both those in the Christian Bible and those considered to be heretical, didn't contain much information about what happened to the central figures in Jesus' life. His followers dispersed after Pentecost and went their different ways but stories and traditions were passed down and collated in the Legends, which became the first popular collection of the lives of the saints. Ben knew it was based on the Dominicans' own books of the lives of the saints, a more extensive, but little read source. Some of the stories were based on apocryphal texts like the Gospel of Nicodemus whereas others came from histories of other saints. There were visions and supernatural occurrences, some claimed to be myth and allegory, but beneath it all was a narrative of the travels of the Apostles. Ben found it to be repetitive, as all the saints performed miracles and then died in some horrible form of martyrdom. Nevertheless it was a good place to start in understanding where the stone of Simon the Zealot might be.

Refreshing his memory with the story of Simon, Ben found that, after preaching in Egypt, the Apostle travelled to Armenia and Persia with St Jude, also called Thaddeus. They converted many people there and were both eventually martyred in Persia. In other texts he found that Simon's relics were scattered all over the Christian empire, from the Vatican in St Peter's Basilica, to Toulouse in France. There was little else to be found here about the movements of the Apostle, so some deeper digging was going to be required. It was time to call in some favors from the Collegium Angelicum in Rome.

Returning to his room, Ben put in a call to the Grand Master of the Order, an old friend he had studied with in Rome many years before. He described what he was seeking. The old man on the phone became wary.

"Be careful, Ben. These are dangerous times to be meddling with stones that hold power, whether real or perceived. Why are you helping this woman, and why is ARKANE involved?"

"I believe ARKANE seeks to keep the stones for themselves, but Morgan and her sister Faye are like daughters to me. They've been marked for a special purpose and I believe I need to help them achieve it." He paused. "I also made a vow to protect them as children and this is as sacred a promise as the one I made to the Church and the Order. I made it to a dying friend whose secrets I keep to this day. I must help them."

The Grand Master sighed.

"Then I tell you this as an old friend, Ben, not as your Grand Master. I shouldn't even be talking about this. The stones first came to our notice when they were sought by Nazi relic hunters during the Second World War. They were clutching at any myth to find supernatural weapons to help them triumph. When they came to the Vatican asking questions, the Order looked into the stones with more interest. I believe they even found some of the stones before they were lost again, but then you know all about that time."

Ben's voice was heavy with regret.

"Yes, it seems those old enemies may be rising again. I have seen the pale horse myself. An organization called Thanatos is using it as their calling card, and they are after the stones, too."

"Then you must take great care for these old ghosts are hungry and violent. We are too old to fight again, but I fear another clash is coming."

"I didn't seek this fight, Enneas. It has come to my door and threatens those I promised to protect. I must do this. What can you tell me about the stone of Simon the Zealot?"

"Our research shows that it was kept by a family in Egypt but the Keepers were corrupted over time, their faith eroded by the spread of militant Islam. The family who held it sold the stone onto the antiquities market in the early 1900s after they were stricken with poverty and disease."

"Do we know who bought it or where it is now?" Ben asked.

"It's rumored that the psychologist Carl Jung bought the stone when he was in Tunis in 1920. He collected curiosities that related to religious myth and the story apparently fascinated him. We didn't know about the comet at the time or we would have sought it ourselves."

"How might that the Jung story be authenticated?"

"We have the testimony of one of his guides from that time but it wasn't a priority for us to investigate further. We lost track of the stone after that but perhaps you should follow the trail of Carl Jung into the deserts of North Africa."

CHAPTER 29

Tel Aviv, Israel. May 24, 4.34pm

MORGAN LISTENED TO BEN talk, fascinated by the journey of the stone of Simon the Zealot. They had Ben on speakerphone, with Martin Klein also connected from the ARKANE headquarters, hoping that between them they could locate the final Pentecost stone. Ben continued his story from what the Grand Master had told him.

"Carl Jung travelled to the oasis of Nefta while he was in Tunisia, North Africa, in 1920. He felt the land was soaked with the blood of Carthage, Rome and later the Christians and evidently it was a powerful experience for him. His memoirs say he felt an alien sense of being a European in a Moorish, desert land. He recounted a powerful dream of being within a mandala of a citadel in the desert, where he fought with and then taught a royal Arab his secrets. Morgan, you've studied Jung's writings in depth. Did he ever mention this Pentecost stone?"

Morgan frowned. "I don't remember Pentecost being mentioned specifically, but Jung was fascinated with stones as well as being obsessed with religious mythology. At his Tower in Bollingen on Lake Zurich, he engraved stones with sacred words and images. He created from his unconscious all the time so I'm sure he would have written about this if it meant something."

Ben spoke again. "If he was in North Africa in 1920, doesn't that mean he was still working on the Red Book?"

"Of course, the timing fits," Morgan replied. "We should look there. It's such an outpouring of his mind at that time."

"What's this Red Book and why's it so important?" Jake looked confused. All three of the others started talking at once, and then quietened to let Morgan continue.

"The Red Book was Carl Jung's personal inner journey written during a breakdown in his life. It's an oversized red leather bound book with cream artist's paper that he filled with calligraphy of his thoughts and paintings of his inner life, visions and dreams."

"Why haven't I heard of it before? It sounds amazing," Jake said.

"It's only recently been published for the first time. He wrote it between 1913 and 1929 and it's truly a work of art. His family have protected it until now."

"So, how could the book help us?"

"Jung painted what he saw in his unconscious and also what affected him," Morgan continued. "There should be signs in the Red Book if he had found something spiritually significant. Jung was a mystic, struggling to reconnect ancient myths with the modern world. He even dreamt about the coming rivers of blood in Europe, which turned out to be the Second World War. He felt his mind was broken, but that left him open to divine inspiration, ideas and thoughts that the rest of us discard in the night."

Martin jumped in then, keen to add his opinion. His voice crackled over the line.

"Many of the paintings in the Red Book are representations of mandala, the circle in the square which represents the inward journey of the soul. There are images of Egyptian myth and particularly of snakes, a spiritual image of renewal and creation as well as the Christian idea of it representing the Deceiver. The snake is a powerful symbol in many ..."

Jake jumped in, cutting off his enthusiastic oratory. "Thanks, Martin, that's enough for now. Could we get images of it, please?"

"Of course, I'll send them now. I've seen the real thing, Morgan. It's amazing! I was assigned to be one of the few physically present when it came out of the Swiss vault and photographed. The colors are so fresh because the family have kept it pristine for years, with hardly a soul looking at it. You're going to be amazed when you see it."

As they waited for the emailed images to arrive, Morgan thought about Martin seeing the actual Red Book. She had an oversized full color reproduction, but her professional jealousy was piqued by his unique experience. Working for ARKANE certainly had its benefits. The images arrived and they opened the first file. Morgan gasped and Jake leaned in closer.

"Is that what I think it is?"

The image showed a square room with turquoise patterned walls and a red and black checkered floor. In the center, a man knelt in worship, his head on the ground with arms reaching towards a small grey object in front of him. From that stone a pillar of fire and flames rose up, filling the room with sparks and smoke, billowing above the man as if about to consume him.

"I've seen that image many times," Morgan said, "but never connected it with the Pentecost stones. It's amazing. Perhaps Jung did experience something powerful, but unfortunately that doesn't help us find the stone. Do you have any more information on where it might be now, Martin?"

"I've pulled satellite images of the desert around Nefta where Jung may have seen the oasis. Perhaps the dream he describes and the painting were actually based on a real experience. There is an ancient citadel near the wadi in the desert constructed in the form of a mandala, a circle within a square. Perhaps he was taken there and had visions or an experience he chose to tell as a dream?"

Morgan looked at Jake, her hopes colliding with doubts as they grasped at these faint possibilities.

"We only have time for one more journey before we must head to America at Everett's request," she said. "He'll give us specific directions once we're there. We have to make a move now to get this last stone, so we need to make a decision. Ben, what do you think?"

The old monk was scribbling on his pad, but looked up again to the camera.

"I think you should try this wadi, Morgan. The stone was last seen in North Africa, but there are no mentions of it in Jung's writings, only this picture which looks to be in a walled place of some sort."

"What about Bollingen? Wouldn't that be a more obvious choice?" she countered.

"Jung's tower has been so highly researched over the years," Ben replied. "Every stone he carved and everything he did there has been completely analyzed by his followers. I don't think there's anything new to be learned there, but his brief period in the desert clearly impacted him greatly and yet very little was written about it. I believe he mentioned that he saw kingfishers at the citadel in the desert and we know that had a special meaning for him. Perhaps that means it was more important than he wanted to tell in his memoir."

Morgan nodded, "OK, it's worth a shot. We don't have any better options at this point."

She said goodbye to Ben, his concerned eyes haunting her as they signed off the call.

"That's it then, we go to the desert of Tunisia." Jake said decisively and shouted to the crew to get things moving, but

Martin called them back to the phone.

"Wait. I didn't mention this before but it's not deserted, Jake. The wadi is a natural fortress and our intel shows that it's currently being used as a hideout and training facility for the local Arab Muslim extremist groups."

Jake sighed, "Sounds like a welcome party to me. Any chance we can slip in and out again without being noticed?"

"Maybe if you can draw their fire away from the citadel, but do you want me to get a backup team organized anyway?"

"Yes, see if you can mobilize Jared Rush's team out of Egypt. They should be able to get there about the same time as us."

As the plane took off Morgan closed her eyes and willed herself to Faye and Gemma, sending positive thoughts to them, wherever they were. She remembered her father teaching her from the Talmud, reading that over every blade of grass was an angel whispering 'grow, grow.' If God cared for each blade of grass, then surely there must be a legion of angels watching out for her family.

The plane leveled out at altitude and the smell of strong coffee made her open her eyes again. Jake set the black nectar down.

"Let's go through the information again. Martin sent the intel on the groups at the wadi citadel and I want to be sure we know what we're getting into."

Martin had emailed them a whole stack of research information on Jung and the North African trip as well as satellite photos of the area and demographics about the local population. He had also included more of the images from Jung's Red Book. Morgan flicked through them and came upon the image of a mandala which reminded her of the one that had been broken during the attack on her office in Oxford. That seemed so long ago now. Her voice was wistful as she said to Jake,

"Some scholars think that this mandala represented Jung's internal journey in Africa. He was immensely affected by spiritual places so perhaps the mandala is some kind of clue to the Wadi citadel? If that's right, the stone would be in the center of the mandala, as it represents the journey into self, a spiraling descent into the spirit and soul of each human life. It must be accessed through the center of the citadel tower."

Jake was also paging through the notes.

"Legend says that Nefta was founded by a grandson of Noah after the flood subsided, so it's important in the myths of many faiths. When Jung went there, it was quiet and peaceful, but from Martin's description it has all changed now. It used to be a Bedouin stopping place, with camels and old men smoking hashish, but now it could be an Al Qaeda training camp, or any other militant Islamic group since they all get labeled Al Qaeda these days. Whatever their provenance, we're going to need that backup team."

Morgan heard the tinge of excitement in Jake's voice and felt its echo within herself. She relished the thought of some action. After days of running away and being on the back foot, she felt an aggression that needed an outlet. Her anger was aimed at Everett, but she would let it out in Tunisia if that was the only way.

CHAPTER 30

Nefta, Tunisia. May 25, 3.24am

JAKE LAY ON HIS belly on a sand dune overlooking the citadel and the sparse camp below. After meeting the backup team, they had crossed over the border from Algeria and were now almost in position. The small group of men were led by Jared Rush, one of ARKANE's senior agents in Africa and a man Jake trusted as a brother. It was good to be out in the field together again.

Jake knew that the city of Nefta was often busy with tourists but only the militants would come this far out at night. The citadel or 'ribat' was one of the fortifications used during the military occupation of North Africa by the Muslim empire. Ribats were built all across this part of the world and had been used as outposts for soldiers. These days they were occupied by a new brand of extremists intent on spreading terror across the world.

Fires burnt around the entrance as guards tried to warm themselves in the chill of the desert night, assault weapons by their sides. Jake noticed that they didn't seem especially vigilant, presumably considering themselves immune to attack as the authorities generally searched for bigger prey in the more dangerous playing fields of Libya and Sudan. Jake used his night vision goggles to locate the side entrance of the citadel they had identified from surveillance footage.

He could see Jared's team moving into place near the front of the castle, ready to draw attention from the side group. Jake checked his watch and looked around to make sure the others were ready. Morgan's body was taut, the black armor tight on her curves. Her eyes were fixed on the scene below and he could sense her readiness in the posture of a warrior. But despite his knowledge of her skill in combat, he still worried about her. That disturbed him, because if he was honest with himself, it was more than an operational concern. Time ticked on. He whispered into his headset.

"Ninety seconds to go. Be ready to move on my signal."

There were five in their side team. Jake and Morgan, then three commandos, Hanson, Margolis and Tien, a Special Forces team borrowed by ARKANE on these types of operation. They all wore camouflaged body armor with night vision goggles, and carried multi-purpose belts with grenades, guns and the tools they might need inside the citadel.

At the agreed time, Jared's team started firing from the dunes near the front of the citadel. Jake watched as the guards took cover and then moved towards the aggressors, drawn away from the tower entrance. Jake and Morgan ran low and fast towards the citadel, holding guns at the ready. The three commandos flanked them. They made it through the outer gate, but then the guards inside spotted them and fired, calling for support as they hid behind the stone fountains within.

The commandos provided cover, throwing grenades and drawing fire, creating havoc amongst the guards. Jake and Morgan ran for the central square tower of the citadel. A man by the main doorway leapt at them with a curved blade. Morgan ducked as the blade swung for her head, then slammed into the man with a rugby tackle, his head smashing against the side of the wall. He lay still as they fell panting inside the main tower entranceway, the sounds of gunfire continuing outside.

Moments later, two of the commandos, Hanson and Margolis, collapsed inside.

"Tien is hurt sir, but one of Jared's team picked him up. They're still engaging the guards outside. They should be able to hold them off but we'll need to get in and out as fast as possible in case the militants call for backup."

Jake nodded. "I guess it means we're safe in here for now. Let's get moving."

Morgan carried the image of the mandala tucked inside her protective jacket as well as photos from the Red Book on her smart phone. She flicked through the images.

"In Jung's mandala, the most precious object is always in the heart, so we should aim for the middle of the tower."

The team looked around. The walls were the color of bleached sand, made up of huge blocks hewn from desert stone and there were corridors in both directions, curling away from the entrance. Both looked as if they headed towards the middle of the citadel.

"So which way first?" Jake asked. "We need to do this fast. Jared's team can handle this small group, but not a full-scale assault."

Morgan stood close to one of the corridors, running her fingers around the rough hewn rock that circled the doorway.

"Look, it's a mark on the wall. A tiny kingfisher, Jung's spirit guide. It must be this way."

Morgan was jubilant. It felt almost surreal to be walking in the footsteps of a legend, a man she had studied and revered for her entire academic life. She held the smart-phone out to Jake. It showed an old man, arms folded and wings outstretched, in the colors of a kingfisher standing over a citadel with palm trees either side with the tangled knot of a snake at his side.

"What's the snake for?" Jake asked.

"Jung used the snake motif in many of his images but don't worry, it's not real. It represents wisdom and of course temptation, as well as the ancient creation story but it's allegorical. Let's go."

The corridor wound in towards the heart of the citadel, a tight stone passageway that grew narrower, pressing in on them so they soon had to walk in single file. The citadel was clearly packed with these tunnels, a maze of stone, spiraling in on itself. At each fork, they checked for more symbols. Other marks were scratched on tunnels going off at tangents but they followed the tiny kingfisher onwards, trusting in Jung's guardian bird. Finally, they reached a circular room, with three archways leading away from the central place. Each arch was richly decorated with stone carvings and Arabic script, totally different from what they had seen so far. They examined the doorways and Jake shook his head.

"None of these have kingfishers on, so which way should we go now?"

Morgan examined one of the mandala Jung had drawn in his Red Book.

"Maybe the clue is in here. The image seems to be a phoenix which was Jung's original family crest. What symbols are carved on the doors?"

"It looks like water, air, and fire."

Morgan looked at Jake, her face uncertain. "It must be fire, because the Phoenix rose from the flames and we're looking for the Pentecost stone which comes from fire."

"Can it really be that easy?" Jake asked.

"It's only the first step from the look of the mandala. There will be another choice before we reach the inner sanctum and the center of the citadel. Let's try it."

They went through the archway marked with the fire symbol. Hanson went first, followed by Morgan and Jake with Margolis behind, whispering, "This is creepy. Why are there no people down here? I would have expected some resistance or someone following?"

"We're not done yet. Just keep your eyes open," Jake said.

Their torchlight flickered on the walls as they walked deeper into the heart of the stone castle. Morgan saw a fat-tailed scorpion lurking against the wall, the segmented tail raised in defense topped by its venomous sting. She walked around it, acutely aware that its Latin name Androctonus meant the man-killer. The path sloped gently but inexorably downward. Hanson's voice came from up ahead,

"I've found the next split. There are another three archways to choose from."

They filed into the tiny antechamber, and gazed at the doorways. They were more intricately carved this time; each symbol an animal that crawled around the doorway in a repeating pattern.

"It looks like the scarab beetle, the snake and the crocodile," Morgan said.

Margolis cursed. "Oh great, it's just like 'The Mummy.' I hate those scarab beetles. We are NOT going down that way."

Jake silenced him with a look. Morgan studied the images trying to work out which way the psychologist would have gone and why the images were chosen.

"This is strange, because Jung used all these creatures in his drawings. He was fascinated with Egyptian mythology, hence the scarab, and also drew snakes and multi-legged crocodiles in many of his paintings. There's no clear direction here. I don't know." She ran her fingers along the carvings. "I think we should try the snake though because he used the image so much."

Jake nodded, "OK, but I'm sending one of the boys in first."

Margolis stepped forward.

"I'm in. Anything to avoid that scarab door."

Jake indicated that he go first and Margolis stepped through the archway. Nothing happened so he took another step, then another one and turned back, "Looks like we're good to …"

Then the ground disappeared beneath him and he plunged through a hole in the floor, his scream echoing through the chamber as he fell.

Jake and Hanson threw themselves down to the floor, reaching for him, but there was no way to grab him in time. His cries grew quieter and eventually faded to nothing. It seemed as if they went on for a long time, so the hole must have been incredibly deep. Morgan stood stunned in the ante-chamber, unwilling to believe the man was really gone. Dying in battle was one thing, but falling to your death in an ancient labyrinth was just crazy, especially as she had sent him that way. It was her decision to choose that path and she felt desperately responsible. She was frozen, looking down at the hole in horror. This wasn't something she had anticipated and it shook her to the core.

Jake shook her. "Come on, Morgan, we have to find the stone and get out of here. Think of Faye. Concentrate: what are we missing?"

He was right, her feelings were a pale shadow of what she would feel if Faye and Gemma went to their deaths. So she flicked through the images again and saw the snake motif, this time realizing the long deep body was an actual pit, not just a representation of creation and the tree of life. It's open mouth was the maw that Margolis had fallen into. After years of looking at Jung in an allegorical sense, she now struggled to make his images fit to the physical sur-roundings. It seemed that they were representations of this place, albeit embellished with Jung's eclectic mythologies.

"Then the crocodile, it must be. Look at this picture, the crocodile chases the round object. It could be an egg … or a stone."

Jake picked up a rock and threw it into the doorway of crocodiles. He threw another one, further this time. Nothing moved. Slowly Hanson stepped through. He inched on a little way, hugging the wall, tapping the floor in front of him with foot outstretched in caution. He shouted back.

"I've found the kingfisher again. It must be this way."

They rushed on, and finally found themselves at the entrance of a square room with a stone plinth in the center, carved with snakes. The serpents wound around it, open mouths gaping with fangs bared. Morgan walked to the pillar and looked at the detail. Each snake's head was finely decorated, a perfect replica of a desert killer almost dripping with venom. Their mouths were portals into the depths of the pillar and she could see something within. It looked like a box. She reached out to put her hand into one of the gaping mouths but Jake grabbed her wrist before she could touch it.

"What if it's another trap?" he asked as she angrily pulled her hand from his grasp.

"It doesn't matter now." she replied. "I have to get the stone. This is the room from Jung's painting. Look at the carvings on the checkered floor. The walls are a faded turquoise. This is where Jung was when he saw the fire coming from the stone. It has to be here."

Hanson made a frantic motion with his hand for them to be quiet. Morgan and Jake stood in silence and then heard the noise. It was a hissing, slithering sound that came from behind the walls.

"We have to hurry," Morgan said, "and I'm getting that box."

She thrust her hand inside one of the snake's jaws before Jake could stop her, her heart hammering in fear and expectation that something would bite at any moment. She grabbed the box and pulled back her arm, a sigh of relief on her lips as she extracted it from the pillar.

There was a clunking sound as if ancient gears were clicking into place. Jake and Hanson pulled their guns and looked around. They waited but nothing happened. Morgan refocused on the box. It was plain wood, nothing special, just something you would pick up in the souk. She opened it but there was no stone inside and her heart sank as she pulled out a piece of thick sketchpad paper. Unfolding it, she saw a crude rendering of the fiery stone image that was captured in greater detail within the Red Book. Jung must have drawn it here and repainted it at a later time. It showed a small square room, just like the one they were in, with checkered floor and carved walls, an almost exact replica of where they stood now. A man prostrated himself before a tiny stone on the ground, arms outstretched in worship, and from the stone emanated a towering pillar of fire. Flames poured from it, embers scattering to the floor. She read the words written on the page aloud,

"'Es ist nicht hier. Es ist mit dem Vater.' It's Jung's writing in German," she said. "It means 'It's not here. It's with the father.' But what the hell does that mean?"

"No time for that now, Morgan, we have to get out of here!" Jake shouted.

She looked up in horror to see snakes coming out of the walls and slithering from the mouths of the carved pillar by where she stood. They were desert vipers by the look of them, and then they heard scuttling and rattling. Appalled, they watched as a wave of fat-tailed scorpions poured out of the same holes, stingers raised in threat. This was a nightmare that made Morgan's skin crawl. Snakes she could deal with but scorpions were alien creatures, their armored bodies skittering across the floor in agitation. She stuffed the box and papers into her jacket, while the men both kicked at the ground, clearing a path to the doorway. The three of them ran out, back the way they had come into the entranceway.

Laying down covering fire to hold the remaining guards

at bay, they sprinted up the steps to the top of the square tower that rose above the citadel. Jake fired a flare high into the air and from the desert out west, they heard the helicopter coming for them. At the same time, they could see Jared's team withdrawing, heading back into the desert where they would rendezvous at the plane. As the helicopter landed the team sprinted aboard.

"We've gotta go now, they've got rocket launchers," Jake shouted. "Go, go!"

Then they were speeding away, flying low over the desert, as the explosions around them faded into the distance.

Morgan stared down onto the silver desert, the moonlight slipping across the dunes, pooling in the smooth undulations across the expanse below. She thought of Margolis and her part in his death. The guilt was overwhelming. After all, she was a Jungian psychologist so surely she could have foreseen the traps that awaited them. Yet all her life, Jung's images had been read as pure symbolism but if those mandala were actually real representations of physical places, what else could that be true of? She looked over at Jake, his face stony in the moonlight. Margolis was one of his men, and they had not even found another stone for their efforts. She needed to get to Faye soon for Pentecost was only a few days away.

CHAPTER 31

Desert, Algeria. May 25, 8.13am

ONCE THEY RETURNED TO the plane, Jake went down the back with Jared to debrief the men. There was a heaviness in the atmosphere, a grief but also a pragmatism. These men knew loss, but Morgan was determined to make the sacrifice worthwhile. She took the image from the box, trying to work out what the words meant. 'It's with the father.' What the hell did it mean? It could be Jung's real father, who was a great influence on him, or his God, but neither of those made sense with the timeline or with Jung's own conflicting beliefs. Morgan sat looking at the words in a trance of concentration, tracing back her studies of Jung and how his career had progressed. He had written so many books with layers of meaning. But an idea niggled at the back of her mind, something she had seen once that lay just out of reach. She calmed her breathing, letting the feelings of guilt subside and focused inwards.

After a time, she sat up sharply, calling for Jake to come back to the main cabin. Her voice was high-pitched with the excitement of realization.

"I think Jung's stone is in America," she said, "at Clark University in Worcester, Massachusetts. It's the last place where he and the 'father of psychology,' Sigmund Freud were still on speaking terms."

"What do you mean?" Jake looked tired and beaten. "This hasn't come up in any of the research so far."

Morgan was determined to convince him.

"Jung and Freud went on a trip together with other psychologists in the early 1900s. They were hosted by G Stanley Hall at Clark University, which is where psychoanalysis was introduced to the Americans. Think about it, Jake. At that point Jung still considered Freud to be a father figure. He was meant to assume the mantle of psychoanalysis in the Freudian tradition, but it was also on that trip that Jung started to go his own way."

"Why's that significant?"

"Jung wanted to include the mystic aspect of the human quest into his own theories. He believed in so many things that Freud dismissed, so Clark University was this turning point, when the father figure was no longer a father. It must be there. Don't you see?"

Jake sat down opposite her, considering what she said.

"No, I don't see. I'm beginning to doubt this whole Carl Jung connection, even with the painting. We've risked enough, Morgan. I'm not wasting time looking somewhere that might be wrong at this late stage. We should explore other options."

Morgan would not be dissuaded.

"But I've been to the university hall where they held their meetings. There was a centennial celebration of the visit in 2009 which I spoke at. There's a bust of Freud, pictures of the men together and most importantly, the twin image to this mandala." She held up the one that had represented the maze they had navigated at the wadi. "One of Jung's drawings was made into a framed image and put into the drawing room where they taught and discussed. It was an amazing time for them all, a life changing event for those men. Jung must have considered it pivotal to his career, so he put the stone there for safe keeping away from the prying eyes in

Europe."

Jake was studying the timeline of Jung's life that she had sketched out and laid on the table.

"But the timelines are confused. How did the image and note get left at the wadi when the North Africa trip in 1920 was after Clark University in 1909? Jung didn't have the stone with him at Clark."

Morgan pointed down at the timeline.

"But look, Jung did return to America in 1924 and must have worked with some of his disciples to hide it then. He clearly wanted it hidden, but he left clues in locations that only his true disciples would understand. If he held the stone and knew the myth, he would have loved the role of the Keeper. He always believed in gnosis, a spiritual knowledge known only to the enlightened few, and he certainly kept secrets."

"So it's Massachusetts, then, you're sure?" Jake said. "Because we've been wrong before and there are only forty-eight hours until Pentecost dawns in America. This is our last chance to get the final stone."

Morgan closed her eyes for a second and when she opened them again, they were cobalt blue steel, the violet slash a deeper shade.

"Yes, I believe that this is what Jung meant. I'm getting this last stone, and then I'll bargain them all for Faye and Gemma. I just want this to be over."

Jake nodded, then moved to the cockpit to direct their journey towards America, to Massachusetts.

CHAPTER 32

Clark University, Worcester, Massachusetts, USA
May 26, 10.02am

THEY ARRIVED AT THE airport near Worcester having slept fitfully on the way over the Atlantic. Morgan drowned her nightmares in several cups of coffee and made a final study of the University plans. Jake organized the small group, Jared and one other man, Morrison, would accompany them, their cover as visiting professors with a hastily constructed back story. Morgan didn't think they looked much like academics, but no one paid them much attention as they arrived at the imposing main entrance.

The red brick façade rose above them, four stories with large windows looking out over spring green lawns. Morgan glanced up at the clock, the Stars and Stripes flapping above it in the breeze. Her body screamed with jet lag. They had covered so many time zones in the last few days, she felt like her soul was still in transit from the desert wadi, and it would be some time before she was a whole person again.

They passed a statue of Sigmund Freud, sitting on a stone bench, book in one hand and cane in the other, a commemoration of the 1909 visit. Morgan ran her hand over the cool smoothness of the statue's head, his austere face giving her pause. What if this was the wrong place? They no longer had enough time to make a mistake. She shook her head to clear the lingering doubt and they progressed into the University.

A meeting had been arranged at short notice citing investigation into Jung's history, so they were escorted straight to the suite of rooms where the professor had lectured over one hundred years ago. It was a place to start at least. Jared and Morrison remained outside to watch the doors while Morgan and Jake went into the main dark wood paneled room. Deep red wing back armchairs sat around a fireplace that clearly hadn't been used in a while. A square table centered the room on a circular rug of Turkish origin.

"It's just like all the offices at Oxford," Morgan said. "Great universities are the same the world over. Look, there's the picture."

Morgan went to the mandala that hung on the far wall, next to the famous picture of the psychologists. It was the same as the one she now unpacked from her backpack, red lines tracing towards the center.

"There's one difference between the two mandala. Do you see it?"

Jake looked closer. "Here, the wasp drawn on the corner."

Morgan traced the tiny intricate image with her fingertip.

"It's strange because Jung didn't use wasps much in his paintings and imagery. It seems out of place."

She paused, deep in thought and then said with surprise. "Oh, the wasp symbol. It must be Wolfgang Pauli!"

"Wasn't Pauli a physicist?" Jake said. "What's he got to do with this?"

"Yes, Wolfgang Pauli was an Austrian physicist who won the Nobel Prize for his discovery of the exclusion principle, a key part of quantum physics. The man was brilliant but deeply troubled and there was a strange myth that surrounded him called the Pauli Effect. It seemed his presence changed matter and made things happen, like experimental equipment breaking as he walked past, but his creativity in science was phenomenal."

"Do you think this Pauli effect had something to do with the stone's power?" Jake asked.

"I'm not sure, but he certainly worked closely with Jung. Pauli had a breakdown and Jung interpreted his dreams. They also worked together on ideas about the paranormal and synchronicity so it's possible he knew about the Pentecost stone and even experienced its power. Maybe he was the one who hid it here."

Her eyes shone with the light of discovery and for a moment Morgan forgot the awful circumstances of why they were there, but then her eyes darkened again.

"Pauli feared wasps. He had nightmares about them and they appeared in the archetypal dreams that Jung interpreted. It's a symbol of what he was ultimately scared of, a weapon of some kind, a destruction of all that's good."

Jake raised an eyebrow. "You think the Pentecost stone might be this weapon?"

"Maybe. We need to find it. Look harder."

They searched the room carefully, looking for some indication of where the stone might be hidden. Jake lifted the mandala picture off the wall but the back was blank. They felt the walls around the pictures but nothing stood out.

Morgan turned around in the center of the room,

"What are we missing?"

Then she saw it. The room was square, with the round rug in the center, with a square table in the center of that again.

"Look, this whole room is a mandala, the circle in the square. The center is where truth lies. Help me move the table."

They managed to drag the heavy mahogany engraved

table to one side, then pulled back the circular rug. Underneath was a trapdoor in the stone floor with some kind of key mechanism. Jake tugged at it, trying to pull it open, while Morgan studied the markings etched in the top. It was engraved as a mandala, with twelve engraved stones spiraling into the center where a groove was hollowed out with a copper ring for lifting.

Morgan looked up at Jake with hope in her eyes.

"This has to be it."

As she bent down to pull the ring, the noise of a scuffle and gunfire came from outside the door. They pulled their guns as the door burst open and six men rushed in, weapons trained on the pair. They were outnumbered.

CHAPTER 33

"No need for any unpleasantness. You," he gestured to Jake, "move away from the trapdoor."

The man who spoke was tall with a rangy athleticism and a shock of grey-silver hair. He wore a black military style jumpsuit with sleeves rolled up. No academic posturing for this team. Morgan could see the pale horse tattoo on his forearm.

"Down on your knees." He pointed with his gun. "You won't be going on this part of the journey. Thanatos wants all the stones and it looks like the good Doctor will be finding the next one for us."

As Jake moved he caught Morgan's eye and nodded slightly, feinting away from her. Morgan hurled herself to the floor, commando rolling towards him. Shots rang out. Jake used the distraction to dive onto the man. Morgan drew her gun but too late. A bullet glanced her shoulder and spun her to the floor where she lay bleeding and weaponless. Jake managed to get in a punch before he was pulled off the man by two others. The leader slammed the butt of his gun into Jake's temple, pistol whipping him to the floor where he lay on the edge of consciousness. Morgan knew their last stand had been useless and now she was alone. The leader walked over to Morgan, leaning over her panting form.

"You just made it harder on yourself."

He put his boot onto her shoulder and leaned into the wound. She moaned, almost passing out from the pain, breathing faster as she tried to stay conscious. The silver haired man picked up Morgan's backpack and checked inside for the precious cargo. With a smug grin, he slung it over his shoulder. "We'll be taking the stones from here. Thanks for looking after them for us."

Morgan rolled to her knees, clutching her wounded shoulder. "But what about the stones Everett has?"

"We'll be getting those too before we return to Europe. The twelve will be together again, but in the hands of true believers, not filth like Everett. He'll pay for crossing Thanatos."

"And my sister and niece?" She dared hope they would be spared.

"I don't have any orders for them," he said. "Clearly they're not important."

They are to me, Morgan thought, breathing a sigh of relief, despite the pain of her throbbing shoulder. It wasn't over yet. The stones were never the important thing for her; it was always about her family.

"Enough talking. Let's get the stone and get out of here." He indicated Jake's prone body to the other men. "Tie him up and leave him in the corner. We're keeping him for interrogation later. He has valuable information about the other ARKANE projects and they'll trade handsomely to get him back. This one's coming with us."

He knelt and pulled up the trapdoor. It creaked on aged hinges to reveal a staircase spiraling down into the darkness. The men put on headlamps and dragged Morgan down into it. Her last glance above ground was at Jake, tied and unconscious by the door, blood trickling down his pale face to pool in the carpet beneath him.

The first man forced Morgan ahead of him. She stumbled in the dark, a cry of pain escaping her lips.

"Why do you need me, anyway? You can find the final stone yourself now."

"We heard about the traps in Tunisia, so we may need you to interpret any symbols along the way."

"Then what?"

He laughed, pushing her faster down the stairs. "Oh, don't you worry about that. There are plans for you as well as Timber."

They finally reached a small circular chamber at the bottom of the staircase. Again, there were three doors, a choice, just as in North Africa. But this time there was nothing was carved on these doors, they were just plain wood. Morgan felt apprehensive about the choice. She had made a mistake in Tunisia and it had cost a life. There was too much at stake, so she was desperate to get it right.

"Which door?" the leader said. All eyes were on Morgan. She hesitated.

"Your friend Jake could have a bullet in the back of his head with one word into this radio," he threatened.

Morgan awkwardly pulled out the mandala picture she had taken from the room upstairs. When she studied it more closely she could see it was slightly different from the original, with layers of information not present on the first version of the image. The mandala curled in on itself, the lines of the spiral colored like a map, with breaks that could indicate choices in the maze. If she followed the openings to the centre, perhaps it would lead them to the stone. The wasp sat in the bottom right of the picture, a beautifully painted tiny nightmare from the mind of Wolfgang Pauli. Her mind raced as she clung to her knowledge of Jung, the doubts swirling about her. But there were no other clues.

"It's the middle one," she said, looking up from the mandala.

"If you're lying to us ..."

"Look," Morgan snapped. "I want to get the stone and

save my family so let's just get this over with. Quit hassling me."

He raised his hands in mock surrender, and nodded to one of the men.

"You heard the lady. Open it."

The door swung open easily to reveal a twisting corridor.

"OK, double time."

The group moved swiftly down the corridor into the blackness. It seemed to go on a long way. Morgan wondered where it would end up and what was above ground here. Why was the stone hidden in this way? Why was Pauli's nightmare pointing them in this direction?

The passage ended in a final door, with the sound of a buzzing hum behind it. An image of the twelve stones was carved into the door with wasps flying around them, weaving a complicated pattern. Stylized flames were engraved at the bottom of the door, reaching up towards the stones.

"This has to be the place," she said, examining the imagery.

"What's that noise?" One of the men said. "It sounds like a generator."

"I think I know what it might be," Morgan pointed to the wasps on the mandala painting and the door. Pauli's weapon was protected by his own nightmare.

"A few wasps won't stop us getting the Pentecost stone," the leader said, "but to be on the safe side, you and I will wait here."

The leader motioned for the other men to go inside. They pulled open the door and entered in formation, guns held high as they walked into the buzzing room. Morgan caught a quick glimpse inside before the heavy door swung itself shut behind them. She saw a plinth in the middle of the room lit from a skylight above. There were dark shapes hanging from the ceiling and a floor that seemed to be crawling with insects.

It was quiet for a few seconds. Then the buzzing grew louder and the sound of gunfire and shouting came from inside. It quickly turned to screaming. The leader grabbed Morgan, and held his gun to her head.

"What's in there?" he shouted as the screaming slowly died, and the buzzing calmed again to a gentle hum. Now there were just the two of them in the corridor, gun held to her head and the man's hand shaking. Morgan's shoulder throbbed with the bullet wound but she felt a strange sense of calm descend as she contemplated what waited beyond the door.

"Maybe they bred an unusual strain of wasps to protect the stone. There are killer wasps in Africa, larger and more vicious than we have here, and guns would have little effect. One of Jung's disciples was a genetic engineer; perhaps they have a hybrid wasp of sorts protecting his secret."

The man pushed her towards the door, gun still pointed at her head. "Well, we have to get that stone, so it looks like you're going in next."

Morgan took a deep breath and thought through her knowledge of Jung and Pauli. There must be a way to get the stone out, because all these devices were meant to allow the true disciple through unharmed. It was only a trap for those who didn't have the right knowledge, the true gnosis. The corridor was a feature in Pauli's dreams, and so was the wasp, but there was something she was missing.

She focused on the circle around the wasp in the carving on the door, racking her brain for the right information. Maybe it represented a way to contain the wasps, or surround the seeker with protection, so the stone could be reached. The mandala seemed to indicate the door itself was a key of some kind. Inspired, she felt around the door frame. On the right hand side was a slight opening: she reached inside and found a key.

Pulling it out, she showed the leader.

"The door wasn't locked. Why the key?" he said.

"The Keepers surely designed some fail safe. Perhaps this activates it somehow."

"Great theory, crazy woman, but I'm not going in there. You go in, get the stone and I'll be waiting here. If you don't come out, then, hey, it's all over anyway."

Morgan swallowed. She didn't like wasps, but then who did? It was a rational human fear. They weren't the stuff of her nightmares but the screams of the dying men who had entered before her still echoed round her head. A trickle of sweat ran down her back as she clenched her fists in determination. She had to face this fear head on because her own life was at stake now, and if she died, Faye and Gemma didn't stand a chance. She took a deep breath, gently pushed open the door, and slid into the room.

CHAPTER 34

INSIDE, THE BUZZING NOISE filled her head and Morgan gasped as she saw what the room held. Wasps' nests draped from the ceiling and dripped down around the walls, hanging almost to the floor. Above them was a distant sky-light and she realized this place must be under the botanical gardens where they could feed, even as they protected their secret. The air was thick with flying insects although many lay dead on the floor with the bodies of the soldiers.

The men had been stung to death, the reaction to the sting bloating the bodies already. It must be potent venom or the volume of stings that killed them with anaphylactic shock. Wasps still crawled over the bodies, crowding on any exposed skin. Morgan could see one of the men's faces frozen in a drawn-out scream as a wasp emerged from his swollen mouth. She shuddered, trying not to imagine the pain of his death but she noticed that the wasps were bigger than normal, with longer stings and the sheer number of them was astonishing.

The buzzing increased at her entrance but the wasps kept their distance for now and Morgan wondered what made them attack. Her eyes darted around the room. She felt the door on her back realizing that there was nowhere to go except forwards into the room. She could see the stone plinth in the middle, similar to the one from the wadi in

Tunisia. There was a box on top of it. The Pentecost stone must be in there, but how to get to it?

Morgan clutched the key in her hand and looked away from the seething mass of writhing gold and black bodies. If it didn't open the door, it must fit in a different place. Then she saw it. On the wall to her right, a good few paces away, three mandalas were carved, each with a keyhole in the center. It was the final test of the seeker. If she moved towards the wall, the wasps would be alerted and would attack. She would have seconds to place the key before they reached her, so there would only be time to try one of the mandalas. She needed to decide which before she moved or she would die here like these men, stung to death, overtaken by toxic shock and venom. Morgan breathed quietly. The wasps still didn't move against her which was puzzling. She looked down and saw a semicircle of light around her from the grille above. It was as if this protected her until she stepped outside the light towards the keyholes. More confident at the task now, she looked again at the mandalas. What was the difference between them and which was the right keyhole?

Each mandala was a highly decorated carving with an image at the center. The paint had faded but Morgan could see that the keyholes were part of the intricate design of each central figure. On the right, a glorious rainbow of color illuminated the Sephiroth, the tree of life. It was a Kabbalistic image that Jung used in his writings and drew in the Red Book. The center mandala was a dark vortex of swirling shades in grey and black with slashes of vermilion. It was a destructive and almost cruel image, the keyhole a dark void at its heart. On the left, a many-legged crocodile spun around the keyhole, its limbs dropping off into a pool of blood below as a man chopped at them with a sword. Morgan shook her head. Even years of study in Jungian symbolism made this a difficult choice because they were all valid in some way. She closed her eyes and focused within.

Doubts and fears flooded her mind, images of Faye and Gemma crying, Jake's bloodied face, the bodies they had left in their wake, and then Elian's bullet riddled body. In the maelstrom of emotion, she knew what it must be.

Having made her decision, Morgan took one last look at the wasps and ran forward with the key outstretched in her good hand. As she stepped outside the light circle, the buzzing became loud and angry as the wasps took flight. She reached the wall and plunged the key into the center mandala as she felt the brush of tiny furred bodies against her skin and winced at the first sting. The mandala represented the shadow self, the dark side of the psyche that Jung believed must be embraced in order to become whole. It had to be the correct one.

A flash of doubt entered her mind as the key plunged in. Then there was a cracking sound and the cavern filled with light. A high-pitched noise made her hunch over and cover her ears. She turned to see the bodies of the wasps drop out of the air, stunned or dead. Morgan wasn't waiting to find out if they recovered. She ran to the center plinth, stepping around the bloated corpses and fallen wasps. She opened the box, took out the final Pentecost stone and ran for the door.

The silver-haired man was waiting, and as she came through, he sprayed a cloud of suffocating fumes into her face. She coughed and fell to the floor, feeling him take the stone from her. Her vision narrowed and she sank into inky unconsciousness. The last thing she saw was the pale horse tattoo, a witness to her failure.

CHAPTER 36

Clark University, Worcester, Massachusetts, USA
May 26, 4.19pm

MORGAN CAME TO IN a groggy state, her mouth dry and head throbbing. She tried to sit up, reaching for her gun instinctively. Then she saw Jake.

"It's OK. You're safe. Relax now," he said.

Morgan realized she was lying on a couch in the study. Jake was looking down at her, his head bandaged. He offered her a glass of water and helped her to sit up.

"What happened? What time is it?"

"It's thirteen hours until Pentecost dawns, and we've got the men from Thanatos restrained outside. We're leaving them for the authorities. While you were down in the tunnels, Jared and I had our own little adventure but how are you feeling?"

She sank back into the couch, visions of the killer wasps and dead men left in the vault swimming before her.

"Physically, like a two-ton truck hit me. Mentally, I'm confused."

Jake sat on the side of the couch.

"What's puzzling you?"

Morgan shook her head.

"I'm finally starting to believe that the stones must

have some kind of power. If a physicist like Wolfgang Pauli protected this one with such elaborate measures, if he was so convinced of its importance, then I have to take it seriously. But at the same time, I don't really care. I just want Faye and Gemma back. Has Everett phoned with the final destination? When do we leave?"

Jake motioned to the other men to leave the room, and shut the door behind them. They were alone.

"Everett isn't getting the stones, Morgan because the myths are true. There is real power in them so we can't have them loose in the world especially with the comet approaching its zenith. You've seen what Thanatos will do to get them. They seek to use the stones to ignite a religious war, a symbol with power to galvanize support of extremists. We can't let that happen."

Morgan's head was throbbing and Jake's words were slow to register.

"What do you mean?"

"I'm ordered to take the stones back to ARKANE. It's my duty to make sure that their power isn't given to Everett or controlled by Thanatos. I'm sorry, Morgan, but you can't take the stones. You can't exchange them for Faye and Gemma."

"No!" Morgan shouted as she sprang off the sofa, rage crushing the physical pain she felt. She was like a lioness defending her pride, her family. She would not give up now when she was so close to saving them. She staggered, trying to get her balance with her bandaged arm.

"Everett is a killer. You know he's murdered in his quest for the stones, which means my sister will be next. I must give him the stones, or he'll *kill* them. Jake, why are you doing this to me after we've been through so much?"

Morgan couldn't believe that Jake would walk away from this. His betrayal cut into her, twisting her guts so she felt a wave of nausea. She reached out to take his hand but he stepped back. She could see he was wavering but his allegiance to ARKANE was too strong for their brief friendship to sway him.

"Those are my orders," he said. "I have to take these stones back to England, to the ARKANE vault, to prevent them getting into the wrong hands. If they are kept apart, then the power cannot be called again. We can get the US authorities involved to help you with Faye and Gemma."

"But there's no time," she pleaded. "Pentecost is only hours away and I can't go empty handed. He'll kill them."

Morgan touched Jake's arm, trying to get him to look at her. He had been a protector on this journey and they had become close, perhaps too close at times. She knew he had already gone further than he needed to help her and she felt a glimmer of hope that she could persuade him to stay. But he pulled his arm away and turned to leave.

"It's over," he said. "Come with me and we'll explain everything to the police."

A flash of anger sparked in her as he turned. At herself for trusting him, and at him for betraying her. She kicked hard into the back of his knee and as he started to fall, she grabbed the lamp from the table and swung it at his head.

"You bastard, you never meant to help me, did you? All the time you've been waiting to get the stones, so you could just take them from me. You've been using me, just like Ben said you would."

Jake blocked the blow as he fell and then twisted on the ground, kicking her legs from under her so they were both on the floor. He moved fast, but she sprang up again ready for his attack, ignoring the stabbing pain in her arm and the blinding headache that threatened to overwhelm her.

"This is crazy, I'm not going to fight you," he said. "I'm taking the stones. We've called the authorities to help you finish this, for ARKANE doesn't deal with the purely criminal side. We just want the stones. You know I would help you if I could."

Jake moved back as she swung at him with her good arm and then launched a kick to his head which he blocked. Backing towards the wall, he could see the fury in her face, blood soaking the bandage from her shoulder wound. She was like an Amazon goddess in her rage and he admired her. Hell, he wanted her. This stunning, fiery woman, lean muscle and curves that attracted him even as she threatened violence. He was torn between Marietti and his duty to ARKANE, the mission and this woman, who he had grown close to in the last weeks. He had been stunned by her intellect, and had spent too long trying to put thoughts of her body from his mind. She grabbed the lamp again and swung it hard. This time it connected. His eyebrow split and blood began to ooze from it.

"Give me the stones, you bastard, where are they?" she shouted, coming at him with a flurry of blows. He hit back at her then, defending himself but still loath to engage in the fight. She blocked his moves but couldn't land any of her own, weakened by the shoulder injury and exhaustion. Then he had to do it: time was of the essence. He punched her wounded arm, sending her twisting down onto the couch again, holding her shoulder and moaning.

"I'm sorry, so sorry," he said. "Forgive me."

He went to her then and held her as she gasped in pain, breathing in the scent of her hair as he rocked her onto his lap, her breasts soft against his chest.

"I didn't want to hurt you, Morgan, but you've got to stop."

She pulled slightly away from him and then head-butted him full on the bridge of his nose. Blood started dripping from it and he wiped it away with the back of his hand. Morgan jumped up, pulling her gun from the side table and pointing it at his head.

"Give me the stones, Jake. You're not important to me,

my family is. I will hurt you, ARKANE, Everett, Thanatos, whoever I need to in order to get them back."

He held his hands up.

"OK, OK. Let me get them for you, just let me up."

"I will kill you if they die," she said, keeping the gun trained on him.

As he got up he dived for her, pushing her arm up so that the shot went wide into the wall. He flipped her over roughly, pinning her down. Morgan lay panting, face down on the floor, angry that she had let him do this. Her reactions were slowed by her injuries but that was no excuse. Jake's knee was in her back, her good arm twisted behind in his vice-like grip. This time he wasn't letting her up.

"Are you finished now?" he asked, twisting her arm tighter. She gasped out a 'yes' and felt him shift, then cold metal clicked into place around her wrist and the leg of the couch. She spat her words at him.

"Why won't you help me? You know Faye and Gemma will die without the stones."

"I'm sorry but you must understand that my mission is to stop the twelve being in one place. That cannot happen so I'm taking these stones back to England today and you're staying here."

Morgan bent her head, crushed by his words, feeling the ache of her bruised body, the helplessness and frustration overwhelming her. She wept then, silent tears that welled up and could no longer be held back. Jake stood, wrenched between his desire to comfort her and knowing that he couldn't see her again, this woman who so fascinated him with her vulnerability and strength.

"I can't help you, Morgan. I just can't. The risk is too great and my duty is to ARKANE, not your family. The power of the stones is too great to let loose in the world. There will be authorities here to help you soon. A call came through from Everett and the coordinates are here on the table. It's near

Tucson, Arizona. I know you'll get Faye and Gemma back, but I can't let you take the stones to him."

Jake placed the key to the handcuffs on the floor so she could reach it by shuffling over and walked out, leaving her alone.

CHAPTER 37

Biosphere 2, Oracle, Arizona, USA
May 27, Pentecost Sunday, 6.32am

As the day dawned, Joseph Everett walked up through the Biosphere to check on the final preparations for his Pentecost enactment. He would wait for the evening when the flames from the pyre would be the most stunning, and he was sure Morgan Sierra would come with the stones. Her sister and niece were the perfect bait. The comet would reach its zenith at 8pm so he would perform the sacrifice then but for now, he wanted to survey his chosen location for the ritual.

The Biosphere had been constructed in the little town of Oracle, Arizona, between Tucson and Phoenix. It was a shining white mini city bleached by the high Sonoran desert, overshadowed by the Santa Catalina Mountains. Joseph was proud to own this place and often brought business colleagues here for meetings to impress them with the complexities of its habitat.

Biosphere 1 was the earth's own living system and Biosphere 2 was a radical experiment based on recreating life on earth. It gave him more than a few business metaphors to use in negotiation. The complex stretched over three acres housing a complete self-sustaining ecosystem, built in the late 1980s as a research facility to investigate the possibility of living in such closed environments in space. The weather could be manipulated and the effects monitored on the five separate bio-systems within. Joseph had kept it running partly as a research facility so it could continue to fund itself.

The main Biosphere experimental area was enclosed in a modern ziggurat of stepped triangular glass and steel panels, each designed to withstand impact from outside and pressure from inside. Joseph walked up the main path, looking down on the ocean complete with coral reef and passing the savannah, mangrove swamp and fog desert. He headed towards the human habitat, a small but self-supporting pod within the tiny world. Several experiments had been carried out where people were locked within the dome, the longest for two years. After closed system research was halted, the Biosphere was eventually sold for development. Joseph had put up the most substantial funding that had bought the Biosphere in 2007 which gave him access whenever he wanted and his own private casita for when he wanted to stay. It was a peaceful place for him, especially at night when he wandered around the ecosystem thinking and staring at the stars through the great glass ceiling. He had even brought a few of the young female researchers here at night. They were keen to see the habitat in darkness, lit only by the stars, and they all knew about his money and connections. The airlocks meant the place was also sound-proof, and they were paid well not to talk of abuses in the dust of the savannah.

The glass panels opened the area to the wide expanse of Arizona sky. The quality of light was stunning inside the complex and, as he walked through the rainforest, Joseph smiled. He particularly loved being there during the extreme weather that the area was famous for. In summer, the heat pounded the land, but when storms came, it was glorious. Web lightning slashed the sky, thunder crashed and rolled down the Sonoran hills, torrential rain bringing the red dust in streams along the roads. The rain on the glass roof was a reminder of the power of nature to destroy and renew again. This was an inhospitable landscape and here Joseph Everett felt peace for today he would use it to welcome a new Pentecost.

CHAPTER 38

En route to Oracle, Arizona, USA
May 27, Pentecost Sunday, 5.35pm

WITH HER SHOULDER PATCHED and out of a sling, Morgan drove towards the Biosphere, going over the plan in her head. After unlocking the cuffs and finding Jake and his team had indeed left, she had escaped Clark University by stealing a baseball cap and jacket from a student locker room. She had pulled the cap low and passed for a student on the grounds, only just missing the FBI team who pulled up to escort her. She knew that the authorities would never make it in time to save her family. She had cursed Jake's betrayal but knew she still had time to find Faye and Gemma, even without the stones to trade for their lives.

Away from the University, she had called Ben and told him what had happened. He had been calm and reassuring in the face of her rage, as if he had expected the deception. He had said not to trust ARKANE from the beginning and sure enough, they had cheated her of the stones and betrayed her trust. She was livid with anger at Jake, ashamed of herself for trusting him. She had almost let him through her barriers, had reached out to him, but her fury would have to wait. First, she must save Faye and Gemma from Everett's fire.

Ben had contacts all over the Christian world and had

sent her to the Teresian Carmelite convent in a nearby town. He had called in a few favors and arranged for the nuns to provide a flight to Arizona, as well as cash for the journey. It was amazing what a spiritual network could arrange at short notice. She had rented a car at the airport and would still be able to make it to the Biosphere by the early evening of Pentecost.

The desert was scrubland near the city, but as Morgan drove out from Tucson towards Catalina and then Oracle, the hills began to overshadow the road. Clouds scudded across the sky, the wind whipping them into peaks of fluffy white. A red-tailed hawk hovered overhead, wings barely moving as it rode the currents. This was a landscape that Morgan felt she knew. It was like the desert around the cities of Israel. She knew the terrain and she understood driving into danger. This was where she felt most alive and it stunned her to feel this way now after closeting herself in the safety of academia for the last few years. Now she channeled her anger at Jake and ARKANE into planning her next move.

At the convent she had collected a number of stones from the garden, roughly the size of the Pentecost stones. It wouldn't fool Everett for long, but it would at least get her into his presence and might buy her some time. She felt the gun in the holster at her back and the cool of the knife strapped against her calf under her jeans. She had swapped the blood soaked top for a Clark U t-shirt. The nuns had dressed her shoulder wound and given her painkillers, but she would need more serious medical help in the next twenty-four hours if she was to recover full use of her arm. Right now, she had to get to Faye and Gemma.

She thought back over the time she had known her sister. She didn't understand Faye's faith or her lack of ambition. She aspired to be a good mother, a wife and member of the church but she seemed to want nothing more than this. In one argument Morgan had raged at her, shouting that she just didn't know what she wanted. How could she give up her own life to just live it for other people? But deep down she knew her sister was like the reeds that grew by the river Cherwell, anchored deep in faith, bending but never breaking in the storms and hail. She remembered Faye had worn that smile of patience and understanding, and poured Morgan more tea, explaining what her life meant in God's eyes. She had a fulfillment in life that Morgan would never understand. Was that why she had taken David from her sister, even for one night?

As she saw the Biosphere in the distance she realized that the guilt would continue to drive her until the end, until they were safely back home.

CHAPTER 39

Biosphere 2, Oracle, Arizona, USA
May 27, Pentecost Sunday, 6.35pm

FAYE STOOD BY THE sink in the Biosphere pod, peeling carrots for dinner. She had kept up a routine of domestic chores to try and behave normally for Gemma, who was playing by the table on the slate-grey carpet. They had been inside the human habitat of the Biosphere for several days now and had not seen anyone since the airlock was closed on them. But it was comfortable enough and there were provisions for a few days, plus books and DVDs for Gemma so she was entertained. They had not been treated badly and were mainly ignored so it could be a lot worse. Since the trip out to the kiln Faye hadn't even seen Everett, for which she was grateful. After that horrific experience she had clung to Gemma, desperate to get her to safety but not seeing any way to escape. Then they were transported here and locked in. Faye was still unsure why they were here, but she held out hope that Morgan was coming to find them. Still, in moments of weakness, the face of the burning man from the kiln haunted her and the flames of memory licked her skin. She shivered. Knowing what this man was capable of, she didn't think it could be a happy ending.

When they'd thrown them in here the guards had said

it would be over soon. She had been tense at first, waiting for the noise of the door opening, the laugh of the bully threatening her. She had kept Gemma close, not letting her out of her sight, barely sleeping for fear of what would come next. But after several days with nothing happening, she tried to relax and treat this as an adventure for Gemma to keep her calm. The whole experience seemed to alternate between long periods of boredom and sharp visceral terror. Then door slammed open and all her fears were realized.

Faye dropped the vegetables in the sink and snatched Gemma into her arms, holding her close. Two men stood at the door, guns at their belts.

"It's time to go. You won't need anything, just you and the girl." They indicated the door. "Get moving. It's time, and he's waiting for you."

Gemma whimpered, sensing her mother's fear. She was almost too heavy to carry now so Faye grasped her hand tightly, walking between the guards into the main dome of the Biosphere. They stumbled through the rainforest section and up to a platform at the highest point, overlooking the mesa, the ocean and out through the glass onto the plain. Up on the top platform, she gasped in horror.

Joseph Everett was putting the finishing touches to a high funerary pyre. Wood was stacked in a rectangle with a bed of thinner logs on top, ropes laid ready to tie someone down. Another man sat in a wheelchair to the side. He was a pale, thin version of the man who had abducted them. Everett beckoned her over.

"Come, come. See my wonderful creation. It has wood from all kinds of holy places. I wanted to make a perfect offering to God on this day of healing and creation, through destruction of course."

Faye whispered, "What do you want from me? What are you going to do with my daughter?"

He gestured at the pyre.

"Surely that's obvious. It will be like suttee, the ancient Indian custom of immolating yourself on the husband's funerary pyre. Of course, your dear husband is not here, but it doesn't matter. I need a final sacrifice for the stones as we call down the power of Pentecost. It will amplify the power of the stones."

He turned and pointed at the wheelchair bound man, who stared vacantly into the distance, untethered to this world.

"This is my brother, Michael. He's going to be healed today and your sacrifice is the catalyst I need to bring the power down to earth."

"No!" Faye cried, pulling Gemma into her arms. She tried to turn and run, but the men grabbed her and held her fast. "Just let Gemma go, then. Please. I'm begging you. She's only a baby."

"I might let her go if your sister shows up and you go quietly. A sacrifice of twins must surely be the most fitting, since we are twin brothers. I shall consider it, but time is running out."

He motioned to the men. One tore Gemma from Faye's arms, and the little girl started screaming, reaching out to her mother. Faye tried desperately to get to her until a man held a cloth over the child's mouth and she passed out. Faye stopped struggling then, surprising the men who held her. She seemed strangely calm as she spoke.

"You're wrong about this sacrifice and the stones. There's nothing in what you speak of in the Bible that relates to the true Pentecost. There's no human sacrifice in the Christian tradition. There's no power except from God himself."

"Ah, that's where you're wrong" Joseph said, his own stone hanging on his chest. "The stones are made from a unique radioactive rock that resonates with the Resurgam comet. It's beyond our knowledge whether they were originally empowered by the death or resurrection of Jesus, but the healing powers of the Apostles came from these stones. The Pentecost fire was forged from the stones, the collective power of the twelve being in one place at the same time but they were split when the Apostles left Jerusalem and today, for the first time in history, they will be together again."

A radio crackled, and a man made a sign to Joseph.

"Excellent, it seems your sister is here. Just in time. We only have a few hours left of Pentecost, the fiftieth day. And she is alone, just as I asked."

Faye sagged then, collapsing to the ground. If Morgan was alone, then it was over and they would all die tonight. Joseph indicated the pyre, and the men hoisted her up onto it, tying her hands to the heavy logs. She screamed then, afraid to die this way. From the end of the huge dome, she heard Morgan's voice calling her name.

CHAPTER 40

MORGAN HAD LET THE men hustle her into the building and then she heard the screams of her sister. She shouted, "Faye" before one of the men backhanded her into silence. They roughly pushed her up through the Biosphere sections, guns tight against her back. As she walked, Morgan scanned the place for possible escape routes and weapons. She noticed that it was a strange mix of natural habitats existing right up against each other under the glass dome, but there was nothing she could immediately use.

As they reached the top canopy in the rainforest habitat she saw Faye shackled on a funeral pyre, Gemma slumped on the ground guarded by men with guns, a man in a wheelchair and, finally, Everett in person.

"Dr Sierra, I'm so glad you could make it. Let me see the stones."

She clutched the bag tightly, wanting him to fight for it.

"You have to let Faye down first. I'm only giving you the stones in exchange for my family. Backup is outside. I'm not here alone as you might think."

Joseph laughed at her bluff. "We know ARKANE abandoned you. No private jet for you this time."

He waved his hand and the man behind her punched her heavily in the kidneys. She went down then, her body exhausted, drained and in pain from the beatings and bullet she had taken in the last few days, but she still held the bag with the stones close to her body. Everett kicked her, hard in the side and she groaned and rolled slowly over. Faye was screaming again, straining against the ropes to see what was happening.

"Please no, don't hurt her."

Joseph leaned down.

"It's time to give them up, Morgan. If I shoot you in the head now, these stones will be empowered by your death. I don't need to burn you alive after all."

He held a gun to her forehead. She let the bag go and he took it from her.

"Excellent, now let's take a look."

He emptied the bag out on a table in front of the pyre to join the stones he already had. There were high-tech gadgets laid out, including a Geiger counter. Morgan knew it was all over then. He realized within seconds that she was trying to trick him and spun around.

"Where are they, you bitch? Did you come all this way just to die?" he shouted in frustration, his voice echoing around the dome. In fury, he ran back, kicking her harder in the ribs, landing his boots wherever he could on her body. He would beat her to death for cheating him out of the stones. Morgan heard Faye screaming her name as she felt her world slipping away.

CHAPTER 41

"I'D STOP THAT IF I were you."

The words halted Joseph. He turned to see the ARKANE agent Jake Timber pointing a gun at the head of the guard in front of him and holding a bag in his hand.

"I have the real Pentecost stones, Everett so it's me you want after all. Just let them all go and I'll give them to you."

Joseph growled deep in his throat.

"I don't bargain for what is rightfully mine."

He ended on a shriek as his frustration spilled over. He grabbed a gun and shot the man Jake held as a shield, at the same time using another guard to stop the bullets as Jake fired in return, killing two guards who raced towards him. A bullet grazed Jake's hand and he dropped the stones, ducking away into the undergrowth of the rainforest as the other guards charged him.

"Kill him!" Everett shouted to the remaining guards as he swept up the bag. "I will have my sacrifice."

Jake ran through the thick foliage that slapped at his body as he pushed into the rainforest. It was dense with liana and palms, dripping with water that was raining down constantly on the ecosystem. The smell of rich wet earth was a tangy reminder to Jake of his time in the jungles of Borneo. He knew he had to draw the men away and lose them in this maze of trunks and vines, then he could double back to the pyre. He had gone directly against Marietti's orders to come here, but he would not leave Morgan alone again. After he had left her in Worcester, he had been haunted by nightmares of his own family, hacked to bloody limbs by a vengeful group of youths high on methamphetamines. If he had been there to protect them, perhaps their deaths would have been prevented, or he would have gone down with them, a fitting place to die. He couldn't care about Morgan's family, but he found himself thinking of her, heading to almost certain death, risking her life for her family as he would have done for his. They were alike in so many ways, yet both so independent he knew they couldn't admit to a mutual need. Still, this time he had made his choice and he would face whatever consequences he had to.

He ducked behind a palm tree, listening to the men crashing through the undergrowth after him. They were almost drowned out by the sound of the wind that was building outside and rattling the biosphere glass. A huge storm was fast approaching. Grabbing a liana from one of the trees, Jake wrapped it around his hands, waiting for the guards to go by.

As the men ran past on the narrow boardwalk, Jake leapt out and wound the vine around the last man's neck. A quick flick and he pushed him off the boardwalk, the man's fingers scrabbling at the constricting vine, dropping his gun in the undergrowth as he choked. Jake bent to pick up the fallen gun as the other man turned and shot wildly at him. He dived for the man's legs, toppling him to the ground. In a wrestler's grip, he flipped the man over and slammed his head hard down onto the boardwalk again and again. The body went limp. Then an agonized scream pierced the noise of the storm.

CHAPTER 42

HEARING FAYE'S SCREAM, MORGAN groaned and rolled over onto her side, sharp pain stabbing through her ribs and into her chest. Wounded but not out just yet, she was lucky Jake had appeared when he did. She fleetingly wondered why he had come back, after leaving in such a definitive way. She could see Joseph examining the stones at the table near the pyre and by the look on his face, they were real. He saw her looking at him.

"It seems we will have our sacrifice today, after all. You and your sister, the twins, are the perfect final offering for the stones. Michael doesn't yet have your energy but he will soon. The stones will heal him and restore his mind and we shall be true brothers again."

They heard shots down in the rainforest, and Joseph smiled.

"I wouldn't expect Jake to rescue you again, Morgan. We'll summon the new Pentecost now. Finally the twelve stones are together again."

He wheeled Michael closer to the pyre. Faye lay still now, her eyes on the little figure of Gemma on the ground. Morgan looked around desperately for something she could use to stop this madness. Joseph placed six of the stones in a bag of netting and draped it around his brother's neck. He paused to wipe some drool from Michael's mouth and whispered, "Not long now. Soon you'll be restored to me."

In that moment, Morgan saw that his fanaticism stemmed from a deep love of his wounded brother, and she understood that both she and Everett would both do anything to save what remained of their family. Then he lit a taper and held it to the bottom of the pyre and Faye began to scream again.

As the flames started to catch at the base of the pyre, storm clouds gathered over the Biosphere and turned the sky black from the nearby town of Oracle to as far away as Tucson in the Catalina foothills. It was as if a heavy lid of cloud had dropped over the area, the shadow darkening to a radius of only a few kilometers. Lightning began to flicker inside the clouds, metallic blue streaks against the burnt orange sky lit with the final rays of the smothered sun. Purple sheets of rain bruised the land, punishing the saguaro cacti as they raised their dusty gray arms to God like desperate believers. Crimson and silver-blue cracks broke the clouds and hurtled to earth. Jagged lightning strikes came closer to the stepped ziggurat of the Biosphere as the earthy grumble of thunder rattled the windows of the adobe houses nearby. High above the clouds, in an event not seen for two thousand years, the eye of the comet storm reached the Earth's atmosphere.

Inside the glass dome, Joseph laughed and shouted up to heaven.

"It has begun. The twelve are reunited and I call down this power from heaven."

Clouds covered the rocky outcrops surrounding the Bio-sphere, their tops shrouded in thick swirling darkness as the wind grew in intensity and volume, pounding the structure and engulfing it in fury. The howling increased as the rain pounded down, wind whipping it into the sides of the struc-ture with increasing speed. The steel creaked and moaned, trying to hold together beneath the ferocity of the storm. Lightning crackled even closer, luminous veins connecting sky to earth as electricity supercharged the air.

The first strike hit the north side of the Biosphere zig-gurat, lighting the rainforest in brilliant magnesium white and the deep explosion of thunder followed immediately. The storm was on top of them. Forked lightning split the sky, visible branches breaking into splinters of light while thick bolts smashed into the glass and steel. Wind tornadoed the building, encasing the Biosphere in its own hellish vortex. Then the first cracks appeared in the glass and spread quickly, raining shards down on the remaining guards below. Joseph seemed unaware of the falling glass, reveling in the power of the storm but his men ran for the exits, unwilling to risk their lives for this madman. Torrents of water poured down on them now, and Joseph held his hands up to the unseen forces as the wind whipped around him.

Morgan rolled over and crawled towards her sister, moving slowly but surely out of the line of Joseph's sight. He was totally manic now, cackling and dancing in the rain and the wind. The stones were glowing as if they were sculpted from volcanic magma, torn from inside the earth. Joseph held the largest in his outstretched hands towards the splin-tering roof. He was oblivious to them now, focused only on the stones and the storm. Morgan climbed onto the pyre behind Faye and pulled the knife from her boot. She cut the bonds that held her sister to the smoldering pyre, the smoke of the wet wood hiding them from Everett. Morgan almost felt pity as she looked down at them, the brothers together, one a silent witness to the other's madness. Then she saw Gemma lying on the ground, soaked by the rain. Pulling her sister off the side of the pyre, they crawled around to where the little girl lay motionless by the edge of the rainforest where she had been dumped by the fleeing guards.

Lifting Gemma and holding the little face tightly to her neck, Faye started for the exit, stumbling a little as Morgan covered her escape. Then Jake appeared, sweeping Gemma into his arms and helping Faye down the stairs. He met Morgan's eyes briefly and she nodded, no time for words. It was enough for now that he had come back for her. They ran down through the rainforest and onto the desert mesa, past the ocean. No one stopped them. The men had deserted Joseph as the end seemed to be in sight and the Biosphere was clearly failing in the face of the tempest. As they reached the exit, the creaking of the structure turned to a mechanical scream as the supports started to break and buckle under the dense rain and hail, lightning superheating the steel.

As they ran from the building, a bolt of pure scarlet scythed apart the clouds above the Biosphere. Morgan turned to see it strike the platform where Joseph stood next to Michael, his hands on the wheelchair. It seemed to flicker around them gently, lighting their limbs and touching their necks where the stones hung then it became a pillar of flame connecting heaven to earth. Growing in intensity, it lit the scene in a crimson glow. Morgan watched, transfixed, as Michael rose up out of his chair and embraced his brother, the two frozen in the ruby light from above that split into a million drops as the rain hammered down. Was it a miracle, she thought, and in that split second, Morgan cast aside her skepticism and believed in the power of the stones, a divine phenomenon ignited by the storm. Then the light around the men exploded and they were lost in the glare. Morgan blinked and the moment was gone. Had she really seen something deep in the flames? She and the others ran out into the rain to escape the destruction as the Biosphere collapsed behind them.

CHAPTER 43

Biosphere 2, Oracle, Arizona, USA
May 27, Pentecost Sunday, 11.52pm

Firefighters and police arrived at the Biosphere, drawn by the storm and the inferno that had been seen across the plains to the town of Oracle. An ambulance crew rushed to meet the group as they emerged from the dome, coughing in the smoke. Jake squeezed Morgan's hand and then disappeared towards the police vehicles. She watched a paramedic work on Gemma as she held her arm around her sobbing sister. She borrowed a cellphone and dialed David's number, handing the phone to Faye when he answered in a desperate tone. They belonged together and only now was her guilt beginning to lift.

Morgan turned to watch as the structure of the Biosphere burnt furiously in the night, the fires still fierce even in the bucketing monsoon. She held her face up to the storm, feeling the wash of cool rain running down her neck, hiding the tears of relief now that her family were safe again.

Hours later, Morgan sat in one of the Biosphere's outlying adobe houses watching Faye and Gemma sleeping on the bed. Faye was wrapped around the little girl, her body a protective shield. Morgan reached out to gently brush a curl from her sister's forehead. She thought of what these two meant to her and how she would have given her life to save them. It was time to go home. But first, she wanted to find Jake.

Standing, she looked at herself in the mirror on the rough wall. Her eyes were bloodshot, skin bruised from the beating and still sooty from the ash. Her arm was in a new sling but her t-shirt was dirty and she smelled of smoke. She smiled. This wasn't Morgan the academic anymore and she was glad of it. Despite Jake's betrayal, he had come back and he had helped her find this side of herself again.

She walked out into the Arizona dawn, the first rays of the sun inching over the horizon. The fires still smoldered but she could see firefighters and police now sifting through the ash. Jake stood at the edge of the debris, his back to her. She could see the strength in his stance, the muscles in his back through the torn shirt. There was so much to say but she knew it would go unsaid by both of them. As she walked up behind him, he turned, silhouetted against the russet sky.

"Hi," Morgan said, smiling up at him.

"Hi yourself. How are Faye and Gemma?"

"They're sleeping now."

They both fell silent and then spoke at once.

"Jake ..."

"Morgan ..."

Laughing, they turned back to look at the shattered ruins, the moment broken.

"They only found one skeleton," Jake said.

"What? How can that be?" Morgan looked puzzled, remembering the vision she had seen. "Nothing could have survived that inferno."

"It's true. ARKANE is working with the police to ID the

body we have but they were twins and the remains are burnt beyond recognition so we don't know which one it is."

Morgan looked at him, "And what about the stones?"

"I'll find them, don't worry. It's time you took your family home."

As they watched the last of the fires burn down, Jake reached for Morgan's hand. Her fingers entwined with his, united for a moment at the end of the storm.

CHAPTER 44

London, England. 2 weeks later.

MORGAN HAD BEEN INVITED to London for a debriefing on the mission with ARKANE Director Elias Marietti. She decided to accept for a sense of closure, and she knew that part of her wanted to see Jake again. There was so much that remained unsaid between them and she had left that night before he had found the stones. Perhaps they hadn't survived the inferno after all?

She was met at the official entrance of ARKANE by Marietti's secretary and taken up to the Director's office. He rose to greet her and indicated a chair. She glanced at the art on the walls, the books on his shelves and saw evidence of the latent power Ben had spoke of.

"You've been a great asset to us, Morgan. Thank you for helping our mission to retrieve the Pentecost stones."

"You're mistaken, Director. It was always my mission. I was never there to help ARKANE find the stones, I only wanted to help my family. You would have sent them to their deaths just to save some relics of the early Church."

Marietti gave a thin smile.

"But you're intrigued by ARKANE, aren't you, Morgan? You saw something in the flames that was evidence of another reality. You know some of what we research here and it fascinates you. We have many mysteries to solve, many unique areas of research you could be part of. There are things happening in this world that you can only imagine, the stuff of angelic dreams and demonic nightmares."

"Why are you telling me this now?" she asked.

"I want you to join us," Marietti replied.

There was a sharp intake of breath from behind her and Morgan turned to see Jake in the doorway. He was clean shaven and wearing a slate grey suit, his white corkscrew scar standing out against his tanned skin. He was a handsome incarnation of the man she had travelled with, who had been beaten, bruised and smudged with ash from the flames of Pentecost. But this man was a stranger, his face stony as Marietti ignored his entrance and continued.

"We need a top researcher who can help us solve some of these mysteries, someone with your expertise in biblical matters and psychology of religion and someone who can hold her own in the field. Of course, you would have access to all our research."

Morgan thought of the database of which she had only touched the surface, the amazing resources ARKANE had and the secrets they protected. Marietti certainly knew how to tempt her professional side. Being back in staid academia for such a short time already, she was already longing for adventure. But then she thought of what Faye and Gemma had been through, of how close she had come to the flames of Everett's fire and the bullets of Thanatos. She started to speak but Marietti held up his hand.

"Just think about it. Right now, you want to see this."

He picked up a plain black case from behind his desk and held it out to her. It was dark wood, inscribed with tongues of fire that were picked out in gold leaf.

"You found the stones?" she said, amazed that they had been pulled intact from the flames. She reached for the case, laid it on the desk and opened it. They lay benign, all twelve, just pieces of rock, each with its own place carved so that they sat snugly. She recognized her own stone, remembering when her father had given it to her, no hint of what powers it might contain.

"This one is mine, you know, and that is my sister's. You have no right to keep these."

"But I think you appreciate their potential power now." Marietti said. "Perhaps it's best that they rest together in our vault. No one will come for you or your family again if we have them."

She traced the outline of her stone with a fingertip. Then she nodded and closed the lid, without relinquishing the box. Marietti stood.

"You deserve to see them laid to rest. Come, we'll go down together."

Morgan glanced sideways at Jake as they entered the elevator. They had still not spoken directly. His eyes were dark and hooded, as if he had withdrawn into his agent self. The Jake she had seen in the ruins of the Biosphere was hidden again. She was confused by his conflicting signals and didn't trust her feelings enough to speak so she stood away from him in the elevator as they descended into the depths of the ARKANE vaults.

Marietti stopped in front of the main vault door. It looked like an ancient portal, but inlaid with modern steel bars, protected by a high level security system. He scanned his retina and entered a passcode. Jake spoke his keywords to authenticate the entry. The doors opened and Marietti waved Morgan inside.

"Few outsiders see this, but I thought you'd find it interesting."

A puff of cool air blew over them from the humidity controlled vault as they walked through the doors. Morgan marveled at the size of the hall in front of her. It stretched into the distance with separate opaque sealed rooms for books, religious artifacts and unknown objects hidden inside.

"This is our treasure vault," Marietti said, "where we keep the most precious and dangerous artifacts. Here are the manuscripts of heresy and occult knowledge, the bones of martyred saints and secrets the world would have us keep."

"Or you would keep from the world," she countered, but followed him down the hallway. Marietti stopped in front of a doorway and led her in. It was dark and cool inside; a dim light outlined boxes, paintings and scrolls all in numbered places around the walls.

"The light must stay dim to protect what is here, but these are secrets that the stones can rest easy with, Morgan."

She didn't relinquish the box.

"After what you've put me through, after leaving me and my family to die and taking the stones, how can you ask me to give these back to you? There's more to ARKANE than protecting religious secrets for the good of mankind, I know that. Why should the stones stay with you?"

Marietti sighed, age showing in his face.

"We couldn't let the power of the stones into the world and you're a resourceful woman. Clearly, you inspired great loyalty in Jake, and you both made it out, with the stones so no harm done. This time. But this is a safe place for them now, especially if you work with us. Think about it. I know you're intrigued by what lies within these vaults and we can give you access. You're a scholar. Knowledge is what you seek." He paused. "... And perhaps adventure as well."

Morgan looked around the vault, at the cornucopia of intoxicating possibility. She bent and gently laid the case of stones down in their allotted place, as if saying goodbye. She backed out of the vault as Marietti followed.

"I've just got my life back," she said. "I've found my family again and have a chance for a normal life. I've seen what you do and I don't want this crazy dangerous ARKANE life. The price is too high."

She looked pointedly at Jake then. He met her eyes with a challenge, saying nothing to stop her. Turning away, Morgan began to walk down the long corridor back towards the elevator. Marietti called after her.

"A war is coming, Morgan. A religious battle where millions may die and ARKANE is the only group capable of stopping it. Thanatos will not give up this easily. We need you."

She stopped for a second, but didn't turn around as he finished.

"Ask Ben. Ask him about your parents and the pale horse of Thanatos. You've heard of the prophecy, that the stones will be together in the end times. Those times are upon us. Ask him, and then call me."

She walked on faster then, away from his haunting voice. Up in the elevator through the levels and into the light of another London day, to be lost in the tourist crowds of Trafalgar Square.

* * *

Morgan and Jake's adventures continue in
Crypt of Bone, available now.

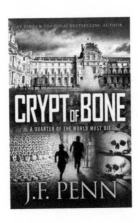

*The prophecy in Revelation declares that
a quarter of the world must die ...*

... And now a shadowy organization has the ability to fulfill these words. Can one woman stop the abomination before it's too late?

ISRAEL. A victim of Jerusalem Syndrome jumps to his death from the top of the Western Wall, his body smashed on the ancient stones. Another disembowels himself under the scrawled figure of the Pale Horse of the Apocalypse with the chilling words, "God told me to do it."

Dr Morgan Sierra travels to Israel to investigate the deaths and becomes embroiled in an international conspiracy that will use cutting-edge technology to carry an ancient curse to mankind, and threaten those she loves.

Morgan joins agent Jake Timber at ARKANE, a secret government agency investigating the supernatural. Together they must hunt down the Devil's Bible, pursued all the way by the evil forces of Thanatos.

From the catacombs of Paris to the skeletal ossuaries of Sicily and the Czech Republic, Morgan and Jake must find the Devil's Bible and stop the curse being released into the world before one in four are destroyed in the coming holocaust. Because in just seven days, the final curse will be spoken and the prophecy will be fulfilled.

ENJOYED STONE OF FIRE?

If you loved the book and have a moment to spare, I would really appreciate a short review on the page where you bought the book. Your help in spreading the word is gratefully appreciated and reviews make a huge difference to helping new readers find the series. Thank you!

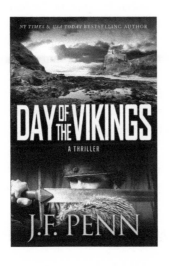

Get a free copy of the bestselling thriller, *Day of the Vikings*, ARKANE book 5, when you sign up to join my Reader's Group. You'll also be notified of new releases, giveaways and receive personal updates from behind the scenes of my thrillers.

WWW.JFPENN.COM/FREE

* * *

Day of the Vikings, an ARKANE thriller

A ritual murder on a remote island under the shifting skies of the aurora borealis.

A staff of power that can summon Ragnarok, the Viking apocalypse.

When Neo-Viking terrorists invade the British Museum in London to reclaim the staff of Skara Brae, ARKANE agent Dr. Morgan Sierra is trapped in the building along with hostages under mortal threat.

As the slaughter begins, Morgan works alongside psychic Blake Daniel to discern the past of the staff, dating back to islands invaded by the Vikings generations ago.

Can Morgan and Blake uncover the truth before Ragnarok is unleashed, consuming all in its wake?

Day of the Vikings is a fast-paced, supernatural thriller set in London and the islands of Orkney, Lindisfarne and Iona. Set in the present day, it resonates with the history and myth of the Vikings.

If you love an action-packed thriller,
you can get Day of the Vikings for free now:

WWW.JFPENN.COM/FREE

Day of the Vikings features Dr. Morgan Sierra from the ARKANE thrillers, and Blake Daniel from the London Crime Thrillers, but it is also a stand-alone novella that can be read and enjoyed separately.

AUTHOR'S NOTE

Thank you for joining Morgan on the hunt for the Pentecost stones. One of my favorite parts of thriller novels is when the author outlines where some of the ideas came from. Now I can share my own inspiration, where research meets fiction.

The Pentecost stones and the Apostles after the book of Acts

Whatever your personal beliefs about God, the Bible is full of inspiration for writers. I have a Masters degree in Theology and I find myself returning again and again to the realm of the spiritual for ideas.

The Biblical book of Acts, Chapter 2, describes the day of Pentecost when the Holy Spirit was poured out on the Apostles of Jesus. They spoke in tongues, preached to crowds and performed miracles. However, there is no biblical tradition of the stones of the Apostles. That is my fiction but it certainly seems to be the last time the Apostles were together in one place as the twelve scattered across the known world. Is it possible they took symbols of brotherhood with them?

In my research, I found that little is known of what actually happened to those twelve men and what is documented is contradictory and confusing. I used multiple sources to try to locate where the likely resting place of the stones might be if they had been left with the bodies of the Apostles. Some are well known, like James and Peter, but others have disappeared into myth, like Simon the Zealot.

A National Geographic article in March 2012 goes into some of the research I also used. More details here: http://joannapenn.com/national-geographic-apostles/

Resurgam comet

The Resurgam comet is fictitious although I based the information on some of the theories around comet Elenin which did pass close to the Earth during the period of the Japan earthquake and tsunami.

The related Biblical verses are: Mark chapter 13, Matthew 27:51-52, 28:2, Revelation 6:12-14

Locations in the book

I have tried to be accurate in the physical description of the locations in the story, most of which I have been to in person. I'm a travel junkie and particularly love places of religious and cultural significance.

> **INDIA.** Manikarnika ghat in Varanasi is indeed where bodies are burnt and Hindus believe they can escape the endless cycle of rebirth. I've been on one of those boats watching the burning bodies. As a Westerner, it was a profound experience that affected me deeply. This first scene was the birth of the idea for the whole book.

> **ENGLAND.** Oxford is my spiritual home and the place I return to in my dreams and in real life as often as I can. Steeped in myth and history, it crops up in every story in my head. Morgan's office in Bath Place is a real location, but it's a hotel. The Turf pub is just behind it.

Blackfriars is on St Giles and I attended tutorials there myself when I did Theology at Mansfield College, but I have taken liberties with the interior and layout. The Pitt Rivers Museum is a wonderful treasure trove of inspiration that you can now roam online as well as in the flesh. In London, Trafalgar Square is well known as a tourist destination, but I don't know what lies beneath it!

SPAIN. Santiago de Compostela does have a silver reliquary of St James and also the largest swinging censer in the world. I found this when roaming the cathedral online and just had to use it as an escape route for Jake. The vision of Pope Leo XIII is from real Church archives.

IRAN. There is a church of St Mary in Tabriz and the Armenian faith is one of the oldest in the world. I took liberties with the actual location as there was little definite information. It seems certain that one or more of the Apostles made it that far east.

ITALY. The Pope does take Mass in St Peter's regularly and anyone can attend. My husband and I stumbled in there for Epiphany in January 2010 and were amazed at how close you can get to him. There is a glass case holding the remains of Pope Pius X, and the statue of Alexander does feature a skeleton with an hourglass. Venice is flooded increasingly more often each year and may indeed be underwater one day, hopefully not in our lifetime. There is a spectacular Pentecost mural in the Basilica San Marco which reshaped the whole plot after our visit there. Amalfi is the supposed resting place of St Andrew.

ISRAEL. Jerusalem is one of my perpetual inspirations, having travelled there a number of times. The church of the Holy Sepulchre is as crazy as I describe and the Ethiopian Coptics did live on the roof when I last visited.

TUNISIA. The wadi at Nefta is a real place but everything about the citadel is fictional.

USA. The founders of modern psychology did indeed visit Clark University in 1909 and there is a statue of Freud on a bench. I visited the Biosphere 2 in Arizona years ago and was entranced by the various habitats. The glass ziggurat came to mind as somewhere that would explode dramatically, and the storms in Arizona make the crazy weather a possibility.

Carl Jung, The Red Book and Wolfgang Pauli

One of my abiding fascinations is psychology, particularly when it relates to religion and faith. I have read Carl Jung for years and almost trained as a psychologist, but that would have been another life.

The Red Book was opened to the public in 2009 and I have a copy myself. It contains a painting by Jung of a pillar of fire spouting from a grey stone in a room as I describe in the book. But of course, I made up the interpretation of the picture.

Jung did travel in North Africa and also to North America and Clark University. He also counseled physicist Wolfgang Pauli on his dreams, the wasp being one of his real nightmares. The relationship of these men to the Apostles of Jesus is fictional.

Any mistakes in the research are purely my own.

MORE BOOKS BY J.F.PENN

Thanks for joining Morgan, Jake and the
ARKANE team. The adventures continue …

Stone of Fire #1
Crypt of Bone #2
Ark of Blood #3
One Day in Budapest #4
Day of the Vikings #5
Gates of Hell #6
One Day in New York #7
Destroyer of Worlds #8
End of Days #9
Valley of Dry Bones #10

If you like **crime thrillers with an edge of the supernatural**,
join Detective Jamie Brooke and museum researcher Blake
Daniel, in the London Crime Thriller trilogy:

Desecration #1
Delirium #2
Deviance #3

If you enjoy **dark fantasy,** check out:

Map of Shadows, Mapwalkers #1
Risen Gods
American Demon Hunters: Sacrifice

A Thousand Fiendish Angels:
Short stories based on Dante's Inferno

The Dark Queen

More books coming soon.

You can sign up to be notified of new releases, giveaways
and pre-release specials - plus, get a free book!

WWW.JFPENN.COM/FREE

ABOUT J.F.PENN

J.F.Penn is the Award-nominated, New York Times and USA Today bestselling author of the ARKANE supernatural thrillers, London Crime Thrillers, and the Mapwalker dark fantasy series, as well as other standalone stories.

Her books weave together ancient artifacts, relics of power, international locations and adventure with an edge of the supernatural. Joanna lives in Bath, England and enjoys a nice G&T.

* * *

You can sign up for a free thriller,
Day of the Vikings, and updates from behind the scenes,
research, and giveaways at:

WWW.JFPENN.COM/FREE

* * *

Connect at:
www.JFPenn.com
joanna@JFPenn.com
www.Facebook.com/JFPennAuthor
www.Instagram.com/JFPennAuthor
www.Twitter.com/JFPennWriter

* * *

For writers:

Joanna's site, www.TheCreativePenn.com, helps people write, publish and market their books through articles, audio, video and online courses.

She writes non-fiction for authors under Joanna Penn and has an award-nominated podcast for writers, The Creative Penn Podcast.

ACKNOWLEDGMENTS

Thank you to everyone who has encouraged me during the writing of the book, especially to all the enthusiastic readers on my blog, TheCreativePenn.com. Your comments, tweets and emails in the last year have made it a journey I've been privileged to share. Your votes for the book cover and comments on the back blurb in particular helped me no end and I will continue to share lessons learned as we travel together on the writer's way.

A special thank you to my proof-readers: Jonathan Bleier, Jacqui Penn, Elizabeth Wilmott, Karen Thomas, Heidi Uytendaal, Damian Cox and Alan Baxter, dark fantasy author at AlanBaxterOnline.com. Your feedback significantly helped shape the final version of the book. An extra thanks to Damian for the brilliant plot ideas and introducing me to the Preston & Child Pendergast series, which enabled me to see a future for Morgan's adventures.

Thank you to Tom Evans, TheBookWright.com who encouraged me to write fiction when I was blocked by the idea that I was only a non-fiction writer. Also to Mur Lafferty murverse.com whose advice "it's OK to suck with your first draft" helped me get the words down. The first draft of the novel was started during National Novel Writing Month and I would encourage any writer to participate if you want a jumpstart: nanowrimo.org

As an independent author in this process, I engaged a number of professionals along the way. Steve Parolini at TheNovelDoctor.com did a fantastic Editorial Review that helped me rejig the structure, plot and fill out the characters. The wonderful cover was created by Joel Friedlander from TheBookDesigner.com. Joel's brilliant blog is packed with information for indie publishers. The print design for the second version of the book was done by Jane Dixon Smith at www.jdsmith-design.co.uk.